TARA

Nelofar Currimbhoy is a gifted writer whose vivid and evocative style has earned her acclaim from readers, critics and the media alike. Her poetry collection *Eyes of the Healer* was adapted into a musical drama by Muzaffar Ali—*Ananda: Eyes of the Healer*—featuring Kabir Bedi as the narrator.

A graduate of Lady Shri Ram College, Nelofar later studied Beauty Therapy at ITEC, London. She currently serves as President of the Shahnaz Husain Group of Companies, playing a key role in its growth. While she oversees the national distribution network, her passion lies in the research and development wing, where she delights in reviving ancient Ayurvedic formulations to be marketed to the world.

Tara follows the success of the bestselling *Flame*.

Follow the author:

www.facebook.com/NelofarCurrimbhoy.Author
www.twitter.com/NelofarAuthor

Also by Nelofar Currimbhoy

Flame: The Inspiring Life of My Mother Shahnaz Husain

≈

'Tara's story stayed with me long after I turned the last page. It draws the reader into a gamut of emotions—love, passion and human failings. An unforgettable read I highly recommend!'

—Muzaffar Ali
Writer and Filmmaker

'In *Tara*, Nelofar Currimbhoy reveals a rare gift for storytelling that is at once lucid and layered, elegant and immersive. With an assured voice and a storyteller's instinct, she weaves a narrative that blends reality with imagination, the spiritual with the mysterious and the glittering with shadow into a seamless mosaic. Her words flow effortlessly, capturing the delicate threads of longing, ambition and the enigma of human connection. Her characters are strikingly alive— flawed, vivid and deeply human—anchoring a plot that simmers with quiet tension and emotional resonance. This is a novel that seduces you slowly, pulls you in and refuses to let go. *Tara* is not just a novel; it is an experience.'

—Vinita Dawra Nangia
Director, Times Literature Festival
Founder-Director, Write India

TARA
THE DREAM CHASER

NELOFAR CURRIMBHOY

RUPA

Published by
Rupa Publications India Pvt. Ltd 2025
161-B/4, Gulmohar House,
Yusuf Sarai Community Centre,
New Delhi 110049

Sales centres:
Bengaluru Chennai
Hyderabad Kolkata Mumbai

P-ISBN: 978-93-6156-705-6
E-ISBN: 978-93-6156-839-8

First impression 2025

10 9 8 7 6 5 4 3 2 1

The moral right of the author has been asserted.

Printed in India

Dedicated to the memory of my hero
My grandfather
Justice Nasir Ullah Beg
Your footsteps have been my guiding light

Contents

Prologue

The 14th-floor penthouse apartment offered a perfect view of Marine Drive curving gently towards Chowpatty Beach at its northern end. Even from this distance, he could see the waves crashing against the embankment, turning into a spray of froth. The pre-monsoon rains had washed the city clean, and it glistened under the halogen lights. Mumbai looked surreal, almost perfect; the night hid away the grime, the urchins, the snarling traffic and the women who walked the streets soliciting passing cars. It also hid away Tara.

An oil painting of her face stared back at him from the wall—*her beauty grossly was exaggerated*, he thought. Her eyes, tilted, followed him as he paced the room. It irritated him.

Tara had left them unnerved. Aishwarya's words kept ringing in his ears. 'My goodness, Vikram, the girl is gone. Can you stop being this obsessed? It's embarrassing. Besides, how on earth would she be at the races in Mumbai?'

'Because we would never think of searching for her here!' he snapped.

'There is a party at the Willingdon tonight. I want you to be at your dignified best. And remember—Tara couldn't join us because she is occupied with her charity.'

'I will play along with your little charade, but do you realize that, as we speak, my wife—your daughter—is absconding?'

That silenced Aishwarya momentarily.

'Vikram, there's family dignity at stake. You've married into the royals—we don't want whispers spreading.'

'Well, the royal wife has vanished! How are you going to explain that to your illustrious glitterati?'

'There are none left, Vikram—you have managed to alienate everyone with your court cases and antagonism.'

'I am allergic to you royals,' he said disdainfully. 'Your pretentious make-believe lives, your set of rules—don't I know what goes on behind your palace walls!

'You are an outsider. I thought you would blend in. But a commoner will always be a commoner. Don't try to understand us born royals.'

'This commoner is going to make you more money than you can dream of, mother-in-law, provided you put your mind to tracing your daughter.'

Vikram turned away and took a long sip of scotch, trying to calm the anxiety churning in his belly. It bothered him—he had seen her. He was sure of it. She stood in a private box ahead of him as the horses raced by and the crowd cheered lustily. Her tresses were unmistakable. He shuffled his fingers, agitated—he could recognize their texture even from a mile away. And then, in the milieu of excitement, amidst the gunshot, the roar of hooves and the rush of it all, she had vanished. He had pushed through the crowds, desperate to follow, but she was gone.

Then again, he never got to see her face. Was it really her at all? Conflicted, he downed another scotch.

In a figure-hugging wrap dress and a derby hat obscuring her face, she was dressed more like the women he entertained on his business trips—unless, of course, it was a disguise. He glanced at the painting on the wall and grew even more agitated.

'Maybe you're right,' he muttered, trying to convince himself. 'Maybe it was someone else,' he said, swirling his drink.

The rattling of rocks of ice against the crystal created a sharp medley. Aishwarya frowned, exasperated.

'I *know* I am right,' she scoffed. 'Now you choose to care about her whereabouts? Really?'

'Well, you could have had a speck of motherly influence on your daughter,' he shot back.

She ignored his caustic jab, focusing instead on adjusting the large diamond-encrusted ruby on her finger.

Vikram glared at her, blowing perfect rings of smoke with his Dunhill. He had the nasty habit of stubbing out halfway only to light up again immediately. He was getting edgy and restless.

Aishwarya held his gaze with cool contempt, but his mind drifted back to the mysterious sighting. It was strange—just moments after spotting her, he had turned back to see her rushing out of the place. A long-haired man had followed. He was not sure if they were together or if it were a coincidence. Something about the scene seemed off. This was far too close a call for Vikram to let go.

Tara was gone, and she was going to wreck everything he had planned.

Part One

1

A Flight to Freedom

The car swerved around the marble fountain and sped through the imposing rusted-iron gates. Touching the four-lane highway, she pressed down on the accelerator. The air carried the soft scent of rain, and she could sense the menace trailing her—a fine spray of desert sand peppered the windscreen, accompanied by an incessant hissing sound that grew louder; she knew the familiar signs all too well—a desert storm was approaching.

She had to make it out of here before she was caught in a cloud of silver dust. Just then, a pair of headlights loomed in the rear-view mirror, freezing her hands on the wheel.

No! Vikram couldn't possibly have woken from his drunken daze to chase after her. Was he having her followed? She replayed his exact words in her mind: 'I want her dead by tomorrow—let her fall off on the morning horse ride.'

She was going through moments of denial—she couldn't believe that Vikram actually wanted her dead. He was the man she had married, the man she had trusted her life with, but then his voice echoed in her mind, loud and unrelenting. The headlights inched closer, almost grazing the side of her car before the Land Rover overtook her and disappeared into the night. She took a deep breath; she needed to relax. Not every car was following her, not every shadow was trailing her.

She switched on the radio, and Michael Jackson's voice rang out through the speakers: 'It doesn't matter who's wrong or right. Just beat it, beat it…'

Her mind flipped through her options. Sanganer Airport was just a few miles away—oh how she longed to get on a plane and fly far, far away! A flight felt like the perfect getaway.

As the airport drew closer, the traffic began to slow down and then came to a grinding halt. She felt jittery as she rolled down her window and called out to a policeman. 'I need to catch a flight. I hope this won't take long.'

'Nakabandi,' he said gruffly. 'We have to check each vehicle.'

Her heart sank. She pulled up to the checkpoint, and a sluggish policeman peered into the car. 'Papers, madam,' he said.

Tara squirmed in her seat. She knew it—Vikram would not let her leave so easily. She opened the dashboard and reached for her driving licence, handing it over to the policeman.

'Pull over to the side, madam.'

'Why? What have I done?'

'There's an FIR against you—for stealing your family jewellery and absconding.'

Her stomach dropped, but she managed to steady her voice. 'You can search my car for the jewellery. And while you are at it, take a look at this.' She turned her face to reveal a deep gash along her cheek.

The policeman frowned and then sighed. 'Go,' he said softly. 'Get away quick, girl.'

She didn't wait to be told twice. Pressing down on the accelerator, she drove on. A few miles ahead, she took a sharp turn down a narrow, dark street, pulling over abruptly. The car jerked to a stop as she slammed on the brakes.

Leaning her head against the steering wheel, she clutched it tightly for support. For a moment, she just sat there, her mind blank. There was no way out, nowhere to go. Friends, family, even the police—none of them could help her now. The stakes were too high, the money involved too tempting. Vikram would find her, and the jewellery theft charge would be his weapon to drag her back.

She pulled out a tissue and lifted her chin. Using a touch of cologne kept in the car, she dabbed her face with it. *Ah, it felt so good.* Staring into the rear-view mirror, she noticed how tense her eyes looked, the gash on her cheek making her appear suspicious. She wrapped a scarf around her head, covering the injury just enough to pass unnoticed.

The head cover felt secure—a small hiding place. She then looked around and stepped out of the car. Pulling her bag, she headed towards the main highway. In the distance, the lights of the airport shimmered, beckoning her. *It is not that far. I can make it*, she thought, determination propelling her steps forward.

Her feet were sore, her breath short, but she finally made the distance. Walking past the glass doors at the airport, she was hit by the cool rarefied atmosphere inside. She took a deep breath—it felt good. She stood still, staring at the electronic flight listings as though it were a menu. The next flight was to Mumbai. Destiny had made the choice for her, and she took it without a thought.

She walked up to the counter. 'I need a ticket for the next flight to Mumbai,' she said.

'Doors close in 20 minutes, ma'am, so you will need to make a dash,' the man replied in a flat, robotic tone. 'Or there's another one in an hour.'

'I need to go now,' she said firmly, then softened her voice. 'I am paying in cash.'

'Return ticket?'

'One-way,' replied Tara—no questions, no second guesses.

The glow of the *Security* sign sent a chill through her. Her pace, her breath caught—but then she exhaled deeply and steadied herself. She slipped off her handbag and retrieved a pair of tinted glasses and a face mask. Hidden well enough, she approached the checkpoint. The officer eyed her warily, clearly expecting her to reveal her face.

She pulled down her glasses and then coughed as hard as she could. 'Just getting over Covid,' she croaked.

'Okay, madam. You go, go! Fast!' she almost screamed, covering her nose with a big, white handkerchief.

Stepping onto the plane, Tara felt an overwhelming urge to throw her hands in the air and scream in victory. This was it—freedom. Relief.

Buckled into her business class seat, she looked out of the window. The man beside her gave a polite nod before burying himself in the day's news. The morning flight to Mumbai was packed, as always, with executives dressed as though they would step straight into corporate meetings on landing.

The Airbus 320 revved its engines, taxied down the runway and tilted its nose towards the sky. As the plane took off, Tara felt cradled in her seat, finally safe. *I have done it,* she thought. *I escaped.* It was a surreal feeling for her—her flight to freedom!

The steady hum of the cruising plane lulled her into a light sleep, but her reprieve was short-lived. With her eyes shut, the memories crept back in monochrome shades—mirthless figures dancing around her—and she woke with a start. Her temple throbbed as she replayed his voice. It echoed down the corridor, slurring with alcohol, menacingly sharp and commanding.

The grip of his hand, the force of his clutch. She cringed at the flashbacks. And then there was the scent—that invasive, cloying perfume. It clung to everything, lingering between them like an unwelcome third presence. She was always there—the other woman—mocking Tara. It was the woman who held his attention even though it was Tara who lay in his bed every night.

Tara knew her smell, her favourite shade of lipstick—a garish red she so carelessly, or perhaps tauntingly, smeared on the edge of his kurta. Tara comforted herself with the thought that she would never have to smell that fragrance again.

Worse than it all, though, was her mother's stoic silence.

The memories brought beads of sweat to her brow, but then, as if heaven-sent, the air hostess appeared with a smile. 'Would you like to have tea or coffee, madam?'

'Tea, please,' Tara almost pleaded.

'Darjeeling or Assam? Would you like it strong or mild, with or without milk? Sugar or plain, or perhaps a substitute?'

The hostess disappeared after taking Tara's order, only to return moments later, looking apologetic. 'I am so sorry, madam, but we have run out of Assam.'

Tara sighed, exasperated. 'Just give me a cup of hot cocoa then.'

'Toned or full fat?' the hostess embarked on her list of choices again.

'You know what? I will have your favourite,' Tara said, her tone weary.

'I have a lactose allergy.'

'Well, I think I might have an allergy at the moment. I'll skip breakfast.'

Tara woke up to the aroma of hot coffee wafting through the plane. It had been long since she had her last meal, and her neighbour's breakfast tray caught her attention—double-fried eggs, a croissant, jams and a mint chocolate on the side. She was regretting her decision.

Sensing her eyes pause on his tray, the man turned to her. 'Can I pass you my breakfast please? I go light on flights.'

'Are you sure?' she asked. 'I would love that,' she quickly added. Looking at the middle-aged man by her side, she thought, *Not all men are bad. Not all women are good.*

Tara helped herself to the breakfast and looked out of the window as the plane began its descent. The Mumbai skyline came into view, the city's peaks emerging through the haze. The sight stirred a hint of excitement and a sense of hope within her. *Hope,* she mused, *can sometimes just be a new place.*

The plane landed with a jerk and then taxied down the runway. Tara stretched on her toes to retrieve her bright pink overnight bag from the overhead locker—the only luggage she had managed to pack in her haste. Around her, people hurriedly reached for their bags, their faces eager as the cabin doors opened.

As she stepped on to the ramp, she observed the familiar behaviour of passengers disembarking—a universal impatience to escape the confines of the space. *We're all just human,* she thought.

Mumbai airport was bustling as always with an air of urgency—people arriving were eager to meet those waiting for them, while departures moved swiftly to catch their flights. Everyone here was in a rush to get somewhere. This massive terminal served as a gateway to the city, a harbour where hope and human enterprise flowed in endless streams. The excitement of those arriving was palpable—Mumbai was not just a city; it was a celebration of life and a philosophy in motion. It taught the art of surviving and thriving in the process. It was a city that said, 'No matter what, I will survive. I will endure my fate.'

Tara waded through the dense crowd, porters pestering her along the way, asking, 'Any luggage, madam?' Blurry-eyed travellers thronged to the exits, pushing their loaded trolleys. Tara moved along with the crowd; a gush of moist air hit her face as she stepped outside, accompanied by the cacophony of taxis and car horns. 'Welcome to Mumbai!' a giant hoarding declared. Tara flagged down a white-bearded taxi driver, who pulled over with practised ease. '*Kahan jata hae*—where to?' he asked in a typical Mumbai lingo that relied on shortened phrase for normal language.

This city does not have time to speak in full sentences, Tara thought.

'Where?' he called out again, impatiently.

'South Mumbai.'

'Address, madam?'

'Gateway of India,' she said hurriedly.

He got off to load her bag into the boot before politely opening the door for her.

The car snaked its way through the dense Mumbai traffic masterfully, the ride feeling like an extension of her flight—only bumpier.

Tara thought for a moment, then pulled out her phone and pressed a number on her speed dial.

2

Landing on a Hot Roof

When Kamala Jaiveergiri threw a party, it was curated to perfection. Tonight, in the top-floor apartment, the royal inhabitants were dressing up for the evening. Divya, as always, limited herself to placing her special handmade candles around the house before disappearing into her room. She knew her mother's pre-party frenzy would soon transform into a dazzling smile as the guests arrived.

Jaiveer Mahal had passed through several owners and names before Rajan Jaiveer, Kamala's husband, an astute businessman, bought it as an intelligent investment. Once, Kamala and Rajan had belonged to Mumbai's 'new royalty'—the super wealthy. In those days, the family stood just a breath away from being listed among the top 10 businesses in the country. But then came the policy changes and the long era of industrial strikes that shook the family's empire. Their fortunes dwindled rapidly.

Rajan now limited his public appearances, preferring to spend time with his ever-growing collection of books. His only indulgence was his beloved Cuban cigars, delightfully named *Romeo y Julieta*. Kamala, on the other hand, enjoyed meeting people and throwing elegant parties—the whirlwind of the social circuit made her feel valued and relevant.

This evening, Kamala had summoned the florist from Colaba Causeway to design the dining table.

'No gladioli,' instructed Kamala. 'They look so plebeian.'

'For God's sake, Mum!' exclaimed Divya. 'How can you even say that? Creating a class—hierarchy for flowers?'

'There is a hierarchy for everything in life, darling. Marigolds cost a few rupees; white orchids are ₹200 a stem. Life works that way.'

'Yet marigolds still adorn the feet of gods.'

Kamala smiled wistfully. How she wanted the next generation to embrace the style and glamour that once defined their family. Instead, she found herself settling for compromises. 'Darling, if you must wear jeans tonight, make sure they are Calvin Klein's.'

'I won't embarrass you, Mum. I will wear the Ralph Lauren dress.'

Kamala looked relieved. 'That's exactly what you would be expected to wear as a Jaiveergiri daughter.'

'It's for you, Mum,' Divya replied softly.

Kamala worked hard to preserve their reputation—not just for her but for Rajan as well. The front of the house was always immaculate to maintain the illusion of grandeur. Her home was a stage, impeccable and carefully preserved for the world to see—a theatrical performance curated from memories of their former life. The flowers, the lighting, the dishes, the priceless shawls draped over stained sofas—all contributed well to the illusion.

It had been years since the family had lived off interests from various trusts, and now it was time for the jewels to be sold off discreetly to foreign buyers. Kamala had retrieved her best pieces from the locker to wear them one last time before the replicas, being crafted by Tania Baruch, who was well known for her perfect reproductions of old pieces, would take their place. For now, the feel of real diamonds against her skin felt good. Kamala wondered how the make-believes would feel.

Her ringing phone broke her reverie. 'Ma'am, this is Hemant Jha from the Blue Valley Wine Company,' the voice crackled.

'Hello, Hemant. I hope you have the best for my friends tonight.'

'Yes, ma'am. I have sent two cases of our finest years. I will also send brochures detailing the origins of the grapes.'

'Hemant, I will serve your wine, but I am not handing out brochures like a saleslady!'

'My apologies, ma'am. Maybe you could just say good things—your personal views.'

'My friends know that I only appreciate the best Italian wines.'

'Okay, ma'am. Then please just let your friends taste ours and decide.'

✯

As the preparations neared completion, Divya sauntered up to her room. 'Arjun, love,' she said into the phone, 'I need to get out of this house. Mum's having one of her suffocating dinners today, and I want to run away.'

'Come, baby,' Arjun drawled. 'I am always waiting for you.'

Divya had met Arjun at Jaipur Law College—that equalizer where everyone was free from the baggage of their homes. In those days, he wore jeans and sloganeered T-shirts that declared his current state of mind. His shoulder-length hair constantly fell upon his face, forcing him to flick it back repeatedly.

The morning she first noticed him, he had pulled his hair into a strange plait and thrown on a kurta. The last chair of the library always worked well for him because no one ever ventured that far into the endless tunnel of books, except for Divya, but she rarely looked up from her laptop. That day, as usual, she had been furiously typing away at her keyboard when, suddenly, she felt hungry. Reaching into her bag, she pulled out a box of homemade *barfi*s that Kamala Devi dispatched to her daughter regularly. The fragrance of reheated ghee and sugar left an intoxicating aroma hanging in the air.

Arjun looked up, then quickly looked away. Divya popped one barfi into her mouth, and then another. Finally, he couldn't resist.

'Hello, I am Arjun, and I am starving. Can I go for that last one? Unless you're saving it!'

Divya giggled, charmed by his candidness. 'Go for it. Why didn't I think of offering it earlier?'

'Would you like to grab a cup of coffee in town?' Arjun asked.

'Not today,' Divya replied. 'I have a friend coming to stay with me. But I will take you up on that offer one of these days.'

She'd packed up her things and walked away. 'Hey, Tara!' she spoke into her mobile phone. 'I will be at the airport to pick you up.'

That was 10 years ago. Time had moved on. While Tara had married her mother's chosen prince charming, Divya spent years fighting to marry the man who was on her family's 'Rejected' list. Arjun was now a Delhi businessman dealing in car spare parts—and that didn't sit well with Kamala.

'He's not a manufacturer, Divya, he is a dealer. And Delhi? It is such a crass city. I would have been fine with Kolkata, but the North gets to me.'

For Divya, the parties at Jaiveer Mahal had become a tiresome chore, a nuisance. She opted for a 'good girl' look—a pink short-sleeved dress by Ralph Lauren as promised to her mother, paired with diamond earrings. It would help her fit in with the less rebellious young women who would be attending the soirée. As she struggled to pull on the figure-hugging dress, her phone buzzed.

She answered, smiling, 'Tara! Hey there!'

'I need to see you,' came a tired voice on the other end.

'You sound worried,' said Divya, her smile fading.

'Divya, I did it finally. I have left home. I feel…relieved.'

'Now life starts for you, Tara,' said Divya.

'I had to get away before he killed me.'

'Where are you?'

'In Mumbai.'

'Come home right away,' said Divya, her hand gripping the phone tightly as her eyes welled up.

Relief washed over Tara, and she felt anchored by Divya's

voice. As she slouched in the back seat of the cab, she noticed the driver stealing glances at her in the rear-view mirror. It didn't take her long to realize why. The city lights flickered across her face—the wind from the open window had blown her scarf aside, revealing her secret.

Tara's finger traced the deep cut running from her lip to her chin. A surge of anger welled up inside her. Vikram's heavy hand had left its mark many times, but this time had been different. The sharp edge of the wedding ring she had slipped on to his finger had sliced her face like a razor—*sacrilege*, she thought bitterly.

The sun dipped into the ocean, casting the sky in hues of peace, and Tara felt a fleeting moment of calm. Somehow it helped to compose her nerves as the cab swerved into the porch of an antiquated apartment complex.

In the city's chaotic development, Jaiveer Mahal had stood the test of time. The pink stone structure, rising four storeys and spreading across two blocks, was a heritage property that embodied Mumbai's multicultural ethos. While the ground floor had been taken over by premium brands—a stylish handbag chain and a few leading designers—the upper floors remained home to some of the top corporate bosses, those who could afford to live at Jaiveer Mahal—a home that was a symbol of professional success for many.

Tara stepped into the antiquated iron-grilled elevator, which rattled laboriously to the third floor. She looked up at the spot fan that was rattling above her head—it felt good to find that some things never changed. She had taken this vertical journey countless times in her teens, but today, it felt like a lifeline—taking her to a sanctuary, somewhere she could wait and brace herself.

She hesitated at the door, which swung open before she could even ring the bell. Divya hugged Tara before she could utter a word. Then she stepped back, her eyes narrowing. The moment she got a closer look at Tara's face, Divya gasped. 'No way is he getting away with this,' she declared. She grabbed Tara's hand and led her friend to her room. 'Let's get you some first aid.'

Divya rummaged through a drawer and pulled out a first aid box. With a large sterile wipe, she gently dabbed the still-raw cut. Tara shut her eyes; she hadn't felt loved and cared for in years now. She had missed it.

'Almost done. Do you want something to eat, Tara?'

'No, Divya. I just need to sleep.'

'You mentioned his violence wasn't the only reason…'

'I got away before he killed me, Divya. I overheard him talking to a hired killer.'

'You should have called the police!'

'He's got his tentacles everywhere.'

'Why did you tolerate him for all those years?'

'I don't want to speak about it. It's terrifying.'

Tara lay down on the bed and Divya covered her with a light duvet. She shut her eyes, but her mind remained restless. The thought of Vikram finding her made her feel like a dove searching for a nook to hide. For now, Jaiveer Mahal was her safe nook.

★

Kamala was nothing if not punctual. Her guests respected her timings, and she expected her family to be dressed and waiting well in time.

'Divya,' she called out. 'I want you down before the guests arrive.'

Tara looked surprised. 'You didn't tell me there was a party at your place tonight,' she said, a little embarrassed.

'Do parties ever stop at Jaiveer Mahal?'

'I just hope they don't,' said Tara, with a wistful smile, remembering the days when she would fly down to Mumbai to spend her vacations in the big bad city of temptations. Back then, she and Divya would make lists of the handsomest boys in town and invite them over along with some of their plainer-looking friends.

'Tara, take a shower, dig into my make-up and wardrobe, and join the dinner.'

Tara hesitated, her reluctance visible.

'It's not the social set tonight,' Divya reassured her. 'Just a few visitors from America and a photojournalist interested in the family history. Besides, it's Vikram who should be hiding, not you.'

That seemed to strike a chord with Tara; she felt a sudden burst of energy and anger surge through her. She stepped into the shower, letting the warm water cascade over her. It felt like a balm to her wounded soul. Her fingers slipped into her hair and she rubbed the sore spot on her scalp, still tender and hurting from Vikram's rough grip.

Stepping out of the shower, she wrapped herself in a plush towel and stood in front of the mirror, hesitating to look up. She dabbed her face, wincing at the sight of the scar. It was raw and jagged—there was no way she would enter the party with that on her face.

Vikram had crossed the line. The injury on her body would heal with time, the pain would go away, but the wound inflicted on her dignity would stay. She did not want it to fade. It felt like a scar from a war—she needed to preserve it till it made her the woman no man would ever dare harm again.

'You look nice and fresh now,' said Divya encouragingly as Tara emerged in her robe. She then pointed towards a young girl standing by the dresser.

'Meet Rosy. Every pretty face in Mumbai has been painted by her,' she said with a grin.

'Divya, please! Give me a break. I am not in the mood to show my face tonight.'

'Fair enough. But let Rosy see if that mark can be concealed.'

'Sure. I would like to learn how to conceal it anyway.'

Tara sat down and submitted to Rosy's skilled fingers, which danced on her face, treating it like a canvas. Layers of corrective foundation and concealer softened the scar's appearance. Gradually, Rosy moved to the rest of Tara's face, and she didn't object. Her tired eyes were brightened with a touch of kohl, bronzer enhanced her dusky complexion and a soft lipstick complemented her full lips. Her lush hair was curled and styled into cascading waves.

'Look up, ma'am,' said Rosy.

Tara stared at her reflection, stunned by the transformation. 'I've never looked so glamorous,' she murmured.

'Stunning is the word,' chimed in Divya.

'She has worked magic,' Tara admitted, pleased.

'Now, would you like to sit in the room by yourself with that stunning face or make an appearance?'

'Honestly, I would rather sit on that beautiful terrace where we used to spend so much time. Not really in the mood to party.'

'Well, you will still need to pass through the living room,' Divya said, sliding open the doors of her wardrobe. 'Pick whatever you like. It's all yours. I promise, you will feel better once you are out there, beyond Vikram.'

Tara browsed through Divya's clothes, which leaned heavily towards high fashion—famous designers and ensembles bordering on the extreme—short skirts, sequined shirts with Swarovski crystals. *This is the wardrobe of a single girl in Mumbai and I am a married woman from Jaivangarh,* Tara thought.

Tara finally settled on a simple soft pink silk kurta with delicate thread embroidery. It felt subtle and understated—something that would make her unnoticeable. She put it on and then worked the hairbrush desperately to tame her mane. Tempted to remove the make-up, she thought of wiping it away but stopped when she realized how flawlessly the scar had been concealed. She did look good with Rosy's artwork on her face.

Tara peeped into the living room, taking a deep breath before pulling the door wide open and stepping inside.

'Who do we have here!' Kamala exclaimed. 'Darling, it's so nice to see you.' Kamala greeted Tara with a light hug, making sure her lipstick was not smudged.

'Thank you, aunty. I hope I am not intruding.'

'You are always welcome here, Tara. Your mother and I haven't spoken in years, but you are still like my child.' She hesitated, then looked at Tara pointedly. 'Your husband is not accompanying you?'

'He's...errrr...he's busy with work.'

'Really! What does he do?'

'He manages the family properties, aunty,' Tara replied quickly.

'Your family's properties, I suppose?' Kamala pressed.

'Yes, aunty. The museum and the lands.'

'Your questions, I am sure, can wait, Mum. I think Tara is exhausted,' Divya interjected, cutting off her mother's incessant questioning.

'Ah!' said Kamala. 'I get it. I am asking too many questions. But then, I always do, don't I? Come, sit with me for a while. It's been ages since I last saw you, Tara.'

Just then, the doorbell rang, cutting the tension that had been building up. The first guests arrived and Kamala broke into her perfect hostess smile.

The guests for the evening poured in, the living room filled with chatter, the din giving Tara a headache. A small Maltese pup sat neglected in the corner, wagging his tail eagerly at her. She bent down and lifted him. He seemed to enjoy the attention and curled into a comfortable position on her lap. *Strange,* she thought, as an unexpected sense of comfort enveloped her. She liked the feeling of his soft fur between her fingers. Something about this blissful creature made her believe in the kinder side of life. She gave him a hug and gently put him down when she noticed he had fallen asleep. She covered him with a blue napkin and he stirred and wagged his tail in his sleep.

The sea breeze swept into the room, its salty coolness drawing Tara to the wide terrace. She stepped out, walked to the edge and leaned against the banister. The breeze caught her hair, making it billow like a sail. It was a clear night, and in the distance, she could see the Naval Dockyard, the Gateway of India sitting at the centre and the dome of the Taj Mahal Hotel shining in the night glow.

Holding up her phone, she framed the Gateway carefully in the centre. Just as she tapped for the perfect shot, she heard another click. Startled, she looked back and saw a man with a large camera, its lens aimed in her direction.

'Hi, I am Kabir,' he said, extending his hand. 'Bored of the party like you.'

Tara hesitated but then decided to be civil and shook his hand.

'Do you want me to send you the picture I took of you with the Gateway?'

'You could delete it,' she replied curtly.

'I get it. I was just tempted—you looked beautiful. I apologize.'

'Well…that's okay, I suppose,' Tara said, shrugging her shoulders.

'No disrespect intended. I am a photojournalist,' he added, tapping the oversized camera hanging around his neck.

'Oh!' she said, feeling embarrassed at her reaction. 'I didn't realize that.'

'Clicking pictures is instinct for me,' Kabir explained. 'If I thought I'd lose one of the best shots I've ever taken, I wouldn't forgive myself.'

'Well, I can understand that,' she said thoughtfully. 'Pictures do capture a constantly moving world.'

'I am on a new assignment now, documenting the musical landscape of this country.'

'The musical landscape?' she asked, drawn into the conversation.

'Capturing sound through pictures is not easy, but then

nothing offbeat ever is.' He paused, sipping from the goblet he was holding. 'Can I get you a glass?'

Tara nodded. 'A red would be nice.'

As Kabir returned with a glass for Tara, the conversation between the two on the terrace continued, a quiet reprieve from the growing din of the party inside. 'I sense a Bengali accent,' Tara ventured, 'but it doesn't match your name.'

Kabir threw back his head and laughed, the terrace lights catching flecks of his hair.

'Well, here's the fun part. My full name is Mirza Kabir Dubey, but you can call me Kabir—or Mirza, if you prefer.'

'I have a choice of names, it seems,' she replied, a wry smile playing on her lips.

'My name represents who I am. Kind of a mix. My father is a Bengali and my mother is French.'

'Hmm… So where does the Mirza come from?'

'My father loved and admired Mirza Ghalib, so he called me "Mirza" and then it just stuck. My mother, on the other hand, came to India to research the poet Kabir and named me after her thesis subject.'

'Mirza Kabir Dubey,' Tara repeated softly.

'Tell me something about yourself.'

'What do you want to know?'

'How about starting with your name?'

'My name is Tara,' she said softly, as if it were a secret. She had to remind herself that Vikram was far away. 'Tara,' she repeated, a shade louder this time.

'Tara,' he echoed. 'Like the stars above.'

She looked at him; he was clearly waiting for her to go on.

'That's all I can say for now.' She had no plans of letting him into her life any more than required. She was tempted to walk back into the party, but she knew that would mean getting dragged into the cacophony of formalities.

'Tara is enough for me for now,' he said easily. 'Tara. I like the way it sounds. Taa-rrra,' he repeated, rolling the 'r' playfully.

'You have a slight accent,' she pressed on. 'What's your predominant culture—French or Bengali?'

'A blend, I guess. The two eccentric poets went their separate ways, so I grew up in France, while vacationing in Kolkata.'

'That explains it.' Tara smiled, perhaps for the first time since she had left home. She wasn't sure if it was the perfect Bordeaux red, the sea breeze or her desire to fly away to another reality, but Kabir made her forget, for a moment, the Tara she had left behind.

'So, where is home for you?' she asked Kabir.

'Home? That's a question I would love to have the answer to myself. For now, home is wherever I put my bag down. Officially, my passport says Paris though.'

Tara nodded but didn't say anything.

'Presently, my bags are down at a charming Parsi homestay,' Kabir added.

Her interest was piqued. She hadn't escaped her husband's battering only to face Kamala's caustic scrutiny for long. 'How much does this homestay cost?'

'It's reasonable; Rustom gives me a special rate and I give the vain old guy his best shots.'

'I would need to stop relying on Kamala aunty's hospitality at some point.'

'You might like the place. Rustom handpicks his guests to curate an eclectic group around his dinner table each night. He likes playing host.'

'Intriguing for sure.'

Kabir reached into his pockets and slipped her a card. 'Let me know if you are interested. The old man only accepts guests through a recommendation.'

Before Tara could reply, the clear chime of a silver bell rang out. 'Dinner is served!' Kamala's voice called.

The guests scattered across the living room and terrace made their way to the dining room, hoping for some great servings.

★

Kamala sat alone in the aftermath of the revelry, looking at the remains of the evening—the empty glasses, overflowing crystal ashtrays and traces of the many perfumes left behind by her guests. She liked to just sit there and go through the evening with Rajan, who was a good listener.

'Did you notice Aishwarya's daughter? She has an injury on her face that not even all that make-up could hide!'

'Kamala,' Rajan replied mildly, 'there could be many reasons. She's a bright girl; I have always liked her.'

'Well, then we don't share the same likes for sure.'

Meanwhile, back in her room, Divya triumphantly produced a bottle of Dom Pérignon, nestled deep in an oversized ice bucket, and two chilled glasses. 'Look, what I have smuggled in for us,' she said, as they changed into their night clothes.

'Ah! No more, please. I am already swimming in that stuff.'

Divya poured two glasses to the brim and passed one to her friend. 'Just a few sips.' She lifted her glass and clinked it against Tara's. 'To our friendship and the future.'

Tara smiled, her eyes misting slightly.

They sat on the floor, their legs stretched out, and chatted into the night. The moon slid lazily across the sky, its silvery glow casting soft shadows in the room.

Kamala came to the door and stood for a moment, wondering if she should interrupt them, but then quietly walked away.

'Now,' Divya said, 'tell me everything.'

'It's been four years now since our wedding. With each year, Vikram and I seemed to drift further apart. The reason is his complete commitment to my mother.'

'Did you say "commitment"?'

'Yes! He manages the family properties, and every waking hour is spent discussing them.'

'You should be a part of it. It's your father's, after all.'

'It's not just the properties. There is the priceless collection at the Maharaj Uday Singh Museum. There are family heirlooms and historical pieces of immense value—more than the properties. Grandpa was a collector—art, carvings, paintings and even some ancient jewellery. There's a Kashmiri shawl in the collection that dates back to the early 17th century.'

'And you, I am sure, want to preserve all that heritage.'

'Without my signatures, they are stuck. And I will not let them sell it off.'

'Brave girl,' said Divya.

'Not that brave. I overheard Vikram hiring a man on the phone...to kill me. They want me out of the way. That's why I fled from my home.'

Divya leaned forward and hugged her friend. 'That loser—look what he's lost. I am going to help you forget him and your mother, and start a brand new life.'

Tara looked tired but as Divya's words sank in, she exclaimed, 'Yes! I will find a new beginning. Perhaps...' she trailed off, sounding slightly confused.

'You won't find a new world, Tara. You have to create one. That's how it works.'

'I don't think I have the inclination or the energy.'

'Tonight, only positivity. Remember all those good times—the fun we had. We are still the same girls, and we can do it all again.'

She lifted her glass and Tara followed suit.

'To tomorrow, a new day,' said Divya.

'To a new sunrise,' said Tara, playing along.

Divya was determined to help Tara walk away—not just physically but in soul and mind—from the abusive marriage she had lived through.

'Now, tell me about that man you were speaking to—the photographer.'

'He's a photojournalist,' Tara corrected. 'But I am done with men for a lifetime. Never again, Divya.'

'Ah, life without a husband is fine, but without men, it would be rather dry. Take your time, Tara. For now, celebrate your freedom.'

The night wore on, and the wine turned delightfully toxic. Their voices grew louder—they were giggling and confessing secrets, loves, passions and fantasies.

'Did you sleep with that professor—Krish Sir?' Divya suddenly asked.

'Yes, yes, yes!' screamed Tara. 'Thank God I did—just not enough though,' she giggled.

'I have never been married, but I imagine sleeping with a husband is a tiresome experience.'

'You know what, Divya? It's a non-experience—repetitive, mechanical... Like it never happened. More like a proprietary right being exercised. Add that to your dictionary.'

'Ah!' Divya sighed. 'I wish you find a love that makes you feel complete.'

'Someone who gives me butterflies in my tummy,' Tara said with a childish giggle.

'I have felt those butterflies and it's all worth it. I have no regrets about the fact that I can't ever be Arjun's wife,' said Divya. 'Look at me—I am what every married man wants to acquire and what every woman envies.'

'Oh, I would do anything to be a mistress,' slurred Tara. 'That's my ambition. I will be someone's mistress one day.'

'I have to thank my family for that. Mom said, "You will not marry this man", so I said, "Fine, I will not marry him". Then two weeks ago, I packed my bags and moved to Delhi to live with Arjun. I have come home just to tell her personally before she hears it from someone else.'

'Well, I have a scandalous marriage,' said Tara with a shrug. She leaned closer and lowered her voice, adding, 'Don't tell anyone this, but I think my husband is having a wild affair with my mother.'

'What are you saying?' Divya was aghast.

'It's okay. It's platonic—an affair of the minds, perhaps. I am not sure, Divya.'

'An affair of the mind can be far more annoying than a man's occasional physical wanderings.'

'Well, he's given me a very good reason to run away in the middle of the night. Haven't you ever wondered why our architects designed such low banisters in our balconies?' Tara suddenly frowned and reached for her bag, pulling out a document. 'Before I forget, this is a power of attorney for handling my NGO. You just have to sign here.' She pointed to the bottom of a page.

'Why are you doing this?' asked Divya, confused.

'There are too many who bank on me. I want you to promise that you will take care of them.'

'I promise,' Divya said, her voice earnest and sincere.

'Thank you! Now let's get back to where we were!'

'And where was that?'

'To the boys who never got us,' said Tara with an effervescent laugh.

3

Curtains Down

Jaiveer Mahal was silent the next morning, as it always was the morning after one of Kamala's hedonistic parties. Kamala sat reading the morning papers on the balcony, sipping cinnamon tea from a porcelain cup, tossing bits of bread crumbs to the birds hopping around her. She enjoyed their company, but, unfortunately, they had a habit of flying away the moment the food ran out—*so much like humans*, she thought wryly.

'Hello, Tara,' she called out as her house guest approached in a robe.

'Hello, aunty,' greeted Tara cheerfully. 'That was a great party you organized last night.'

Kamala seemed to like that. 'Thank you, love. Last week, I had all the young aspiring actors over for dinner. It was lovely.'

Tara nodded and Kamala's gaze narrowed. 'Tara, when you are in my home, please remember I don't allow anyone to walk around in robes.'

Kamala's pointed tone irked her; clearly, she wasn't welcome here. Tara returned to her room and changed her clothes. As she looked at the mirror, brushing out her hair, Kamala's words echoed in her mind. Kamala and Tara's mother had been at war for years. Tara wondered if Kamala sensed a shade of her archenemy in her. This was not home for Tara and she had hardly ever felt so small. She was done being a burden, a responsibility, a mere thing to be handled and taken care of.

As she bent to put the brush down, her eyes fell on a thick embossed card. In sleek gold lettering, it said 'Rustom's'. Tara remembered Kabir's kind face; there was an earnest air about him. But then, didn't they all seem like that in the beginning? Should she consider it?

Now dressed in jeans, a T-shirt and slides, Tara made her way to the kitchen for coffee.

'Oh, at least you're dressed now,' Kamala remarked, her face hidden behind the newspaper.

Tara forced a smile but said nothing. As she turned towards the counter, Kamala spoke again. 'Say, Tara, do you want to borrow a pair of proper shoes from Divya? I've seen our maids wearing slides like those. It doesn't look nice, you know.'

That was it.

'Aunty, I am so grateful for your hospitality, but I will probably be moving out soon.'

Kamala didn't respond, her face still buried in the papers. She did not even make the slightest attempt to ask Tara to stay longer.

Tara was right. Her best friend's mother was waiting for her to leave their home.

★

The cab pulled into the iron gates of the old colonial mansion on Nepean Sea Road. The half-moon driveway led to a porch framed by rounded columns. Surrounded by skyscrapers, Rustom Mansion stood like a charming relic of the past in the heart of Mumbai.

Tara rang the bell and waited till a young man opened the door. 'Welcome to Rustom Mansion,' he said as he ushered her in.

'I am here to meet Mr Kabir Dubey,' she said, recalling his name partially. 'He is expecting me.'

'Hey, Tara! I am right here; was waiting for you,' said Kabir, stepping forward.

'This place looks charming. I hope you can help me with a room,' said Tara.

'Glad you approve! I will do my best,' he said and then

turned to the young man. 'Neville, I need a room for my friend.'

'Has she been invited by Rustom?' Neville asked.

'No, but do tell Rustom I have recommended her.' Then he added, 'Very highly.'

Neville made a quick call and returned. 'Rustom is delighted to invite the lady on your recommendation.'

Tara looked relieved and turned to Kabir. 'Thank you for being so helpful.'

Kabir smiled. He hadn't ever managed to figure out this old Parsi man. He was not quite sure whether Rustom ran the homestay for money or simply to surround himself with interesting people. What Kabir did know was that preserving Rustom Mansion was a passion for its owner.

Tara walked through the spacious lounge with high ceilings and intricately carved wooden edges. A crystal chandelier hung in the centre, adding to the grandeur. The floor was polished to perfection, the chequered black-and-white pattern of the marble gleaming.

Rustom Mansion reminded Tara of the home she had left behind. She felt a pang of pain—the word 'home' cut through her like a sliver of glass. She was running away from it, yet, ironically, it was nestled in her heart.

She gave Kabir a slight smile before ascending the long staircase to her room. She pushed open the heavy door and stepped inside the freshly painted turquoise-blue suite, her eyes taking in its ambience. It gave her the sense of a place that had been transported from another era. She liked the old mahogany bed; it had a strange spongy feel—a soft, caressing hold that came with overuse. Its musty, woody aroma soothed her. As Tara lay down, the sea breeze gently caressed her face like a soothing balm. The life that she had left behind—those nights of agony and shame—had ended and she finally felt at peace.

For now, Tara was content. No ghosts from her past, no memories, no dreams—just silence and complete tranquillity. Curled up like a baby, she drifted into a deep, serene sleep in her new bed far away from home.

4

Stars for Breakfast

Sunlight filtered through the curtains. Tara stirred, her eyes fluttering open. For a moment, she was confused as she looked around; then she realized that she had woken up in a new room and a new bed, yet felt a sense of absolute serenity.

Her fingers moved to the side table but before she could lift it, her phone rang, giving her a start. She glanced at it and froze, her face turning pale. Vikram had not given up. He had called her 25 times through the night. 'Vik' and a picture of his smiling face glared at her from the screen. Her hand trembled and the phone slipped from her grasp, falling to the ground. Its insistent ring continued for a while and then died.

Rising to her feet, Tara walked across to the window and flung it wide open. There it was—the ocean, stretching limitlessly, its salt-spiked breeze bracing. She wanted to forget where she'd come from and didn't care where she was going. She just wanted this moment to herself.

Tara looked out at Mumbai through the veil of mist that blew from the sea—the city in its purest form as people slept, exhausted and intoxicated. She watched the spotless empty roads, silent and strange, devoid of cars and big red buses. She stayed at the window till morning broke and watched the grind of the city, its wheels churning slowly, coming to life. Fisherwomen strode down the streets confidently, their hips swinging rhythmically as they carried baskets of fresh catch. Newspaper boys on bicycles flung dailies with perfect precision into sundry balconies. Children, with huge backpacks, gathered at bus stops. Somewhere, a sheepish playboy tiptoed back into bed before his wife noticed him missing.

A knock on the door startled her.

'Laundry?' called a voice.

Tara looked at her watch and rushed to change into her tracksuit. The smell of fresh bread wafted through the window, and she suddenly felt very hungry. Heading downstairs, she spotted Neville directing guests towards the open-air feast.

Breakfast at Rustom's was like being at a British garden party. Neville moved around with an oval tray, placing hot croissants, butter cubes wrapped in paper and home-baked scones on every table.

'Would it be eggs for you, ma'am?' he asked Tara politely.

'I am a vegetarian,' she replied with a smile. 'But I would love some hot coffee and a platter of fruits.'

'Coming right up, ma'am.' He nodded and then added, 'Before I forget, Rustom has sent an invitation for you to join his table tonight.'

'The chosen one!' Kabir's voice startled her as he appeared by her side. 'Can I join the lady?'

'Of course,' Tara said, relieved to find she wouldn't be eating alone.

'So, what's this about being the chosen one?' she asked, rolling her eyes.

'Rustom invites selectively, so consider yourself very lucky,' Kabir explained.

'Well, then, I am honoured,' Tara replied, smiling.

'How are you today?' he asked, looking into her eyes. 'Tara, you've told me very little, but if I can be of any help, please let me know.'

She met his gaze steadily, her walls firmly in place.

'I get it,' he said quickly. 'I won't ask you anything until you want to tell me yourself.'

Noticing the pensive look in her eyes, Kabir smoothly switched the topic. 'Ah, the stars,' he said, pointing towards the sky.

Tara looked up at the blue morning sky. 'Stars in the daytime? Is that supposed to be funny?'

'I have been reading about the invisibles around us. Trust me, they are there. Millions of them. But you can't see them because the sun outshines them all.'

'Hmmm… Your conversation is always quite fascinating, I must say. Stars for breakfast,' she teased, giggling at his attempt to lighten the mood.

'We are always under the stars, Tara, even in daylight. Just know they are watching over you all the time,' he said, poetically.

'Yes, I guess they are always there, above us,' she replied, looking up at the sky thoughtfully.

'You and I are also stars. Stars who left their hemispheres, set out on uncharted paths and then—boom—we collided.'

'Nicely explained.' Kabir had managed to bring a smile to her face once again.

'How else do you explain two people from opposite ends meeting? It's destiny, and one never questions it.'

'I do believe in destiny, but not in surrendering to it,' Tara replied, a touch of warmth in her voice.

'I believe in reincarnations as well, but I have a different view on it. I think one person lives many lives in a single lifetime. All those reincarnations happen right here, right now. You were someone else somewhere else, but for me, the woman I see before me was born just last night.'

He casually lifted the camera hanging around his neck. Tara flashed a smile as he clicked.

'I know you from this moment onwards,' he said softly.

'You certainly have appeared as a surprise friend and saviour, Kabir,' she said, defining their connection. 'I would have suffocated under Kamala aunty's glare otherwise.'

As she spoke, Kabir watched her expressions change—he was smitten but understood she needed time and, perhaps, he did too.

'Look at these,' he said, holding out his camera. 'I took these photos last night.'

Tara leaned in eagerly. His camera lens had stripped away the layers of make-up and captured the scar on her face.

'I had a fall,' she said.

'It's okay. We all do, and we heal soon enough.'

Tara wondered if this man had a sense of her or whether Divya had filled him in.

'The hardest to heal is the heart,' Kabir continued, as though speaking to himself.

'What's the most heartbreaking thing that can happen in life?' she asked, trying to draw him out.

'When someone goes away but their memory doesn't.' He stopped himself abruptly and tentatively reached out, his fingers wrapping around a loose strand that had fallen out from the bun at the nape of her neck. 'May I?' he asked.

She smiled back and didn't object. His fingers grazed her bare skin and she felt an odd sensation. His touch felt alien, yet so warm. Rather boldly, Tara turned to meet his gaze. The intensity in his eyes was palpable; the blue in them seemed to give way to the deep black of his dilated pupils. She felt his thumb brush against the pulse beneath her ear, tilting her face slightly.

'Perfect,' he murmured.

Her lips parted, but before she could say anything, something came over his face. His hand fell away just as naturally as it had risen. Clearing his throat, he smiled faintly and wordlessly resumed showing her the pictures.

'You mentioned you are here to photograph music,' she commented, regaining her composure.

'Yes,' he said. 'The next few weeks are going to be an adventure. From the music of red-light districts, where traditional instruments are used, to tracks made on modern systems for the films, I will go wherever my camera takes me, trying to capture the sounds. Challenging experiment!'

'How does one capture sound in a picture?'

'Come along with me and find out. Unless you have other plans,' he said.

Tara hesitated. Could she trust him? She had married a man whom she thought she knew completely, and he had shattered every rule in the book. She looked into Kabir's face and mulled over her thoughts. It was time to follow her instincts. *I have a good feeling about him*, she mused. *He's got kind eyes.*

'Yes, I will join you,' she told her new friend, the one who asked no questions.

Kabir smiled, resisting the urge to ask the question that lingered on his lips. He wondered what had made this beautiful woman come alone to Mumbai. *Who is she?* 'It's not my story to tell,' was Divya's cagey retort to his questions.

Tara looked down at her phone; it felt like a menacing presence. She dreaded the next time it would ring. Her fingers moved nervously over the keys before she slid them across the screen. The phone switched off with a click.

'I once wanted to remain untraceable, so I pulled the SIM card out,' Kabir mentioned casually.

Tara could feel him solving the jigsaw of her life. She pulled out the SIM, broke it into two and dropped it into the teacup.

Kabir nodded.

Tara was now untraceable.

Lifting her handbag, Tara stood up abruptly. 'I need to get some work done, so I will see you later.' With that, she walked away, leaving Kabir staring after her, confused.

If only there was a way to access my bank account, she thought as she stepped out of Rustom's. She knew she had to get to it before Vikram froze it.

As she walked down Nepean Sea Road, the sight of a big red bus stopping at the junction tempted her. She checked the route on the chart displayed and hopped on—a small act that made her feel liberated. Memories flooded back to the days when she would come down to the big city for a wild break, away from the restrictions of home—when Mumbai buses were her second home. She leaned across to an elderly man and asked for the nearest branch of her bank and was relieved to hear it was just a few stops away.

★

The bank manager had the air of confidence typical of their profession—crisp and reassuring—the kind that makes you leave your money behind with them in the belief that they will multiply it.

'So, Tara Kumari ji, what can I do for you today?'

'I'd like to access my account, but unfortunately, I have left my ATM cards back home in Rajasthan. I can give you my account number, though.'

'That's fine, madam. Everything is electronic these days.' He bent down and typed in her details into the system. 'Just give me a moment,' he said.

As he scanned the screen, his eyes narrowed and he leaned closer to the monitor. 'Madam, there is an LOC associated with your account—a look-out circular.'

'A look-out circular?' Tara echoed, bewildered.

'Madam, we like to protect our clients' privacy, but a look-out circular forces me to inform the...the authorities...' He hesitated and then added, 'That you have tried to access your account.'

'I haven't done anything to warrant that.'

'I am sure it's a misunderstanding, madam,' he mumbled. 'Please wait here a moment. I will consult with my seniors on how best we can handle this.'

Tara's stomach tightened. She could almost see the bank manager returning with a group of policemen and getting her arrested. She imagined being shoved into a van and taken to a lock-up. She looked around the empty cabin and decided to get away from the place.

Tara walked through the bank's large hall, feeling tense and exposed—as though every eye was on her. Moving swiftly, she emerged out of the building and flagged down the first cab she spotted.

Once inside, Tara's thoughts churned. She could feel Vikram on her trail and that made her feel like a hunted animal. He had planned it all quite meticulously, stripping her of her lifelines. By now, he would surely know her location. Vikram was smart; he knew she would try to access her accounts. The bait had been set perfectly.

Her eyes drifted to her hand, to the diamond on her finger catching the sunlight. She asked the cab driver to stop as they neared the busy Colaba shopping strip. Stepping out, her eyes scanned the shops' windows till she found what she was looking for—a jewellery store, its display laden with precious stones and intricately carved gold pieces.

The armed guard at the door gave her a scrutinizing look as she entered, stepping into the cool, air-conditioned interior. An hour later, when she emerged, the ring was no longer on her finger.

For all her efforts to keep Kabir at bay, she wanted to get back to him and ask him to take her far away—somewhere far beyond Vikram's reach. Suddenly, she felt a need for him.

It was time now for her to find her wings.

5

Rustom's Table

Tara lay in bed, staring up at the fan twirling laboriously, when the sharp buzz of the intercom broke the silence.

'Hey! You must be hungry, I bet,' came a voice.

'Ah, yes. Can't say I am not,' she replied.

'Well, you need to be at the dinner table by eight. The old man likes punctuality.'

Tara dressed just enough to look presentable and then walked down to the dining hall. She stepped inside and held her breath, blown away by the ambience. The dimly lit chandelier cast soft amber light on the polished teakwood floors. Piped music floated through the air, mingling with the lively chatter of Rustom's guests—some seemed to know each other, while others looked new to this wonderland.

Rustom Mansion was one of the wealthiest homes in the city. Once at the centre of the textile trade, the family had dwindled, with children moving abroad and the business shuttered. Rustom Jehangir had been a lonely man until he turned his mansion into an ingenious invitation-only homestay, where he filled his life with interesting people. If you were creative or intriguing enough, you would be invited.

Tara was curious as she entered Rustom's dining room, and she wasn't disappointed. This live dinner theatre was everything she could have imagined.

Dressed in a tuxedo and bow tie, Rustom Jehangir Bulsara was the very image of a '60s film star, who had aged gracefully with time. Slim to the point of appearing gaunt, his hair was unapologetically silver. A walking stick rested against his chair—an extravagant, intricate masterpiece with a sharp gold trim and an enamel top—a sound match for the man who walked with it. There was no doubt that Rustom was part of the old guard, living in a state of opulence he wasn't entirely aware of.

'This is Tara,' Kabir introduced his new friend to Rustom.

'Good evening, madam,' he greeted her with a smile, extending his hand. 'Tara, we have a code here. A first-time guest sits at the head of the table,' he continued, guiding her to one end of the long rosewood table.

Tara sat in the chair that Rustom had pulled out for her and took in the elegant detailing of his famous table—tall, slim candles in silver candelabra casting a warm glow on a floral centrepiece; the polished silverware and starched white napkins laid out added a touch of timeless charm.

Rustom took his seat at the opposite end of the table. The other guests, noticing that their host had taken his seat, quickly disengaged themselves from their conversations and moved towards the table, wine glasses in hand, searching for their name cards.

A long-haired, jean-clad youngster, barely out of college, sat down on one side of Tara. 'Hey,' he said, smiling cheerfully.

A lady in a crisp khadi sari and an intricately painted bindi smiled at Tara as she sat down on her other side. 'New to Rustom's?'

'I am,' Tara replied.

'Welcome to the adventure,' the woman said with a kind smile.

From his seat near Rustom, Kabir glanced at Tara, giving her a reassuring smile. She smiled back formally, comforted by his presence.

The butler poured a dash of wine for Rustom to taste. All eyes were on the host as Rustom waited patiently for the wine to settle before he started swirling it. Picking it up, he took a deep whiff before taking a solemn sip—his guests waited. Slowly, he tipped his head back and swallowed, then carefully set his glass back down and nodded. The butler recognized his cue and proceeded to pour the wine for the rest of the guests.

'To Tara,' Rustom declared, raising his glass. 'Thank you for finding me worthy of hosting you,' he added humbly. As the others raised their glasses, Rustom continued, 'One of my missions is to resurrect lost recipes. So don't be surprised if what you find on your plate looks unusual. I assure you, I only serve what is edible.'

Tara's gaze dropped to the crockery with the family crest. A flood of memories surged—the dinner table at home, the insignia proudly displayed on every teacup. The memory unnerved her visibly. The young boy beside her enquired, 'Are you okay?'

Tara turned towards him with a polite smile. 'I am fine,' she replied casually.

'You are sweating a lot.'

'That's because it's hot,' she said dismissively.

The meal began and Tara discreetly checked if she still remembered her years of dining etiquette. To her relief, she was doing far better than the boy next to her, who was sneaking sideways glances every time she reached for her cutlery. Tara chuckled to herself.

Just as their main course was over, dessert was served along with an aperitif.

'If it's all right with you, would you just leave the bottle here?' the young boy asked the server.

'Why, will you be serving us tonight, Rana?' Rustom chuckled. 'Well, go on then. Let's see how you made money in graduate school.'

Rana returned the old man's smile, running a hand through his choppy hair. 'Of course, Rustom, make me serve, why don't you?' It seemed as if this easy banter was an inherent part of their relationship, in whatever strange way it might have been forged. Like a good sport, Rana draped a cloth over his shoulder and, with an almost professional finesse, swathed the lower half of the bottle in his neighbour's crisp napkin.

'This Martini Rosso is an excellent choice,' he began, adopting the airs of a connoisseur. 'The dryness of vermouth cuts the

decadence of the last course and cleanses the palate for dessert.'
He paused, then added with a cocky lift of his brow and a
cheeky smile, 'Except, Rustom, aperitifs are served before dinner,
my friend.' With a dramatic flair, he moved around the table,
stopping at each guest to expound on the virtues of vermouth.
'If you notice, the slight—'

'Rana, be care—'

'Just a minute, Rusto—'

Before he could finish, Rana tripped. The bottle of wine
hurtled down the length of the table, spinning wildly before
crashing against a plate. It ricocheted, spilling wine all over the
white tablecloth until Kabir stopped it with a steady hand.

'I was going to say be careful,' Rustom said gravely, though
his twinkling eyes betrayed his mirth. 'There is a loose tile there.'
The servers rushed to clear the mess, scooping up shattered pieces
of glass. Rana hovered sheepishly behind Mr Nair, a geologist,
dabbing at the man's wine-splattered collar. 'I'm so sorry,' he
kept mumbling.

'Look at what you've created, though, Rana,' Rustom mused
from his seat.

Tara looked at Kabir quizzically, who gave her a subtle nod,
as though urging her to wait and see.

'It's the path of a mistake,' Sacha, an artist seated beside Kabir,
chimed in. He was dressed in a pair of tan chinos rolled up at
the ankles and a black shirt with tiny watermelons printed on it.

'Why, yes!' Rustom looked at Sacha, a look of inspiration
crossing his face. 'You're right, Sacha!' He got up and ambled down
the table. 'This is the beginning—the sowing of the seeds… Look
at the little droplets.' He moved Tara's glass aside to reveal tiny dots
of wine that had fallen from the rim of the glass on the tablecloth.

'And here—this is excitement, the propeller of action.' He
pointed to a row of three tiny stains, evidence of Rana's enthusiastic
misstep.

Continuing to where Mr Nair sat, Rustom gestured to a sprawling blot of wine. 'And this…this is the moment. The striking of inspiration. That great instance when you lose control of your creation and it takes hold of you…of itself. Magnificent!'

Tara was bemused. Rustom, of course, was no great art critic, but she appreciated his inquisitiveness and his fearless will to try. She pondered it and realized that this man wasn't all wrong. Who was she, after all, to decide what constituted art? Years of rigid training in miniature painting under her very strict teacher at the family museum had made her quite dispassionate about the subject, but here, Rustom seemed to have a free rein, unfettered by convention. *These were wine stains, for God's sake!*

'And that, my friends,' Rustom concluded, 'is the climax. A complete rupture of pre-existing sensibilities. It is what it is, existing in itself. No questions asked. The dénouement, if you will.' He looked up then, a small smile playing on his lips, directed at no one in particular.

'Wow, Rustom! Didn't know you had it in you,' remarked Kabir.

'You might want to save this tablecloth before it's sent out for dry-cleaning!' quipped Sudha, one of Delhi's well-known philanthropists.

Rustom replied with something that Tara didn't quite catch. Her eyes followed the quirky old man as he returned to his seat and fell into a conversation with Sacha.

Tara leaned back in her chair and wondered how she had ended up here. Unpleasant memories began to surface and she felt her throat constrict. With a deep breath and firm resolve, she straightened in her seat. She would take things one day at a time, but first, she was going to relish the éclair with apricot jam filling in front of her.

Across the table, Rustom looked pleased with his collection of guests that night. 'Tonight, we have an eminent research scholar from Banaras Hindu University, an artist, a philanthropist, a geologist, a pianist, a photojournalist, and of course, the great music maestro.'

All eyes turned to a man with a rather crisp French beard and long hair that fell in tight, shiny curls. He wore a denim shirt over a white lungi, a string of beads adorning his wrist.

'Guru Darshan Das, fondly called Guruji,' Rustom continued, 'is a maestro, yet he spends his evenings teaching children from the nearby slums to play the sitar.'

'Rustom, dear friend, you are so kind. Living here has given my art great spiritual avenues. Your home has an aura… A history that inspires me,' Guruji replied with a smile.

'Guruji,' Tara ventured with an eager smile, 'I do play the sitar, but if I could have some lessons with you, I would be honoured.'

He smiled and seemed to consider her for a moment. 'Come tomorrow and let's see if you have the patience to learn from me,' he said.

As dinner concluded, the group moved to the informal lounge for some coffee, the guests still immersed in conversation.

'How about some pure melody tonight?' Rustom suggested, looking at Kanishk Puri, the pianist.

'My pleasure,' said Kanishk, walking up to the grand piano. He paused, fingers poised above the keys, then glanced at their host. 'This one is for you, Rustom.'

Then, he began to sing: 'In this world of ordinary people, extraordinary people, I am glad there is you. In this world of overrated pleasures and underrated treasures, I'm glad there is you.'

The lilting words from Julie London's album seemed to please Rustom. He raised his glass to the pianist. The room fell into a hush, the melody casting a spell over the guests. Rustom broke the reverie, rising to his feet in applause as the tune faded—and, as if awakened, the entire room followed suit.

Tara sat in a corner, more a spectator than a participant. The opulence of Rustom Mansion reminded her of Jaivangarh Palace. She ached to catch a plane back and claim her place in the home she had left behind. Yet she knew all too well that home could often be a dangerous place for a woman.

While she remained wrapped in her thoughts, a new guest entered the lounge and sat down next to Guruji. There was an unmistakeable camaraderie between them. The newcomer suddenly stood up and wandered towards what appeared to be the smoking area. He lit a cigarette and inhaled deeply. The white kurta he wore defined his shoulders rather well and the sheer material did little to hide the hard lines of his chest. A diamond glinted in his left ear. As he ran a hand through his salt-and-pepper hair—more pepper than salt—Tara noticed his long, elegant fingers.

Her breath hitched. She knew that face too well. She had seen it before, almost every night in her room, on her large television screen.

Through the haze of smoke, Vivan Mehta raised his eyes and looked at Tara. He took in her luminous eyes, strong black brows, sharp chin, slightly pointed nose and the full lips set against a warm, swarthy complexion. He found her presence compelling.

As their gazes met, Tara held her breath. He seemed just as handsome; the greys at his temple and the slight lines on his forehead made him look older—and all the more appealing.

Embarrassed that he had noticed her staring at him, Tara looked away quickly. She moved to join Kabir, who was deep in conversation with the research scholar. Yet her mind remained on Vivan. When she glanced over her shoulder, she found him still watching her.

'Can we leave, please?' she whispered in Kabir's ear.

'Good night, ladies and gentlemen,' Rustom announced his exit. 'Please carry on with the evening.'

'Let's go, please,' Tara insisted and a reluctant Kabir escorted her out.

As they stepped out of the room, Tara turned to Kabir. 'Vivan Mehta. The actor. How is he here?'

Kabir shrugged. 'He is a disciple of Guruji. Rustom's dinners are a life-changing experience. You are never the same after a week at his table.'

He was right. Tara's life would never be the same again.

6

Café Colaba

Colaba Causeway, Mumbai's famed foreign goods market, was a treasure trove of flashy mobile phones, duplicated Rolex watches and cheap Chinese fabric displayed on makeshift platforms that vanished into thin air at the slightest whisper of a police raid. It was the common man's haven of attractive goods at unbeatable prices. Bargaining was the lingo of this marketplace, and only a novice would fail to haggle.

'How much?' asked Kabir, picking up a bright blue Nokia phone.

'Two thousand.'

'Forget it,' Kabir waved him off and began to move ahead.

'Come on, sir. You say how much you'll give.'

'You tell me. You are the chap who is selling, aren't you?'

'Okay, sir, ₹1,500. Swear on my mother, you will not get a better price. I am only making ₹100 on it.'

'Better price, please,' urged Kabir.

'Swear on my—'

'Okay, old boy, no more swearing on your family. You've got me.' Kabir pulled out his wallet and handed over the cash as the delighted vendor activated the phone.

With his new purchase in hand, Kabir walked down to the Irani restaurant where he was meeting Tara. She had gone to Guruji's for her first lesson. He glanced at his watch and realized he was early. Nausheen, the owner's son, lounged behind the counter with a bored look on his face until he spotted his favourite customer. He hadn't forgotten the day Kabir had requested to take a picture of him with his family for a feature on Mumbai's second-most iconic phenomenon—the Irani cafés (the first being the *dabbawala*s).

A small set of Iranians had moved to Mumbai several generations ago and had dotted the city with Irani restaurants, which in time became an institution. Quite surprisingly, they did not serve Iranian food but offered a mix of tea, snacks and hearty meals. Halfway between a café and a restaurant, they were the perfect hangouts for a city that was always on the move.

'What would you like today, Kabir sir?' asked Nausheen.

'I am waiting for my friend. But tell me, how have you been?'

'Good, sir… But you might not be served here in a month from now.'

'You can't be serious.'

'My elder brother Nadeem wants to sell the property to Pizza Hut. Says our time is over.'

'Is that him? That grumpy fellow over there?' Kabir asked, pointing to a huge man sitting at the far counter, eyes buried in the cash box.

Kabir walked over and leaned on the counter to make eye contact. 'Hello,' he said cheerfully with a smile but was met with a stone-faced nod. Undeterred, he pressed on. 'Nadeem, this city is fast losing its classic properties to the land mafia. Look at the ambience of your place, its colonial chairs and long ceiling fans. It is part of the city's history, etched in the heart of every Bombayite.'

'Tell them to match the builder's price, then,' Nadeem replied curtly, hammering out the next bill without looking up.

Kabir moved away and took his table, calling out for a cup of tea. He hoped Café Colaba would always be here for him. Opening his copy of Pablo Neruda that he had carried with him, he began to read, losing himself in the verses until he felt her hand on his shoulder.

He looked up at her face—there was something vulnerable about her, a child-like quality. Seeing her made him feel that the world was pure and innocent, as though she were his perfect escape to another reality—much like the one he often sought through his camera lens.

She slumped into the chair across from him, an exhausted expression visible on her face.

A waiter appeared to set down Kabir's cup. 'Tea?' he asked Tara.

'Sure, and some sandwiches would be nice. I am rather hungry,' she replied.

Kabir placed the order and turned to her. 'How was your first music lesson at Guruji's?'

'Like an out-of-body experience.'

'So... You want to tell me about last night's escape?'

'What escape?'

'You know exactly what I'm talking about!' he chided gently. 'Leaving the moment Vivan Mehta came in. Do you know him?'

Tara met his gaze with clear eyes. 'To a man who has been my support in a new city, I can't lie. But the truth is embarrassing.'

'It's your choice.'

She took a deep breath. 'Okay, I will confess. As a young girl, he was my first crush. I thought I would outgrow the infatuation, get over a celluloid image, but it remained with me. Even as I grew older... Even till last night—except he was no longer a celluloid image. It is surreal when you've had someone's image floating in your mind for years, someone you've had absolute adulation for, and then that person suddenly appears in front of you, as if they stepped out of a screen and walked up to you! It is disconcerting.'

'Oh, really? He's played quite a big part in your life for someone you never met. But then, illusions are so much more exciting than reality.'

'I believe in the illusionary world. Vivan Mehta was a part of mine.'

'What do you like about him? What does he have that I don't?' Kabir asked playfully.

'He has my father's eyes. That same mix of blue-grey-green I can never quite pin down. Eyes I could never forget.'

'Aha! I could pull off that colour with a good pair of contact lenses,' he teased.

'You have so much that he doesn't,' she replied with a sincere smile.

'If only we could roll all the best qualities of good men into one perfect being, wouldn't that be great?' Kabir grinned.

'Perfection is rather self-defeating. It gets boring,' Tara mused. Her fingers instinctively moved to the spot she used to wear her ring. The absence felt strange, sort of like a reflection of the emptiness in her life. It was perhaps a sign—a symbol of breaking away from her past.

She looked up at Kabir, his compassionate eyes tempting her to divulge every word that was swelling in her mind, but she hesitated. She needed time to escape the past completely; it was all too fresh in her mind. Walking back through those memories would singe her.

'I am sorry to shatter your perfect illusions, but Vivan Mehta isn't just an actor anymore. He is now a hard-headed mafia man, deeply connected to the land sharks—a fixer for shady political and real estate deals. That's how he finances his passion for films.'

'I wish you hadn't told me that. I don't need to know the real man, do I?'

'I understand, but you would have found out eventually. He is trying to grab the mansion out of Rustom's hands. I am sure you have realized by now that Rustom is sitting on quite a piece of real estate.'

This, Tara had no trouble believing. Mumbai was infamous for its real estate prices. 'I have known people like that. They look for the vulnerable and swoop in at the perfect time,' Tara commented with great vehemence.

Kabir raised an eyebrow at her reaction but knew better

than to ask questions. Instead, he steered the conversation into lighter waters. 'Rustom has had a raunchy past. He was called "Romeo Rustom". To live up to his fame, he is rumoured to have climbed the steeple of St Anthony's Church to hang streamers for his girlfriend's birthday.'

'Rustom Valentino,' joked Tara, trying to visualize their grey-haired host as a wild young man. 'You were right when you spoke of the many lives we go through in one lifetime.'

'Despite the stories, he's a good man.'

Tara relaxed, her guard lowering as she reached absent-mindedly for Kabir's cup and took a sip of his tea. Realizing what she'd done, she blushed and set the cup back down.

A smile played on the corner of Kabir's lips. He reached for her hand and slid the Nokia into her palm.

'What is this?' Tara asked, surprised.

'A new phone and a new number. I'd like to be able to contact you when I'm not around.'

Something warm spread through Tara's chest, a feeling she quickly tried to squash down. With a half-smile that often graced her face when she was trying to hide her feelings, Tara took the phone and turned it on. A notification lit up the screen: the calendar app displayed a tiny icon of a full moon with a red ring, indicating that it was Karva Chauth.

The sight jolted her. She stared at the screen, her thoughts suddenly unravelling. *Am I married or not? If I am married, then why am I not in my home?* Rustom Mansion had become her temporary sanctuary, a place of comfort, but she understood that time was running out. The road could not be her home forever, and that was the truth.

The waiter appeared with their order and placed it on the table with a flourish.

Kabir watched Tara push a bite-sized sandwich around her plate.

'What is the matter? Are you on a diet?' he teased gently, hoping to ease the tension on her face.

'It's Karva Chauth today,' she replied, holding up her phone's illuminated screen for him to see.

'It's what?'

'It's the day all married women fast.'

'So you are married,' Kabir said, his tone deliberately measured.

'Yes, I am married, Kabir,' she replied. She waited for him to respond, but instead he clenched and unclenched his hand. He exhaled slowly and then turned to face her. His expression betrayed the many thoughts that ran through his mind.

'Do you still care enough to fast for that man?' he finally asked.

'I hate that man.'

'Then why fast for him? I don't get all this.'

'Don't try to,' Tara replied simply. 'Since I was a little girl, I was taught that this fast holds a person's lifeline. There are beliefs we live our lives with, Kabir, and they don't follow logic.'

'I am confused, Tara. Doesn't seem to me like you had a good husband,' said Kabir.

Without looking up, Tara picked up the small sandwich and brought it close to her lips before placing it back on the plate.

'Stick with your belief,' sighed Kabir. 'Just a few more hours to go, after all.'

'Oh, Kabir,' she said, reaching across the table to give his hand an affectionate squeeze. 'Why is faith so compelling?'

'Well, that's why they call it faith. No questions asked,' replied Kabir.

★

That night, Tara stood on the small balcony outside her room. The reflection of the full moon shimmered in a bowl of water as she performed the ritual motions mechanically. Once done, she dug into the sandwich Kabir had carried for her all day.

She glanced at Kabir, who stood by the door, and he got a sense of her feelings—she wanted him to hold her. After a moment, he turned and left, walking down to his room. Inside, he unlocked his phone and stared at a picture of someone he had left behind. For a fleeting moment, he was tempted to return to Tara's room and tell her about his life back in France. But the timing felt wrong.

Upstairs, Tara brushed her hair and sat down at the small writing desk in her room. Opening her diary, she wrote until she had emptied her thoughts on to the blank pages. She needed to tell someone the truth, and her diary was patient and silent till the day she would feel ready to let its contents light up the sky. The day she felt was coming closer.

7

Streets of Desire

The night sky hid many facets of the city, and the underbelly of its oldest nightlife hub was one of them.

'You still have time to bail out,' said Kabir, glancing at the elegant woman beside him.

She smiled and lifted her chin. 'I am a tough girl.'

'Well, get ready with your toughest side then,' he replied, unconvinced.

The heady cocktail of stench and scents that preceded Kamathipura was intoxicating. If a perfumer were to shut his eyes and guess the ingredients, it would send him into a 90° twirl of confusion. The pungent tang of sweat and body fluids mingled with the soft fragrance wafting from an attar seller's stall; the sharp sweetness of chewed paan leaves clashed with the smoky trail of burning incense, leaving a strange, lingering taste on the tongue—tinged with the briny breath of the sea.

Rows of women, young and ageing, perched behind barred windows like exotic birds in cages, their hair adorned paradoxically in chaste white strings of *mogra*, the aphrodisiac of flowers.

Tara wondered how men of all ages risked death and disease each night to seek bodily solace in these streets. She looked at the women and noticed their tired eyes and joyless grins, which had long forgotten how to smile or feel ripples of joy in their bellies. The gaudy make-up shone under the halogen lights, giving them a plastic doll-like, surreal glow.

The smudges on Vikram's shirt flashed through her mind—the tell-tale marks of a lipstick shade different from her own. She felt a wave of discomfort wash over her, her pulse racing at the sight of this decaying environment, the utter despair and the dismal pain of this montage. She could almost smell the dying and rotting dreams in this place where women sold their bodies for money.

It was known that many had ended up here spurned from the glamorous world of Bollywood—runaways from small towns lured by the glitz of Mumbai's arch lights.

Tara looked decidedly unsteady, and Kabir held her by the shoulder, realizing that this was probably more than what she had asked for.

'You really shouldn't have come along,' he said, shaking his head.

'Why not?' she retorted stubbornly. 'I have no problem being here.'

Kabir smiled, seeing through the brave front she was trying to put on.

'Alright, the address is up here. Are you ready for the climb?'

Tara peered up the steep cemented staircase dimly lit by a soft blue glow. She lunged forward, her determined stride leaving Kabir amused.

At the top, a hefty man in a khaki pathani suit greeted them with a lurid smile. 'Hello, sahib,' he whispered, his voice oily. 'Is it for both of you?'

Kabir pulled out a slip of paper from his pocket and read the name on it, hesitantly. 'I am looking for Heeralal. Arvind bhai sent me...'

The man's expression shifted instantly. 'Salaam, sahib. You must be Mr Kabir Dubey. Please accept my apologies—I mistook you for a customer.'

'I understand. This is, after all, peak business hours,' Kabir replied dryly.

The man laughed nervously, then led them inside.

The room was lined with rows of cotton mattresses and bolsters, the bright pink walls plastered with prints of Aishwarya Rai. The Bollywood star's radiant smile made Tara feel decidedly uncomfortable. Seeing her favourite star trapped in this seedy place, she had an irrational urge to peel the images off the walls, as if rescuing her.

A small brass pedestal in the corner held a huge clay vase filled with bright plastic flowers. A brass globe inlaid with coloured glass was suspended from the ceiling. As it rotated with the soft breeze, it cast shifting patterns of tinted light across the room. A sort of mood builder.

Finally, Heeralal appeared, a small-built man with beady eyes. 'Arvind bhai said you would like to take pictures. By all means, sir. What bhai says is law for me. He sends me my best customers,' he rattled off.

'I am looking for natural shots—just capturing the night as it unfolds.'

'Of course, sir. Take as many pictures as you like. You can also meet the young ladies if you want to.'

'I would like to talk to them a bit. Just get a sense of their lives here.'

Just then, a woman walked in with a swagger that was unmistakably alluring and seductive, yet also forbidding at the same time. It was obvious she knew the importance of holding back, which was imperative to the art of giving. The chalky white compact she wore did little to conceal her perfectly flawless skin. Her large eyes were lined with a deep black eyeliner that extended at the corners in a '60s-style flourish. Her mouth, perhaps a bit too small for a seductress, was accentuated with bright red lipstick. A carefully placed black beauty spot near her mouth added to her allure, and when she spoke, Kabir couldn't help but notice her cultivated tone.

'Salaam,' she greeted softly, her fingers gracefully cupped in front of her face, with a slight bend of the head in a traditional gesture of respect. 'Heeralal, did you offer our guests some sherbet?'

Her tone left no doubt that she was the mistress of the establishment. Heeralal mumbled an apology and rushed out to fetch the drinks.

'We have a reputation to uphold, sahib,' Salma Bai continued, making eye contact with Kabir and completely ignoring Tara. 'There is a reason we are known as the finest *kotha* in Kamathipura.'

A slim girl, far too young for such a setting, walked in with a glass of red liquid and a copper jug placed on a floral acrylic tray. Her eyes remained lowered all the while. Salma Bai raised her hands and took the tray from the girl; serving, it seemed, was part of her craft.

She lifted the glass in her hands, her brightly painted nails matching the drink's colour, and offered it rather ceremoniously to Kabir.

Kabir accepted the glass and took a sip. She looked at him for a response. 'Very refreshing,' he remarked, feeling her gaze on him.

'It is a special rose drink I make for my valued visitors. The recipe was passed down by the previous keeper of this house. It contains 40 different herbs blended into a rose base and it has been known to energize even the most tired souls.'

'It is truly invigorating,' mumbled Kabir.

As if just noticing Tara, Salma Bai turned to her. 'And for you, madam,' she said, pouring a greenish liquid from the copper jug, 'here is the refreshing *khus*.' She then set the jug aside on a tray near her and passed the glass to Tara with almost no eye contact.

Salma Bai had eyes only for men. She stared at Kabir with rapt attention, her gaze not leaving his face for a moment. She spoke sparingly but with precision, her tone carefully modulated to make Kabir feel as if he were the only man in the world she would ever want to be with. Like a seasoned chess player who had mastered the strategy, she knew that to captivate a man, she first had to make him feel like a king.

She surveyed his face, assessing her progress. Salma Bai hoped that Kabir would become a regular, now that he had experienced the potent concoction in which she had mixed a tablet of Viagra. She had heard that everybody in America was taking it.

How little the Westerners understood the true pleasure of such enhancements. The pleasure of taking it unknowingly was what made the difference. In her view, she was doing the men a favour by making them feel that inexplicable sense of pride in their virility, which they often attributed to her presence. She allowed them a little win, only to ultimately conquer them.

Kabir found his experience photographing nude models in the Bahamas or capturing the stunning beauties of Paris Fashion Week every year to be far simpler than this situation. This encounter, in comparison, was proving to be more complex. He pulled out a handkerchief from his pocket and dabbed his forehead, overwhelmed by the intensity of the moment. His reaction didn't go unnoticed by Salma Bai.

'You are certainly a fascinating lady, Salma Bai,' he mumbled.

She liked what she heard. She liked what she saw. But the rules of the game were strict. Every man was a customer, and until he asked for something, it would be kept out of reach.

Kabir felt disarmed by her complete control over her environment.

Tara, on the other hand, felt irritation prickling at her nerves. She tried to rationalize it, but it was proving impossible to define. She couldn't be jealous or possessive about a man she had met two days ago. Could she? Her heart pounded as she watched Salma Bai play her game, waiting for the kill. It reminded her too much of the evenings she had watched her mother charm Vikram while she looked on helplessly. Tara's stomach churned.

★

The night deepened, and a crowd began to gather on the floor seating. The crackling speakers blared the timeless *mujra* number from *Pakeezah*, 'Inhi Logo Ne Le Lina Dupatta Mera'. Salma Bai's face lit up with appreciation as one of her more talented girls glided into the room.

Dressed in a bright magenta *ghagra* shimmering with *zari* embroidery, she lowered herself in a graceful salaam, her gaze demurely avoiding the audience. Her face was partially visible through a delicate net veil, stopping enticingly just above her lips. She began to sway gently to the music, her movements sensuously slow and seductive at first and then building momentum, keeping up with the escalating tempo of the music.

Finally reaching a crescendo, the dancer crossed over to the next level and performed her best act with a flourish, moving in Sufi-like twirls, endlessly rotating—each revolution more engaging than the last. The men erupted in applause, roaring their delight.

'*Wah*! Thirty *chakkars*!' Salma Bai declared, awarding her disciple with attention and praise. The room was now echoing with compliments for the performer as every eye stayed fixed on the young dancer.

Kabir was observing it all through his camera lens, capturing the rhythm, the echoes and the orchestra the dancer had managed to create with the *ghungroo* on her feet. Was this simply the Pigalle of the East? As Kabir looked out of the window, he realized how wrong he was. Through the sheer curtain, he could see men being led into sleazy back rooms. He wasn't sure if it was just his imagination, but he could swear that, beneath the crackling of the stereo, he had heard faint cries—moans of pleasure or pain, and some shrieks too. The young faces looked exhausted, their body odour beginning to mix with the sandalwood incense that burned all around. There was a veil of pain in everything he saw, even in the dancer's eyes.

Salma Bai turned her attention back to her special guest. Being an artist in these lanes was unrewarding, and she longed to get her story out into the world. 'So, sahib, where did you say this article will come out?'

'In France. The magazine is called *Le Monde*.'

'Okay. I will tell you my story as long as you promise it will never be printed here.'

'You have my word,' Kabir assured her, adjusting his recorder.

Salma Bai described her privileged childhood in an affluent Andheri household. She had attended a good school and had been ahead of the other students.

'Always first in my class. Yes, always,' she insisted, flashing a confident smile. 'You see, I was destined to be a winner, and even now I am the best in my trade...'

As she narrated her story, Kabir expertly clicked away, capturing the shifts in her expressions as she spoke into the tiny recorder he had pinned on her shoulder. In a matter of moments, the emotions on her face changed several times. At one point, tears welled up in her eyes when she recalled how, as a young and vulnerable girl, circumstances had led her to the streets of desire.

On the dance floor, the young performer revelled in the applause and admiration of the audience. Tara, seated cross-legged on the mattress, followed her movements, her body swaying to the music in perfect synchrony.

Intrigued by the only woman sitting among a group of lusting men, the young girl smiled coyly at her. As their eyes met, the dancer playfully waved at Tara.

Tara glanced at Kabir, but his attention was fixed on Salma Bai, his camera lens capturing her face. Irritated, Tara stood up abruptly and joined the young dancer, her feet stamping the wooden floor, her hands flailing, her body moving in perfect tandem with the sensuous beats.

The monsoon crackled through the skies over the city, a streak of lightning lit up the room and a gush of rain-scented wind swept in through the open windows as Tara felt herself transported to another night when she had danced in the fields of Jaivangarh, risking Vikram's wrath. She moved in frenzy, becoming the dance itself. The young performer was taken aback and tried to outdo the challenger on her dance floor, but eventually conceded, stepping back in awe.

Kabir sat frozen, shocked and confused. The unflappable Salma Bai also seemed to be holding her breath.

'You didn't tell me that you had brought this girl to join our establishment,' she finally spoke. 'She is a trained dancer, it seems.'

Kabir's face turned crimson as he strode towards Tara, grabbing her hand and pulling her away with a forceful jerk. Like the tip of a knife revisiting a gash, the memory of Vikram's grip on her hair came back to haunt her. She wrenched her arm free from Kabir's grip and fixed him with a piercing glare before walking out of the room.

She wasn't going to let any man hold any power over her again—not today, not ever.

Without even a cursory goodbye to his hostess, Kabir rushed out following Tara. Weaving his way through the narrow, crowded staircase, brushing past rows of men, he made it down to the street.

Salma Bai watched him leave, her lips pursed in annoyance. This was not the kind of defeat she tolerated or even accepted. *He will return*, she told herself, and turned to Heeralal to get feedback on the heavyweights worth spending her time on. The night was still young, after all, and there was a lot of work for her to handle.

Kabir looked around and was struck by the rain-drenched empty road. Tara had vanished. His first reaction was panic. Sheer panic. His eyes darted up to where rows of girls leaned out of windows, their plunging necklines and painted faces coercing passers-by. This was no place to lose a decent young woman.

He ran, colliding with cyclists and hawkers. Makeshift stalls glowed under streetlights. Brightly coloured boxes of condoms glinted like treasures, prominently displayed in stacks. 'Kohinoor, Queen of the Night. Take one along, sir,' a voice called out. 'Better than a lifetime of problems.'

Kabir pushed past flower sellers and food vendors that lined the street. Finally spotting a stray taxi, he waved it down and jumped in even before it had completely stopped.

'Nepean Sea Road, Rustom Mansion,' he screamed. 'Go really fast!'

As the cab sped through the rain-soaked city, his mind raced. *She's gone*, the thought echoed painfully. Just as suddenly as she had appeared in his life, she had disappeared. He couldn't bear the thought of losing her. He wanted to see her more than anything.

Reaching Rustom Mansion, he bolted up the steps and banged on her door, which swung open. Inside, Tara lay on the mahogany bed, her silhouette unmoving, face down.

'Why did you leave?' he demanded. 'Tara, you scared me. Answer me!' he said, bending over her.

She turned to face him, her eyes swollen and red. 'I don't owe you an answer, Kabir,' she said coldly.

'Sorry, but you do,' he shot back. 'I was responsible for you back there. You can't dance in a place like that. You can't vanish into the night in a red-light area! And what the hell are you? A bar dancer? Tell me now, who are you?'

'How dare you?' screamed Tara, her emotions rising. 'You've done a lot for me, and I am grateful. But Mirza Kabir Dubey, I am a free woman now and no man will ever clip my wings again! I will do what I want with my life!' Her voice broke as tears rolled down her cheeks.

'Don't cry, baby,' Kabir's voice softened. 'I was worried about you. You are the bird whose wings I will never clip. I want you to fly, but I want you to be safe, baby.'

He tried to hug her but she pushed him away. He reached for her again and in that moment, she crumbled. His lips found hers, and she clung to him, holding him as though she would never let him go.

They fell back on the bed, and Kabir gently peeled off her inhibitions one by one. The sound of rain and the distant crash of waves filled the room, their rhythm matching the beating of their hearts. Finally, he kissed her belly, and she smiled softly. A million butterflies seemed to stir within her, their wings fluttering; they escaped into the night sky, soaring free through the open window.

8

Auction at the Ballroom

'Going once, going twice, going thrice!' The wooden hammer came down with finality. 'The pink solitaire dating back to 1852 now goes to Mrs Insha Patel.'

A ripple of excitement swept through the mirrored ballroom, the buzz of whispers mingling with the faint clink of champagne flutes. Two gloved attendants positioned a painting by M.F. Husain on an easel. The artist's legendary horses sprang out of the canvas, their hooves pointing towards the audience, their manes flowing. The image seemed suspended in perpetual motion as though time had surrendered to the artist's hand.

The anticipation in the air was palpable. The auction felt like a thrilling game on the brink of a free fall, where winning depended on having the nerve to climb up a steep hill of currency notes. Tara surveyed the room, which was filled with the city's wealthiest connoisseurs of art and collectables. Men in sharp suits and women dressed in garments from top design houses were dispersed throughout the room. Defining different interpretations of elegance, some were draped in traditional weaves.

To her surprise, the coveted Husain was taken home by the most unexpected contender—a diminutive Gujarati man in a plain white dhoti-kurta, his unobtrusive personality belying his obvious wealth. His wife, in a crisp cotton sari, looked quietly pleased, as if accustomed to such events in their lives.

Tara had stayed awake the previous night, her stomach turning at the thought of being recognized at the auction. But she woke up with a steely resolve—she had to stop running. That morning, she had dialled a number she had avoided for too long.

'Tara! My child, I have been worried sick. Where are you?'

'I am safe, Mummy. Please tell Vikram this—I have written my truth and plan to entrust it to someone who will reveal it if I am even touched.'

'Tara, why are you saying this?'

'There is no point, Mummy. Your son-in-law can do no wrong in your eyes.'

'Trust me, beta, and come home.'

'No, Mummy! I can't trust you simply because you trust him,' she said with finality, and hung up.

It took her a moment to shake off the cloying sweetness in her mother's voice—one she had learnt never to trust.

She had then rummaged through her bag for something good enough to wear to the big event. A deep purple chiffon dress with tiny Swarovski crystals sewn in, which she had hastily stuffed into her escape bag, seemed perfect. Parting her hair to one side and looking into the mirror, she thought she ought to fit in. But as she got out of the cab to step inside the Taj Hotel, she felt a little unsure. She paused for a moment to brace herself; then, setting her shoulders straight, her arm holding on to Kabir's, she entered the plush ballroom. That evening, her steps were measured, her eyes resolute.

'This is my first time at an auction,' Tara confessed.

'And I am here because of Rustom.'

'Really?' she asked, surprised.

'He wants me to put up his antique gold Rolex anonymously. His funds are fast dwindling.'

'The one he had on his wrist at dinner?'

'Probably its farewell dinner,' quipped Kabir as they entered the ballroom.

Rows of sofa chairs occupied the space, and servers weaved through them, balancing trays laden with flutes of champagne. Grabbing one, Tara downed the bubbly liquid, then another.

The liquid courage helped her silence the voice that warned her to stay invisible. Once, she wouldn't have hesitated to attend an event like this with Kabir. But then again, Kabir would never have been a part of her past life.

Kabir looked down at the catalogue, his eyes scanning the pages, imagining Rustom's watch featured there. He didn't like the thought of it, but nothing would deter the old man from preserving Rustom Mansion.

The auctioneer's voice boomed through the room. 'Ladies and gentlemen, the next item is an 18th-century sitar used by Lady Snowdon, wife of the Viceroy, and a patron of Indian music.'

The ancient musical instrument played by the slender fingers of an English lady fascinated music lovers in the audience. The bidding started and reached a point of competitive one-upmanship—the flaw in human nature that all auctions relied on. Kabir's eyes gleamed with fascination. 'I need to get some shots of that musical masterpiece,' he whispered in Tara's ear.

Tara looked around, as though she had landed on a distant planet. The night she fled, the future had loomed over her like a sinister monster, ready to devour her. In her wildest imagination, she could never have dreamt she would end up here. That night when she escaped, her life had been written once again. Tara turned to Kabir and gave him a smile. If smiles could speak, this one was a thank you bordering on a deeper emotion. She had needed this escape to another reality more than anything.

'The auction house now presents a spectacular pair of diamond and emerald earrings with gold encasements, an heirloom from a Royal collection dating back to the early 18th century. The reserve price is ₹90 lakhs.'

A suspended screen caught a close-up of the intricate design, while a gloved man moved with a velvet tray that carried the earrings, showcasing them to interested buyers, before resting it on a stand.

Tara looked stunned for a moment, her face turning pale,

her nails digging into her palms, as an audible gasp left her lips.

'You look so pretty in those earrings, Mummy!' she could hear herself say as she ran up to her mother, admiring the diamond and emerald earrings in intricately etched gold encasements.

'Oh, do I now?' Her mother had arched her eyebrow. 'A bit over the top, if you ask me. I am planning to exchange them for Cartier's newest diamond band.'

'But I want to wear them, Mummy. I will wear them one day. Nani is wearing them in that beautiful portrait of hers.'

'You may absolutely not!' came the stern answer. The vehemence in her voice had taken the young girl by surprise. 'I want to get rid of them.'

'No! Promise me you won't sell them! Promise me, please, Mummy!'

'Promise,' her mother had said, looking at her daughter straight in the eye.

Obviously, her mother had broken her promise to Tara.

Aishwarya had little regard for heirlooms; they were of value to her as long as she could trade them for branded pieces. If it had been for financial reasons, Tara might have understood, even forgiven. But it wasn't; there was plenty spread around in investments and properties. It was just an obsession to exchange old family pieces for the latest Cartier jewels!

'Ladies and gentlemen, I hope you have had a good look. The diamonds are eight carats and the emeralds are uncut.' The gloved hands moved deftly, tilting the stand so every angle was visible. 'Ninety-one,' a bidder called out.

'Ninety-five,' countered another.

A lady in a slim-fitting suit put up her hand. 'A crore.'

Tara felt flushed and her hand moved instinctively forward, as though to seize what was rightfully hers. She looked around and quickly put her hand down, realizing the gesture could be mistaken as a bid. But it was too late! The auctioneer had caught the motion. An open hand, in the language of the auction, signalled a number. She was in the game now.

'We have one crore fifty from the lady! Come on, ladies, it's a royal heirloom,' persisted the auctioneer. 'Any other bids?'

Tara dug her nails into her palms. She was in deep trouble. There was a pause; the auctioneer was looking at her. She felt a flush, her fingers moving to the small, gold Ganesha locket that her father had put around her neck. And then, the frozen moment moved ahead with one more bid.

Kabir appeared beside her, his voice a hushed whisper. 'Did you just bid?'

'I didn't mean to,' Tara muttered, shrugging. 'My hand just moved towards it.'

'You sure want them badly, then. Wish I had the money,' he teased.

'It's mine, Kabir. It's mine.'

'Yours?' he asked, confused.

'One crore sixty,' someone called.

Tara took a deep breath and squeezed Kabir's hand.

'Ouch,' he squealed. 'What was that!'

'We have one crore and sixty. Do we have another bid?' the auctioneer called out.

'Seventy,' a deep voice declared.

'A generous hike, sir. Any more bids for this royal treasure? Going once, going twice…' The gavel struck. 'Sold! The royal treasure goes for one crore and seventy lakhs.'

'I need to get Rustom's watch registered for the next auction. Meet me in the lobby when it's over,' said Kabir before slipping out.

Tara nodded, but her mind was stuck on her earrings. She turned around, desperate to see who had claimed her family heirloom. The man was obviously waiting for this moment and gave her a slight, cocky smile. Vivan Mehta nodded and raised his champagne flute at her.

She felt the roof sway as her head began to spin. She steadied herself, while her mind raced. *Why?* she wondered. *Why is Vivan Mehta trailing me?* His presence bothered her. She wanted to turn back again but resisted—she knew his eyes were still on her. She could feel them piercing her back, and a strange shudder ran down her spine.

The lights in the room suddenly brightened. Tara hadn't paid attention to the rest of the proceedings. Restless to leave the place, she stood up and casually glanced back, but the chair where Vivan Mehta had sat was empty. He had vanished.

She was not quite sure if all this was a coincidence. His bid for the earrings she had instinctively pushed her hand up for played on her mind, unsettling her. Tara skipped the elevator and rushed down the carpeted stairway of the hotel, anxious and confused. The lobby teemed with people, and her eyes darted around until they found the person she had been looking for. Kabir sat lounging on a chair, examining the shots he had captured. He broke into a smile seeing her. *Home*, she thought, *could just as well be a person*. Kabir had become her home for now.

As they drove along Marine Drive, the cool monsoon breeze filled the car. Tara closed her eyes, letting it wash over her, as if it could cleanse her of the evening's memories. She wanted to blow away the memories of the auction—the past that came back to haunt her. 'Can we stop by the sea for a while?' she asked, staring out at the vast, dark ocean.

'The lady's wish shall come true,' Kabir replied, instructing the cab driver to pull over.

In the distance, tiny little lights flickered as the skyscrapers lit up for the night. Tara looked at Kabir. Only a week had passed since her traumatic days in Jaivangarh, yet she felt as though she had known him for a lifetime.

'What are you thinking?' he asked softly.

'That I feel as if I have known you forever. Perhaps, from another life.'

His expression grew tense. 'You don't know the truth about me.'

'Shh,' she said, raising her finger to his lips. 'Right now, I don't need to. Please. This moment is the only truth I want.'

Gingerly, she rested her head on the edge of his shoulder and closed her eyes. She wanted to ask no questions, so she wouldn't get answers that hurt. That moment was her idea of perfection, and nothing could spoil it, not even the truth.

Later that night, as he slept, Tara lay awake, her mind raining thoughts. She walked to her desk and opened her blue diary, penning her feelings.

What are we? Friends? Lovers? Perhaps both. Or maybe neither. Is it possible to find friendship—or even love—in such a short span of time? I don't know how to define my relationship with Kabir, or if it even needs a name. Yet, there is something liberating about that—that it has no specific, definable name. Whatever it is, whatever we are, it is enough. It's bliss.

I am not seeking a label—a wife, a mistress, a girlfriend. It's the intensity between the two of us that is sacred, almost spiritual. He was my saviour, and I his destiny. How did I fall for a man who reached out to me with a Nikon Camera? And how could he love a woman with nothing but her name?

Our love is like a tuft of cotton floating in the sky—directionless, essentially formless, forever moving, innocent of its future and oblivious to the storms that may lie ahead. It doesn't know if the winds will carry it to a distant shore or guide it home. I am that tuft of cotton, and I surrender to the winds.

She shut her diary and went back to bed. Slipping in gingerly beside Kabir, she placed her hand on his arm; he turned over in his sleep and murmured her name. She had given him her body before, but that night, she also gave away her soul.

Kabir was gentle; he didn't push her. He sensed that she needed warmth and security more than anything else at that moment. In the turquoise room of Rustom Mansion, curled up beside him, Tara found the love that had eluded her for years.

Kabir's arm wrapped around her waist, pulling her closer to him. Tara nestled against his chest, her face buried in his neck. He pressed soft kisses on the crown of her head, and they lay like that till sleep enveloped her.

Eternity. This was eternity. She felt it even as she slept.

9

Floating on Bombay Nights

He watched her from the corner of his eye. Unravelling Tara had become Kabir's quiet obsession. This intriguing woman, still a complete mystery, was shedding her layers and growing more confident by the day.

Sitting straight on a tiny stool in front of the dresser, Tara held the brush gracefully, dusting a light blush on her cheekbones. She was in no hurry, her movements deliberate; she paused, pouted, considered, and only when she was completely satisfied did she allow herself a small smile at her reflection.

Kabir expected her to turn around and ask how she looked, but she seemed entirely unaware of his presence. Opening a paper bag filled with assorted flowers, she threaded them on to a plain white cotton sari with ingenuity. She then gingerly lifted up the sari and left the room. When she appeared dressed in her creative masterpiece, Kabir let out a low whistle.

'My God, you gorgeous woman,' he gasped, taking her hand and leading her to the garden below. As the sun dipped below the horizon, he clicked her from every angle, capturing her against the backdrop of blooming flowers and the amber glow of twilight. She looked like an extension of the garden itself—in fact, the most exquisite flower among Rustom's long rows of floral delights.

Later that evening, as Kabir paced the driveway dressed in a sharp tuxedo, he glanced anxiously at his watch. The films were at the core, at the very heart, of popular music, and tonight promised to be a party that would be remembered. 'These are going to be some of the most important photographs in my feature.'

'You have got your lucky charm with you,' Tara smiled.

When the chauffeur-driven car arrived, Tara slipped into the back seat with the poise of a woman accustomed to life's finer luxuries. Kabir, in his black, formal suit, his unruly curls slicked back and neatly clipped, played the part of the debonair Bengali-French man to perfection.

The car glided through Marine Drive and then turned into the narrow streets leading to the iconic Gateway of India—a symbol of history and grandeur. Evening strollers dotted the promenade: there were families with children and couples holding hands. Amidst the lively backdrop, a red carpet stretched towards a jetty.

Kabir helped Tara out of the car and handed over their invitation to the concierge dressed in an embellished black-and-gold uniform, surrounded by rows of bouncers on either side. Tara looked up at the magnificent Gateway, where once Queen Victoria was received after her ship made its way to the jewel in her crown. Though fascinating landmarks of history appeared in India often enough, this one had a warmth that made it a favourite spot for the city.

They boarded the boat, its luxurious interior promising a wonderful evening ahead. As it surged forwards, slicing through the waters, Tara felt a rush of excitement and clutched Kabir's hand instinctively.

'Thank God I met you,' she whispered.

'We were meant to meet, my darling. It was written in the stars.' His eyes glanced up.

The ocean sparkled like a silken blue sheet, lifting and dipping with the breeze. The ship ahead was a vision to behold—all dressed up to the hilt for the party and shimmering due to rows of fairy lights that seemed to whisper, 'Come, celebrate with me. Leave behind your worries, if only for one night.' Tara felt the invitation seep into her very being.

As the speedboat reached the ship, she got to her feet and stepped carefully on to the jetty. Her pencil heels teetered precariously as she made her way up the winding ramp to the grand ballroom.

Inside, men in dark formal suits and women in intolerably high heels, with plunging necklines speckled with glitter, slit skirts showing off toned thighs and backless blouses paired with chiffon saris were scattered in groups—conversing, laughing and savouring the night. In the centre of the room stood the gorgeous Ash, and Tara couldn't help but stare. To her surprise, the actress smiled at her. Tara approached her and whispered some compliments that seemed naïve and revealed her complete awe of the woman.

Ash simply smiled back politely, and then, to Tara's delight, said, 'I love your floral sari. Who is your designer?'

'My designer? I don't have one, yet.'

In Mumbai, that answer was a sign that the woman did not want to share her secret.

On a grand stage, a vibrant poster of Ajay Kapoor's latest film towered above the crowd. This was Bollywood at its finest—a world where dream merchants dared to invest millions into creatively woven tales on celluloid screens. Here, street performers became superstars while millionaires could be reduced to nothing. Homes were lost to banks, and mistresses were often given more social acceptance than wives. It was a cruel world where survival meant knowing how to swim in a tank full of sharks.

Kabir felt concerned; he wanted to ensure that Tara was comfortable. However, he needn't have worried—Tara stood at the centre of a group of people, holding court. She was smiling, perhaps a bit stiffly. Her heart felt almost still, as though she was walking through her own dream—where she was both the dream and the dreamer. She wanted it to last; could she suddenly wake up in her bed, with Vikram's stale breath on her face? She pushed the thought away and went back to sipping the fine champagne in delicate sips.

✮

His eyes had been following her all evening. Shakti Mathur had made a vocation of finding, wooing and exploiting new talents till they broke free of him; then he moved on in search of fresher pastures.

A new bird on the wire, he thought. He was sure he had never seen her before, yet, she did not have the hesitant look of a newcomer, which he had learnt to recognize so well by now. No self-conscious tugs at clothes, no eagerness to be caught in the flash of tabloid cameras, no uninvited introductions—just a quiet confidence, as though she was drinking in the evening.

For the first time in his career, Shakti was confused, and he didn't enjoy it. 'Do you know her?' he asked the man next to him.

Vivan Mehta turned to look at the woman in the white sari. He ignored Shakti's question and walked up to her.

Tara saw him approach and her expression shifted. The French wine she had been sipping slowly was starting to cloud her head. Was she seeing him through the television screen from her bed? He was like a figure from a film, pulling her into an alternate reality. His voice, deep yet sometimes soft and playful, ricocheted against the confines of her bedroom as she turned up the volume to drown the uncontrollable laughter of Vikram and her mother.

'Dance,' Vivan said casually.

Was it a request or a command? She wasn't sure, and before she could reply, he took her hand and led her to the floor.

She moved hesitantly, unsure. But then her steps grew steady, swept away by the music. Vivan guided her through a blend of tango and waltz. Was he really holding her and dancing? Did celluloid images really come to life? She forgot that Kabir had escorted her; the grand ballroom could well have been empty—

with just her and Vivan. She completely gave in to the music.

A soft clap broke the spell, followed by another, and soon the room was reverberating with rhythmic applause.

'Where did you learn to dance like that?' Vivan asked.

'I am learning music under Guru Darshan Das. Maybe it is his influence,' she replied, brushing off the compliment.

'Of course,' he mused. 'I often visit Guruji for inspiration when I run dry of ideas. He's a frequent guest at Rustom's, so am I.'

From across the room, Kabir observed her, part of him still deciphering what she was all about. *The many seasons of the woman*, he thought. He tried to convince himself that he wasn't jealous; after all, he hadn't known her long enough to feel that way. He was just glad to see her in this moment of revelry, enjoying the evening. But his concerned eyes never left her. He knew Mumbai, and this young woman was vulnerable, fragile like a butterfly that could be swept away by a gust of wind.

'You are quite a dancer. Good on your feet,' said Vivan as he escorted Tara off the dance floor. She smiled back at him nervously. Then, with deliberate slowness, he reached out and plucked a flower from her sari. He brought it to his nose, inhaled deeply and then tucked it into the lapel of his jacket.

Tara froze, taken aback and feeling helpless, until Kabir appeared by her side.

He hadn't missed a thing. 'Please return the flower to the lady,' Kabir said, his tone sharp, his smile caustic.

There was a moment of tension as Vivan stared back defiantly, calculating. Then, like a seasoned chess player who knew the art of retreating to ensure a win, he removed the flower from his lapel and handed it to Tara.

'Your friend seems offended. But I only meant to compliment your beauty,' he remarked, smiling. With that, he vanished, leaving behind an air of mystery.

As the evening wound down, the boat ferrying the guests back to the shore swayed gently on the water. The revelry had ebbed, leaving behind sleepy faces and muted conversations. Tara and Kabir stood at the edge, holding the railing.

Tara's thoughts were swirling. Vivan Mehta—a man whose films had once been her solace during her darkest days trapped in the palace—had held her hand and danced with her tonight. But reality felt surreal. There was something about his presence that left her feeling disturbed. Reaching for Kabir's hand, she rested her head on his shoulder. He put his arm around her—the touch gentle, a soothing balm—and she knew he was there for her.

★

The night had been sleepless, with turmoil and conflicting emotions. Relieved to see the early morning light, Tara made her way down the avenue, eager for Guruji's lesson. The strains of her sitar were more than just music today—it was a soul-searching experience. The notes flowed, resonating with her emotions. With her eyes shut, she let the music take over, transcending the turmoil within. Guruji did not disturb her. His sixth sense told him that his student needed solitude. He understood the inexplicable connection—between body and mind, heart and soul, emotions and music, melody and the musician. Perhaps it was this rare insight that made him the greatest of all maestros in India.

'Now play to the sea,' he said, his hands lifting dramatically as though invoking the elements themselves. 'Today, there are no rules, no ragas to follow. Just play to nature.'

Tara opened her eyes and turned her gaze to the horizon, where an orange molten sun was rising from behind the vast expanse of the ocean, framed by the rhythmic crash of waves. Inspired, her music broke free, untethered, flowing with a liberty she hadn't experienced before.

Guruji, his head swaying gently, smiled as he watched a

peaceful expression grace his student's face. The long, flowing cotton curtains fluttered in the breeze, and the marble floor, laid down years ago in the mansion, remained cool beneath the bare feet that walked on it.

Tara felt light, almost limp with peace. It wasn't just music that she was playing; it was an outpouring of unexpressed feelings, a symphony of her emotions.

At the far end of the hall, a tall man dressed in a crisp white kurta-pyjama walked in silently. He seated himself on a low couch and lit a cigarette. As he exhaled, rings of smoke floated into the air, blurring his view of Tara. He flicked the ash of his cigarette into a half-empty matchbox, his eyes fixated on her.

Tara sensed his unbroken gaze pierce her and opened her eyes. He sat motionless, the cigarette dangling from his lips, and then suddenly he clapped.

Guruji turned sharply, and his deputy crossed the room and whispered something to the visitor. Guruji did not appreciate visitors who took liberties, not even if they were Bollywood stars.

'Film stars!' grumbled Guruji. 'I do not appreciate loud clapping during my lessons.'

Vivan rose smoothly. With a glance at Tara, his expression unreadable, he slipped out as quietly as he had entered, and then vanished.

✫

Tara walked briskly along the narrow footpath. Her mind replayed Vivan's appearance, who had appeared and disappeared like an apparition.

In the distance, dark clouds loomed on the horizon, rolling towards the city. She glanced seawards and stopped in her tracks. A phenomenon she had only heard of but never witnessed unfolded before her: the monsoon rains were advancing over the ocean, a moving wall of water surging towards land.

She stood transfixed, awestruck, till the first raindrops fell on her hair and a gust of wind whipped her sari around her. The sudden reality of being soaked snapped her from her reverie. She spun around, desperate for a cab, wondering how they always seemed to vanish when one needed one the most. Drenched, she walked as fast as her feet could carry her, chanting Kabir's name in her mind.

A soft screech of tyres made her freeze. A sleek, metallic-blue sports car glided to a halt beside her. The door swung open, and he held his hand out.

'Get in, please,' he said softly.

She recognized his muslin kurta and deep piercing eyes, and her heart felt faint. Tara hesitated and slid into the seat.

'So, where can I drop you? Heading back to Rustom's?' asked Vivan.

'Drop me off at the corner of Nepean Sea Road, please,' she said, sidestepping the conversation.

'And I suppose you will walk the rest of the way in this rain?' he said, grinning.

'I will manage fine.' Tara nodded, a hint of unease in her voice.

'Don't worry. I am not going to whisk you away.'

There was no humour in his words, almost as if it was exactly what he wanted to do. He remained completely silent during the drive, yet an energy that transcended words filled the space inside the Mercedes Coupe.

When they arrived, Tara bolted up the winding staircase to her room. The spiral structure seemed to mirror her spinning head. She was tired and confused, and her hands trembled as she fumbled with the key. She didn't have to try too hard; the door opened and Kabir stood in the doorway.

'Kabir!' she sobbed, collapsing into his arms.

'What's wrong?' he asked.

'Nothing,' she whispered. 'Nothing at all. I was just...thinking of home.'

Kabir searched her eyes; he knew she was hiding something from him. Suddenly, she seemed vulnerable. The swan who had dazzled the party had flown away, leaving behind a scared young woman looking for shelter in his arms. He held her tight, stroking her hair gently. He didn't ask any questions.

That night, they made love with an urgency. It was as though Tara was begging him to save her from something he had no clue about—he just seemed to know how to heal her for a while. Kabir understood there was much more to her—many stories that she had hidden. And he was waiting, patiently, to unravel them.

Long after he had fallen asleep, Tara lay awake. Tears of guilt and confusion rolled down her face. She didn't like keeping secrets from Kabir, yet she felt a strange ripple inside her as Vivan's image, with a cigarette dangling from his lips, filled her mind.

She recalled every moment in excruciating detail: his intense gaze as he watched her from across the room; the quick puffs on his cigarette; his slight sideways glances in the car; the complete lack of conversation that made the drive almost an erotic experience; the undercurrents of chemistry that moved in the tiny space, like ignited waves; his sinuous muscles flexing as he leaned across to help her open the complicated coupe door; the weight of his eyes following her as she exited the car; his scorching gaze on her wet back.

She held Kabir's arm tightly and silently pleaded, 'Help me, Kabir. I love you so much. Don't let me go. Don't let him take me away from you. Away from myself. Rescue me, Kabir. Rescue me, please. Take me away from here.'

10

Racing Horses

'Wake up, Tara, wake up.'

She stirred and opened her eyes to find Kabir leaning over her. 'You should start dressing. We have a big event this morning,' he reminded her.

She smiled and stretched languidly, giving him an affectionate peck on the cheek. Kabir always had a way of making her believe everything was fine, that life was good. The night was over and she had only one thought on her mind—that she would never hurt Kabir. She resolved to remove every trace of Vivan from her life.

'I will be ready in perfect time,' she assured him, slipping out of bed.

Kabir turned his attention to his camera and began cleaning its lenses. The world, for him, was often framed through those lenses, so they had better not be hazy. Yet over his shoulder, he couldn't resist stealing glances at Tara. She was studying herself in the mirror, like an artist assessing her own canvas. He was tempted to click her but decided to let her have her personal moment.

There was a quiet grace in the way Tara collaborated with the mirror to transform herself. A faint smile played on her lips, as though she approved of what she saw. Her blush pink, off-shoulder dress hugged her slight curves with elegant simplicity. A wide-brimmed, off-white derby hat perfectly framed the soft waves of hair cascading down her waist. Stylish white pumps completed her look.

Tara felt beautiful and she liked the feeling—a sense of self-worth she had missed for long. Adjusting her hat for the final touch, she looked in the mirror and paused. As she raised her eyes, she caught Kabir's gaze and realized he was watching her.

His grin stretched so wide she feared it might split his face.

'You are going to steal the races today,' he said, breaking into a wolf whistle.

She burst into giggles, cheeks flushing as warmth spread through her. Kabir had a way of making her feel seen and heard. It was a stark contrast to Vikram's disinterest—the way he looked right through her as though she didn't exist. Kabir's presence in her life was something she would never regret. He made her feel alive, appreciated and precious.

'Is this good enough a disguise?' she asked, slipping on oversized sunglasses.

'I wouldn't recognize you if I passed you on the street,' he teased, wondering when she would be ready to tell him more.

She sensed something in his eyes—the weight of unspoken questions. There was so much left unsaid between them, so many shadows in her past she had yet to reveal. *I will tell him everything, but not today. Maybe tomorrow.*

'I need to tell you about my life, Kabir. Then you will understand why I need to hide. But for now, I need this time with you to stay magical—untouched by anything else. Away from reality, maybe for just one more day,' she said, sitting down next to him.

'I have been waiting, Tara. It's time you tell me everything. I am sure I could help you in some way.'

'Tomorrow. I promise.'

'Let me put on some music before I go in to dress. What's your choice?'

'Anything peppy will do.'

He flipped open the laptop and clicked on a song. 'Done.'

Tara's heart stopped. She remembered the last time she had heard the song, and she never wanted to hear it again.

Kabir hummed along, 'It doesn't matter who's wrong or right. Just beat it, beat it...'

'That's not my favourite,' she said.

'I know I'm bad, but you don't have to make it so obvious!' he laughed.

'You are definitely good enough to sing for me. Just not that number,' she replied quickly, masking her uneasiness with a smile.

★

Even dressed in a deliberate disguise, Tara felt anxious at the prospect of stepping into the bustling crowd at the races. She hoped that in the chaos of women vying for media attention, she would go unnoticed; her broad hat and large sunglasses ought to help her blend in and pass off as just another spectator.

'Rustom has a private box at the races for his friends. No one will spot you,' Kabir reassured her, his voice a calming balm.

When Tara looked at the mirror again, she barely recognized herself. Tara Kumari of Jaivangarh had vanished, replaced by her perfect reincarnation.

Kabir emerged from the dressing room in a tailored grey linen suit. His unruly curls that usually sprang up in all directions had been tamed, falling gracefully around his face. Tara couldn't help but smile at her gypsy gentleman.

'What's the verdict?' he asked as he walked over to her, planting a quick kiss on her forehead. The familiar scent of his cologne— notes of wood and spice—lingered between them.

'Like a million bucks,' she teased.

Sliding his arm around her waist, he said, 'Off to the races,' with a mock flourish. His carefree jest made Tara laugh, and she suddenly felt excited about going to the derby. She was all set to take on the world and everything that came with it.

They went down to the lobby, which was abuzz with racegoers.

'I'll arrange for a car,' Kabir said, stepping away, as Tara sat down in one of Rustom's elegantly carved chairs.

Neville, who was rushing around arranging transport for the

guests, saw Tara and remembered something he shouldn't have forgotten.

'Oh, madam, I am so glad I saw you. I have a package for you—it's been in my locker,' he said, hurrying away and returning with a lush, wine-coloured velvet box. 'I was instructed to hand it over personally.' He gave the box to Tara.

Heart pounding, Tara opened it. Nestled inside, against the soft velvet lining, lay the earrings. She let out a breath she hadn't even realized she was holding. Slowly and carefully, she pulled them out and placed them in the palm of her hand. They felt heavy with the weight of history. The uncut emerald and eight-carat diamond earrings had been passed down through generations. She could visualize them on her mother's ears, her own childhood voice asking, 'Can I have them when I grow up?'

Although part of her felt they belonged to her, that she was their rightful owner, she was embarrassed to receive them as a gift from Vivan.

Tara felt tempted to try them on just once. Putting them on, she glanced at the mirror in the lobby. The earrings fell gracefully along her long neck, the emerald perfectly complementing the soft blush of her dress. They were, after all, a family heirloom; they had to sit well on her. *If Mummy could just see me wearing them!* She decided to wear them to the races before returning them to Vivan. The cab arrived and Tara joined Kabir outside. The driver, noticing the lady in a hat and a man in a tuxedo at 11 a.m., guessed instantly. 'Off to the races, I see. Are you going to be betting today? I have all the inside information,' he said.

'No, buddy. I will leave gambling to those who don't mind losing,' said Kabir, grinning.

'Wah!' the cabbie replied. 'That's a good one. But there is no game, sir, where you can only win. Not even life.'

'True,' he said to the philosophical cabbie, and, switching on his phone's music, let Mozart's soothing strains fill the cab.

Tara and Kabir made a good-looking couple, and as they arrived at the Mahalaxmi Race Course, they drew glances. Cameras flashed and Tara looked down, well-shielded by the brim of her hat.

Kabir was surprised to see Neville, who, miraculously, had reached before them despite leaving later.

'Do you have a twin?' he asked the young manager, amused.

'No, I just happen to have the talent to be in two places at once,' Neville quipped with a rather triumphant grin, gesturing towards his trusted Lambretta that had snaked through the city traffic with ease. 'Follow me,' he said.

The races had started by then and every eye was trained on the tracks. Rustom's private box was steeped in history and privilege. His great-grandfather had donated generously enough to ensure generations of the Bulsara family had a perfect view of the tracks from a private space.

The sound of hooves thundering on the tracks filled the air as Tara and Kabir entered. Rustom stood by, binoculars in hand. This was Rustom's moment; he enjoyed derby day, when he could lean against a past that remained preserved for him.

Neville assumed his position against the banister, his eyes following the storm of horses going past them. A waiter circulated with a tray of champagne flutes.

'Too early for me,' said Kabir, but Tara reached for a glass. She was still a little nervous.

The race concluded with a surge of cheers. Rustom turned to his guests, holding up two fingers in a victory sign, indicating that the horse he had bet on had won. He looked pleased.

'Look who we have there,' Kabir said, pointing to the row ahead. 'The editor of *National Geographic*. I am not pushy, but that's one guy I need to meet.'

'Go ahead, Kabir. You absolutely must,' Tara encouraged.

'Will you be okay?'

'Of course. How lost can I get in an exclusive enclosure?' she said with a giggle. 'It's a playpen for grown-ups.'

Kabir chuckled and moved away, approaching the tall, bespectacled man. He extended a hand and tried to gently steer him into a conversation.

'Stunning.' The voice was so close that she could almost feel its echo in her head. Tara turned sharply.

His eyes followed the curve of her neck, where her earrings glistened. Although she had half-expected him to be here as Rustom's guest, she wasn't prepared for the intensity of his scrutiny.

'It is kind of you, but I cannot accept them, Vivan,' she said hesitantly.

'You don't know me well enough, then. My gifts are never returned,' he murmured.

Her eyes darted through the crowd, searching for Kabir. Vivan was the sweltering fire that threatened to consume her, while Kabir was the calm river—and she seemed to need both.

'Who are you looking for?' Vivan's voice was almost a whisper. He was a player, trapping her in mind games. With his free hand—the other held a champagne flute—he reached out to brush a loose lock of hair off her collarbone, his eyes lingering on his gift.

At that moment, Kabir returned, and Tara looked at him as though seeing light after travelling through a dark tunnel.

Vivan extended his arm. 'How are you doing?' he asked.

Kabir shook his hand, his eyes briefly flicking to Tara, sensing the tension between them.

Vivan turned to Tara and gave a slight smile. 'The royals are seated up there,' he said, pointing to a private section ahead. 'I'll be there if you need me.' Then, leaning closer, he added, 'I think I know something,' before walking away.

But Tara barely heard him. She was staring straight ahead.

It wasn't just any royal seated in the private section. It was the maharani of Jaivangarh.

And beside her was a man.

The two were bent towards each other, as if they were talking about something important.

Then the man nodded and turned around.

Tara was staring straight at Vikramjit Rathore.

11

Girl Gone

Pacing the length of his room impatiently, Vikram sipped his scotch, hoping it would calm the churning in his belly. Aishwarya Devi's words kept ringing in his ears.

'My goodness, Vikram, the girl is gone. Can you stop being this obsessed? It's embarrassing.'

But he couldn't shake it off. He had seen her. He was sure of it. Amidst the chaos of the races, as the horses thundered by and the crowd cheered, there she was—straight ahead of him. Her tresses were unmistakable—he could recognize them from a mile away. He rubbed his fingers, reliving the silken touch, and then his hand clenched into a fist.

And just like that, she had vanished. Was it really her?

'Maybe you're right,' he muttered, trying to convince himself.

Yet it was strange—just moments after spotting her, he had turned back to see her rushing out of the place. A long-haired man had followed. He was not sure if they were together or if it were a coincidence. Something about the scene seemed off. This was far too close a call for Vikram to let go.

Tara was gone, and she was going to wreck everything he had planned.

Slipping out of the room, Vikram called Dhruv Jhabwala, the man he could rely on for handling uncomfortable situations—especially when they came in the way of his business deals.

'I need you to do something for me,' he said tersely.

'Anything for you, sir.'

'I think Tara is in Mumbai. I need you to find out.'

'Consider it done,' Jhabwala replied. 'What am I supposed to do once I find her?'

'What do you do with thorns in your side, Dhruv?' Vikram asked.

'Pull them out.'

'Well, there's your answer,' Vikram said, cutting the line.

A sudden pang of guilt passed through him, but he smothered it with thoughts of the project's sheer magnitude. He stared at the ceiling, a growing unease gnawing at him. Then he dialled Jhabwala again—his wife deserved a dignified death.

His lopsided concern for the rules of the game was purely instinctual.

Dhruv Jhabwala had several virtues, but patience wasn't one of them. Buttoning up his paisley-printed shirt, he threw a casual blazer over it, dressed for business as usual. Sentimentality, he had learnt early on, had no place in land deals. Years of muscling people out of their homes had given him a Teflon coating that deflected any stray emotions.

Recalling his phone call with Vikram, he thought of how arrogant the old boy had sounded.

'Put her in her place, Dhruv. But remember, she's a Rajput. And she's my wife. If you so much as lay a finger on her, things won't play out well for you.'

The misplaced vanity of fading royalty never failed to amuse him. *A man who had bought his influence through marriage, now issuing threats!* He chuckled at the thought.

But business was business, and things needed to be done— sometimes not gently. Unless you knew that, there was no way to get ahead in the rat race. Jhabwala was good at doing what needed to be done. Hesitation had no place in his world. First, though, he needed to pacify his impatient investor.

He dialled a number. 'Vivan bhai, I have good news for you.'

'I have told you before, Dhruv, you are not permitted to give me bad news anyway,' Vivan Mehta replied, his tone sardonic as he looked at the small child knocking on his car window.

'The Desert Water Park and Hotel project looks all set to close. There was a family member stalling it, but we got lucky! She's come to Mumbai and is likely hiding here. Once I get her, our way ahead will be cleared.'

Vivan was silent, his mind cruising through possibilities.

'Send me her picture,' he said finally, his voice slow and deliberate. A strange feeling stirred in his chest.

'Why? Are you setting up her obituary?' quipped Jhabwala.

'No. Because I think I may have gifted her a priceless jewel.'

'So, you have met her in Mumbai?'

'Send me her picture *now*,' said Vivan, his voice impatient.

It irked Jhabwala how easily Vivan could raise his voice at him and get away with it—all because Vivan twisted the arms of the bureaucracy, made the right phone calls and paved the way for Jhabwala's skyscrapers to rise from the rubble.

Jhabwala was usually secretive about his projects. He revealed his hand only when every move was already set in motion. But he needed to placate this man for the moment.

'There, I just sent you her picture.'

Vivan Mehta glanced at the photo of the young woman in a sari. It was unmistakably her. The white hat and long emerald earrings she had worn to the races did little to camouflage her strangely determined and somewhat enigmatic expression. He took a deep breath, staring at the ceiling of the car.

'Vivan, did you give her a look-over?' Jhabwala's voice pulled him back.

'What does "look-over" mean? You could be a bit more respectful when referring to a woman,' the actor snapped.

'Oh, sure, as you say, Vivan. But have you seen her anywhere?'

'No, Dhruv, I haven't.'

'Okay, I'll start the search then. I will let you know when I have sealed the deal.'

Vivan ended the call. This was probably the worst business decision of his life. Yet the idea of Asim's hands on the pretty Tara churned his stomach.

No! he thought. *Not Tara.* There were better ways to earn his money. This softening in his heart—he didn't like it at all. These were the early signs of weakness, the sort that created a loser. Business and emotions had to stay separate.

The traffic lights turned green, and as his car crawled forward, he reached into his wallet and handed a ₹500 note to the child still at his window.

Meanwhile, Jhabwala was already on another call. 'Asim, is the car ready?'

'Yes, sir. It will be waiting when you come down.'

'Fantastic.' Running a hand through his gelled hair, Jhabwala headed for the door.

In the hotel lobby, Asim waited with his briefcase. Jhabwala remembered the day he had hired this man—mild-mannered and willing to do absolutely anything. Desperation drove people like Asim, and what a useful thing it was—desperation. It pushed people beyond moral boundaries, suspending humanity itself.

'I need you to find Tara Kumari of Jaivangarh. She is in Mumbai, most likely in South Bombay. I don't know much else. Find her, get rid of her,' said Jhabwala, his voice cold and final.

Asim Ebrahim had never fully grown accustomed to taking orders like these. Yet, as a loyal foot soldier, he could not do much but acquiesce. That day, he felt more exhausted than ever.

Tara's face floated through the city; Asim's informants carried her picture, scanning the faces of each guest at every guesthouse and hotel, eager to be the first to report back to 'Big DJ'. It was a network that rarely failed him—a domino effect of foot soldiers spread throughout the city. The search for Tara was in full swing.

He had paused briefly to pick up a can of his favourite orange drink when his phone rang.

'She is staying at Rustom Mansion,' said the voice on the other end.

'Confirmed news?' asked Asim.

'Confirmed, sahib.'

'*Shabash*, beta. DJ will reward you.' Asim hung up and pressed the accelerator. The furious shopkeeper chased after his car, cursing the customer who had sped off without paying for his drink.

Disregarding traffic lights, he sped through the city, his focus singular. Finally, he slowed down near a *bhelpuri* seller, a permanent informer, and pulled out Tara's picture.

'She is inside there right now,' the vendor replied, pointing towards Rustom Mansion. 'Has not stepped out in four days.'

Rustom Mansion. She was there for sure. He dialled Jhabwala.

'Sir, I have found her… Yes, sir, by tomorrow I will finish the job. Consider it done, sir.'

Two days later, Asim sat in his car, parked outside the last relic of architectural grandeur on Nepean Sea Road, still waiting for a sighting. His eyes never left the formidable doorway that only let in people invited by the old man himself.

Jhabwala was losing his nerve. Time was money in his world, and delays were unacceptable. He decided to take matters into his own hands and dialled a number.

'Rustom, I am coming for dinner at your table tonight,' he declared.

There was silence on the other end. Jhabwala could sense the hesitation in the old man's voice when he finally replied.

'Okay, Jhabwala,' Rustom said, his tone resigned. He sighed, slouching back in his chair. 'Neville,' he called out. 'The builder is after the mansion again. Check our list of invitees for tonight.'

Nothing stoked Jhabwala's fire more than the prospect of an easy win. He had put off taking Rustom Mansion away from the old man for long enough, but the Jaivangarh deal had strangely brought him back to this coveted piece of real estate—a 5,000-square-yard plot of prime land overlooking the Arabian Sea.

The thought made Jhabwala snigger as his car pulled into the driveway. He spotted Asim pacing outside, red-faced and sweaty.

'Alright,' Jhabwala said, flashing a rare smile. 'Let's get this done.' He rang the bell and waited. After a moment, Neville opened the door and asked them to wait in the lounge.

Jhabwala sauntered inside, his sleek black briefcase in hand, eyes scanning every guest who passed by. He smiled to himself. He wouldn't have to search much further. Tara Kumari was probably a few metres away. He couldn't wait to surprise her at Rustom's dinner table.

★

Rustom's table was set for the evening. The whites chilled in iced decanters while the reds sat open, breathing—just the way Rustom liked his wines served. The table was adorned with freshly cut flowers and soft flickering candles; Rustom's favourite—Mozart's *Symphony No. 40*—played softly in the background.

The host walked in, a little unsteady and subdued, his usual cheer missing.

'Good evening, guests,' Rustom greeted. For the regulars at his table, that was the cue to take their seats.

Tara settled into her chair, the music, lighting and the feeling of being part of Rustom's coterie making her feel comfortable. She took quick sips of the aperitif wine placed before her and eased her nerves. She reached out for a second pour.

Across the table, Kabir caught her movement and gently shook his finger, indicating that she should slow down. She giggled in defiance and reached out for another glass, revelling in her rebellion.

Kabir smiled, his eyes tracing her, contemplating the twist of fate that had brought them together. He couldn't hear her conversation too well from across the table, but he could see her throw her head back and laugh at the young designer's jokes. *At least the girl is enjoying herself,* he thought.

The empty chair at the table caught his attention. It was unusual, given Rustom's well-known obsession with punctuality. A portly man walked in, his overpowering cologne making him an unlikely addition to the gathering. Rustom turned around and gave the late arrival a look of disdain, deciding this guest did not deserve an introduction.

Dressed in his hallmark electric blue jacket with a touch of diamanté on the collar, Dhruv Jhabwala took the chair across from Tara. She felt her breath catch in her throat. Her gaze locked on to him, and her heart felt as though it would leap out of her chest. This was not the wine working; she was actually sitting in front of the man she feared the most. She reached out for another glass of white wine and downed it.

Tara clutched the Ganesha locket resting on her collarbone. Something deep within her shifted. She felt herself lose her inhibitions as fear gave way to defiance, fuelled by the strength of her Rajput lineage. The faces of those who had wronged her flashed through her mind—powerful men whose hands had twisted her life, her soul, her very existence and made her flee her home. But they no longer held power over her.

When she looked up, her eyes locked on to Jhabwala's again, this time burning with a fiery intensity that made him feel strangely uncomfortable. He had no idea how to respond to it.

'Ladies and gentlemen,' Tara addressed the room. 'May I introduce to you Mr Jhabwala—a builder, a promoter and a man who loves to turn farmlands into skyscrapers,' she said.

Jhabwala remained silent.

'So, Mr Jhabwala, are you here to get me?' Tara asked, a slight, playful smile on her lips.

'Tara,' he said finally, finding his caustic tongue. 'Don't embarrass me.'

'Are you carrying a gun, Jhabwala? Because if you are, I'll need to call the police.'

Jhabwala laughed. 'Little Tara, you don't understand how these skyscrapers come to be. Entire *bastis* vanish to make room for them, and the police are shareholders.'

Tara's voice rang out loud and clear as she said, 'Ladies and gentlemen, Mr Jhabwala believes he can buy anyone—establishments, governments, people. Yet, sir, you couldn't buy the poor farmers on my land, and you never will.'

Her last words were quieter, almost as if she was convincing herself. The liquid courage was quickly fading as the fear of Jhabwala's presence returned.

Her phone, which had been buzzing incessantly throughout, rang for the fourth time. She ignored it again, but Rustom gave her a kind smile and urged her to pick it up.

'Go ahead, Tara. Rules are meant to be broken sometimes. Someone really wants to speak to you.'

Hesitantly, she answered the call. A muffled voice warned, 'Tara, leave now. There is a man there to kill you, waiting in the corridor. Run fast. Take another route to your room.'

'Who is this?' demanded Tara.

'Take the emerald earrings along,' the voice added before the line went dead.

Tara rose from her seat, her legs shaking. 'Rustom, will you please excuse me? I don't feel too well,' she managed, giving Kabir a pointed look.

'Go ahead, dear. Take care of yourself.'

Jhabwala watched her leave, his eyes trailing as Tara walked out of the room, with Kabir at her heels. He reached for his glass of champagne. It was time to celebrate the beginning of Desert Water Park Hotels.

Kabir and Tara moved swiftly through the corridors, her hand clutching Kabir's tightly. Spotting Asim near the main hallway, she quickly ducked behind a wooden partition, her heart pounding. With frantic steps, they made it to her room, her hands fumbling with the key. Once inside, she bolted the door and looked at Kabir, who stood there, anxious and confused.

'Let's get out of here right away.'

'Tara, you need to tell me what's happening. Now!' he said, sounding aggravated.

'I promise I will tell you everything, but right now, you have to trust me.'

Kabir stared at her. He didn't know her full story, but he trusted her completely. He nodded.

Tara threw clothes into a bag—both hers and his—whatever she could find, along with the emerald earrings. Then, using the service staircase at the rear of the mansion, they escaped into the bustling street. The chaos of the city outside somehow felt safer than the elegant confines of Rustom Mansion.

Tara turned to Kabir, as though his eyes could shelter her in some way. 'Take me away from here,' she begged.

'I will take you away. You will be fine,' promised Kabir, holding her.

They flagged down the first taxi that came their way. 'To the Gateway of India,' Tara instructed the driver.

'Let's take a boat to the island. It's the safest place to be,' she told Kabir.

★

The last boat out of the city was virtually empty except for a group of tired office-goers. Tara kept her head low, scared of being seen. Kabir held her tightly, stroking her hair, rocking her back and forth gently. He was her protector, her anchor. She buried her face in his shoulder, her tears forming a damp patch on his T-shirt. Gradually, her sobs grew softer as anger replaced fear.

The boat docked at Alibaug with a jerk. The weary travellers dragged themselves off, searching for transportation. Kabir and Tara looked around, contemplating their next move. The neon light of a small motel nearby brought a sense of relief. The Comfort Inn was everything its name promised. The small room, although generously sprayed with air freshener, still had the musty smell of the ocean. Tara dropped herself on to the springy couch, leaning her head against the armrest.

Kabir expected her to fall asleep; instead, her tears flowed afresh.

'My life is in danger Kabir,' she said, her voice cracking. 'I want to tell you who I am and why I am running. I want to tell you about my family... About my father, whom I lost and still dream of. I want to tell you every word, Kabir.

'Tara, I want to hear it all. You need to let it out... I can see you are hurting inside. Why are you running? Who are you, and who made you the woman you are today?'

'Tonight,' she whispered. 'Before I sleep. Else, I won't be able to shut my eyes.'

That night, she stood by the window, speaking to the winds as if they would carry her story away and ease her pain. He noticed that her eyes would often be shut, her words incoherent with emotion but always laced with honesty.

She spoke of her search for her father, her aloof mother and the husband who had committed the most treacherous betrayal.

Kabir listened without interrupting, letting her speak till she had emptied herself of every thought, every word. At times, she seemed breathless and her voice faltered.

He walked up to her and pulled her into his arms, hoping his embrace would soothe her. He had never fully understood the extent of the problems she was in or the depth of her determination to fight back. Now, he understood her better. Tara was a remarkable woman—a lamb and a lioness in one.

'That night at Kamala aunty's terrace, Kabir, you appeared to rescue me. It was written in our destinies. We were heading towards each other all along. The good and the bad were just part of that journey.'

Tara moved to the table and opened her laptop while flipping through the pages of a worn, blue leather diary beside her. Her fingers flew across the keyboard, her face intense. She seemed to be writing something that meant a lot to her. Her eyes reflected anger, pain and even resignation at times.

Kabir wanted to stop her, to convince her to rest, but instinct told him that this moment was her catharsis. That he needed to leave her to herself. Sometimes, waking back was the toughest part of life, but tonight, she had to.

✱

The sun crept over the horizon, its warm light flooding the room. The ocean outside was peaceful, with seagulls flying over it. Tara woke up to see Kabir smiling at her. His gentle hand on her shoulder meant more than words ever could.

'Kabir,' she said, 'thank you. Thank you for being by my side.'

He set a steaming cup of coffee on the table beside the bed. 'I think you probably need this.'

They sat together, sipping the strong elixir Kabir had brewed in the noisy electric kettle. They chatted about plans that would secure her life, and about the museum and the lands she loved dearly.

Holding her diary in her hands, Tara smiled. 'This is my strength, Kabir.'

She rested her head on his shoulder, her lips murmuring faint words that soon faded into silence. Kabir realized Tara had fallen asleep out of sheer exhaustion. He sat still for what seemed like hours until he felt her stir again. When she finally opened her eyes, there was something different in them.

'You look peaceful, Tara. Very calm.'

'I feel lighter,' she replied. 'Unburdened. And now, I have you to guide me. Before, it felt like I was going through a maze in circles—running but not getting anywhere.'

'You cannot run from them forever. Build a place of strength and then confront them. You have to smile in the face of the lion, Tara.'

Tara straightened up. She liked the sound of those words. She let the thought settle in her mind before saying, 'You are right, Kabir. I have to control these monsters. I have to stop running.'

'Start by moving the courts immediately. At the same time, rally the people of Jaivangarh. I have strong media contacts in Delhi—the seat of power where even the influence of wealth will not work.'

'The builder lobby has a tight grip—a stranglehold on our systems.'

'But public opinion is stronger. You'll need an out-of-the-box approach.'

'Will you help me, please?'

'I promise I will,' Kabir assured her.

'I have a plan, Kabir. But you won't like it, I know.'

'Just don't do anything that puts you in danger,' Kabir said, then paused. 'Look at the stars,' he continued in a soft voice, peering out of the window of their motel. 'They are all shining for you, Tara. Remember, even in daylight, they will still be up there for you.'

12

Tara's Story

The night of catharsis had cleared her mind. Yet reliving the memories had left her indignant, with no intention of sitting idle like prey. When fear is replaced by anger, it creates an inferno, and Tara now felt its heat burning within her. She had looked into the eyes of her worst fear and survived. The memory of Vikram's smug expression and her mother's unflappable elegance played over in her mind, fuelling her rage. It angered her that they continued to enjoy their lives, getting away with all they had done.

She hadn't smoked in a long time, but that day, as she walked down to the lobby, she bought a pack of cigarettes and lit one. The first drag reminded her of Jaivangarh, her days of angst. She inhaled deeply, feeling the bitterness. Going through her options, she decided that waiting for them to find her wouldn't be the best one. She had to make the first move—one that would expose them completely. An empty purse and a blocked bank account wouldn't get her anywhere; she needed to start earning. She opened her bag to check the remnants of her money and found a shiny gold card with a number scrawled across it. There was no name on it. *Strange*, she thought, until it struck her—Vivan had slipped it to her with a grin, saying, 'Call me if you ever need me—or better still, if you don't.'

It had seemed frivolous at the time, but now it felt like hope staring her in the face. The pieces of the jigsaw were falling into place. Her next move was in her hand. Holding the card tightly, she dialled the number. The phone rang for a few seconds before someone finally picked up, but they stayed silent.

'Hello, this is Tara.'

'Oh, hello, Tara,' came the voice. 'I am glad you called.'

'Vivan, I need your help.'

'Where are you?'

There was a split-second's hesitation before she decided to gamble. 'I am at Alibaug but I will be heading back to the mainland soon.'

'My car will pick you up from the Gateway,' he said, leaving her no room to object.

She ran up to her room and found Kabir still in bed. He rolled around sleepily.

'You're up early,' she said. 'You've put me on the right track, Kabir. I made a call.'

'A call ?' asked Kabir.

Hesitating, she said, 'To Vivan. I have a plan, Kabir. Trust me. I need to see him.'

'Go ahead,' he nodded, avoiding her eyes.

Tara looked at herself in the mirror. If she was meeting Vivan, she wanted to look her best. *He only does things for pretty women,* she thought. A touch of lipstick, her favourite black kajal and a hint of blush were enough to make her look beautiful without showing the effort. For all her desire to be free of male dominance, the thought of meeting Vivan excited her. She gave herself one last look in the mirror and suddenly felt more confident. Power, she had heard, was exciting; power over power seemed even more exciting.

✯

She stood waiting with the morning office crowd coming from Alibaug to work in the city. A black Audi pulled up in the distance. A tall, muscular man dressed entirely in black stepped out and walked up to her. 'Madam, you are Tara ji?'

'Yes, I am.'

'I am Joseph. I have been instructed to bring you to meet my boss.'

'Where is that going to be?'

'His location changes frequently, so it is hard to say,' he replied cryptically, adding to the enigma surrounding the man Tara was going to meet.

The car wove through the dense afternoon traffic, eventually crossing the sea link that tied the two ends of the city together. Tara watched as the scenery began to change. Buildings grew sparse, traffic thinned and the foliage became lush and tropical. The road narrowed, leading towards the ocean.

In the distance, she spotted a lone island connected by an iron bridge. The car moved down the private access road, gliding smoothly as a boat on calm waters. Then suddenly, it became steep and the car ascended the incline at full speed.

Tara bit her lip in a sort of strange anticipation, the sort of thrill she remembered from her first roller coaster ride at Disneyland. The mix of excitement and stress gave way to guilt and she called Kabir. Almost immediately, she changed her mind and cut the call, choosing instead to send a short text informing him she would be back later that evening.

As the car took a sharp turn, an imposing mansion came into view. Perched at a towering height, the structure seemed other-worldly, far removed from the mundane chaos of the city. Vivan Mehta's private haven had an ethereal feel to it. It looked like a historical monument, with grand columns and intricate architectural details.

The tall wooden doors opened electronically as Joseph punched in a code. They entered a capsule-like enclosure where another layer of security awaited.

'Boss said no security for the lady,' Joseph informed them.

The beady-eyed man at the console, dressed in black overalls, gave Tara a long look before entering another code.

Tara caught her breath as the final door opened, revealing a spectacular expanse. A balcony, the size of a large hall, jutted over the Arabian Sea. Soft strains of ragas played on the sound system, syncing perfectly with the rhythmic crash of the waves.

Vivan sat on a lounger, gazing at an expanded screen image of Tara staring out to the sea. She looked beautiful. Although he was immune to good-looking women after years of being surrounded by them, this girl was different. There was something about her he couldn't quite lay his finger on—a special quality he couldn't quite define—and that bothered him. What was it about her that set her apart? His eyes narrowed as he focused on her face. She was feline, exciting and as unpredictable as the wind. Although she had come to him, he knew she would not be easy for him to grasp.

'Hello, Tara,' he said, approaching her.

She turned, startled despite expecting him.

'Sit down and tell me why you look so worried.'

'I need to earn, Vivan.'

'I can give you a loan.'

'I don't accept loans. I need to earn,' she replied, her chin tilting slightly—her trademark gesture of defiance and resolve. It intrigued him, giving him a sense of what drew him to her.

'What can you do?'

'I want to join your line of business.'

Vivan threw his head back and laughed. 'Join my business! You are quite amusing. This enterprise was started in 1620 by my ancestors during the Portuguese rule in Mumbai.

'"Vivan Mehta" is a pseudonym I adopted when I joined the film industry. My real name is Daniel D'Costa. I am a Christian of Portuguese descent. My family once sailed the high seas carrying spices—more precious than gold in those days.'

'Fascinating,' Tara remarked. 'Almost like a fairy tale.'

'Not quite. It's hard as nails. The business has evolved, but the pressure remains brutal. It is not for you, my lady.'

'I am hunted, Vivan, and nothing appeals to me more than

having unassailable power that I presume comes with your trade. It will be my safety net to survive.'

'Something tells me that's not the only reason.'

'Perhaps you are right,' she admitted, momentarily confused, as though reassessing her own motives.

The sun dipped low over the waters, and the lilting strains of ragas changed their tunes—softened, mingling with the gentle sounds of the waves.

'The man with you, Kabir—the one who picked a fight with me—'

'He is my saviour and friend.'

'And lover?'

'Maybe.'

'My apologies. I am stepping into your personal space.' He looked at her, and for a fleeting moment, she thought she saw a spark of jealousy in his eyes. 'Don't worry. I play a fair game.'

'I didn't know we were playing games.'

'Let me tell you something, Tara. I never go to a woman. She has to come to me.'

Tara stayed silent.

'What is that in your hand?' he asked, suddenly noticing the file she was holding. 'Not an application to join the underworld, is it?' he grinned.

'I was hoping to avoid that, but perhaps it is time. Vivan, I wanted to share a thought with you—'

'I suggest a watermelon martini,' he interrupted playfully. 'You'll find your thoughts clearer after drinking it.'

'Sure,' she agreed.

'I have a story here. It is my story,' she said, holding out the file. Her grip on it was firmer than she had realized, as though she couldn't part with it.

'Trust me,' he said, prying the file from her. 'I will not share it without your permission.'

'I don't expect you to do this for me, Vivan. But if you find the story interesting, I would like to act in it.'

'You would?' he said, his eyebrows rising slightly.

'Yes. The attention this film would generate could expose the ruthless people threatening my village and stop their plans. Let them be judged by the people who watch this film.'

Vivan tilted his head, a slight crease appearing on his forehead. 'You are like an ocean, young lady,' he said. 'Your mysteries never end.'

He opened the file, his eyes moving across the lines, his face intense. His long, slender fingers turned each page slowly, and Tara knew she was being revealed a little more.

She turned towards the glass wall that separated her from the sky, the notes of *Summer Wine* floating in the air. Dark monsoon clouds gathered over the city, and Tara followed them with her eyes, trying to distract herself. A small boat packed to the hilt was leaving the harbour, vanishing into the encroaching darkness. She felt a sudden urge to join them, to escape to the end of the sea.

As Vivan continued to read, his eyes moistened. For a fraction of a second, he paused and looked up at her, as though creating a connection between the pages he was holding and reality. Then he bent his head again, reading until he reached the last line. When he finished, he set the file down gently and studied Tara's face in silence. Tara waited, expecting him to speak, but he closed his eyes instead, replaying her story in his mind.

Part Two

13

The Man with Amber Green Eyes

Excitement coursed through Vivan. Tara's story had to be made into a film—it demanded it. But that meant a second read, to make sure that it truly was a story worth telling.

This is my story. My love, my passion. The people who made me and those who unmade me. It is my celebration of life—not just mine, but of all those I included in it. Those who are unheard. I want to be their voice.

Vivan was touched by the short and candid introduction. It created an instant personal bond. 'I like your opening lines, Tara,' he said, glancing up briefly before diving back into the pages, completely riveted.

His image is the most treasured memory I carry with me. And it's never gone away.

The man who had shaped her, made her into who she was. He was indelibly etched into her soul. She remembered him vividly, not just through her memories, but also through the stories her mother had shared—tales of days before her birth. She had painted and embellished those images in her imagination, gilding them like precious artefacts. The man she called 'daddy'.

Gaj, as his friends called him, was the epitome of the contemporary aristocrat. A royal by both birth and inclination, he bore his ancestral heritage lightly, wielding it with effortless charm and advantage. That day at the Mumbai races, he arrived in a crisp white linen shirt, tailored jeans, and a nine-carat diamond stud in one ear—its size and sparkle left the city's women spellbound, as did his elfin amber green eyes. His sleek, leonine black hair was casually pulled back, accentuating the deep, distinctly flirtatious cleft in his chin.

Sundays often found him at the Mahalaxmi Race Course, indulging in his twin passions: speed and horses. The enclosure was a spectacle of Mumbai's elite—models, millionaires, imposters and journalists mingling beneath the snapping cameras. Women, dressed to outdo one another, flaunted their finery. Waiters moved through the crowd, serving pink champagne and strawberries to the young textile magnates gathered in their plush private section.

Gaj's grandfather had donated the 225 acres of land that now made up the iconic Mahalaxmi Race Course—a gift celebrated by generations to come. That day, amidst the glitter and glamour, the film industry, as always, had a quiet presence. The elegant Madhuri Dixit, resplendent in a chiffon sari, stood in a private box with a small group of friends.

While the social scene at the races was always pleasurable for a single man, Gaj's mind was preoccupied with Badshah, his prized stallion, who was being prepared for his first race there. The atmosphere was electric. Bets were being placed on a buzz, a rumour, a reputation, a whim; a comment was enough to sway the big bucks in favour of a particular steed. The favourite, undoubtedly, was Badshah. But a whisper about another contender—a first-time entrant at Mahalaxmi and an international winner, Silver, owned by Princess Aishwarya Devi—was causing a stir.

Oblivious to the financial upheavals, the bankruptcies and the instant millionaires they were about to create, the rows of prized horses basked in the attention, lapping up the pampering, the extra hugs and caresses from their owners, who, with a 'good boy' and a pat, were pleading with their steeds to do their best. Gaj gave Badshah a final brush-down, his palm gliding over the stallion's glistening coat. Leaning in, he whispered words of encouragement and Badshah threw his head up excitedly, as if understanding every nuance of his owner's touch and voice.

The bell rang out, signalling all owners to leave the enclosure.

Gaj turned back for one last look, meeting Badshah's steady gaze. He knew his loyal friend had absorbed his silent thoughts—a connection that fascinated Gaj to no end.

The starting shot rang out, electrifying the entire racecourse—from the horses to the crowd in their Sunday best, from the bookies to the cold-drink boys. The air itself seemed to shift as the gates opened and a dozen horses sprang on to the turf. A din of excitement rose through the air as the synchronized rhythm of hooves pounded like the drums of an advancing army.

As always, Badshah started slow. Silver, the white mare, surged ahead, her energy palpable. But soon, Badshah, in his characteristic style, preened his neck and shot forward, his muscular legs rippling in the sunshine. Silver was not far behind, and for a few long moments, they were neck and neck, their rivalry commanding the crowd's rapt attention. The tension peaked as they rounded the final bend. With an unmistakable burst of energy, Silver pulled ahead, and Gaj fell back in his seat as Princess Aishwarya Devi let out ecstatic screams of joy. Silver had stolen the day.

Cameras swarmed the suave princess as Aishwarya rushed down to hug her victorious mare. Silver pranced in delight, basking in the adoration and attention. Gaj watched the spectacle unfold from a distance as he made his way to the stables. Badshah stood there, his head lowered, avoiding eye contact. Somehow, he knew he had lost.

Gaj gave him a pat and whispered in his ear, 'You did well, Badshah. The lady was worth it. That, my friend, was a strategic loss.'

With that, Gaj turned, his thoughts already focused on how to manoeuvre an introduction to Princess Aishwarya.

★

The sea-facing apartment on Marine Drive felt like a world apart. A pianist played a gentle melody for the guests, the music punctuated by the occasional pop of a bottle of bubbly. The hostess moved gracefully around the room, receiving her guests with a broad smile. Rosie Palampur was basking in the celebration of her friend's victory. From their early days as rivals at the London School of Economics—standing on opposite sides of fiercely competitive debate teams—to their evolution into pub-hopping buddies who surfed London's nightlife till the wee hours, they had come a long way.

Rosie waited as a projector flashed the highlights of the euphoric day. Aishwarya stood watching, clad in a pristine white muslin kurta, her sleek, jet-black hair cascading freely, an ancestral sapphire hanging casually around her neck. Her deep, black eyes were fixed on the screen, reliving every moment of her triumph. As Silver crossed the winning line, Aishwarya cheered and the guests joined her, erupting into loud applause; the energy of victory was infectious, its heady after-effects still lingering in the air.

In the corner of the room, Gaj watched her silently, waiting till she noticed him. When their eyes finally collided, she smiled at him. He responded with one of his own, feigning surprise.

'Hello, I am Gaj Singh,' he said politely, walking towards her and extending his hand. 'And you, of course, are the winning lady.'

'Have I seen you before?' she said, trying to place the face.

'Oh yes, sure you have.'

Her eyebrows knitted as she tried to remember.

'Not long ago, at the races today, in fact. I am Badshah's friend, I would say.'

Aishwarya smiled warmly. 'Badshah is a beauty,' she said indulgently.

'He is. And the next race will be his for sure,' said Gaj, tilting his chin up.

Aishwarya let the loser have his moment, her eyes inadvertently drawn to the mole on his perfectly contoured upper lip. *Quite disconcerting*, she thought.

The night wore on, and the winner and the loser found themselves seated together, discovering an uncanny similarity in their lives. Both were Rajputs; both had attended elite schools in England; both were enmeshed in the tightly knit circles of Rajasthan's royal families.

Gaj spoke animatedly about his plans for a museum of ancient arts and Aishwarya listened, fascinated. The light from an 18th-century Czech chandelier cast a soft glow over the pair as they lounged on a plush white couch, their feet propped up on the table before them. Around them lay the spoils of the evening— empty glasses, half-eaten plates of snacks, scattered cushions and stains on the rare Persian carpet. The ocean outside played its own nocturnal melody, shifting with the tide.

As they talked late into the night, sharing their plans, hopes and dreams, a bond emerged; it was as though they were both headed in the same direction.

★

Six months into their whirlwind romance, Gaj Singh arrived at Jaivangarh Palace to marry his beautiful opponent. The grand convoy of elephants, camels and horses created a mesmerizing sight. He arrived riding his beloved stallion, who was dressed in an ornate 18th-century saddle and a diamond-and-ruby headpiece, with a red plume springing from the centre to complete his look.

Gaj patted Badshah affectionately. Despite the blaring music, the mobile kerosene lights and the fireworks, Badshah's instincts for communicating with his master remained as sharp as ever. Playfully, he shook his head in response to the happy moment.

The bride's family waited in eager anticipation as Gaj dismounted. He leaned close to Badshah and whispered, 'We did it, buddy. We won the race.'

14

Here Comes Life

The plush velvet bed embroidered with an emerald insignia did little to ease the agony gripping Aishwarya's body as she pushed to release the life trapped within her. Rosie, holding her friend's hand in support, winced as Aishwarya's nails dug into her skin.

'You are doing well, Ash. You are doing so well,' Rosie assured the maharani.

A row of nurses in white uniforms stood ready, murmuring words of encouragement. But this was Aishwarya's moment—hers alone—the moment she would earn her place as a creator. Her face flushed red, her eyes bulging, chest heaving.

'One more time! Just one more push, please,' urged the head nurse.

Summoning a final burst of energy, Aishwarya threw her head back and pushed with all her might. A sharp, piercing cry filled the room.

'It's a girl,' announced Dr Rathore. 'And she has beautiful eyes.'

'Show her to me,' gasped Aishwarya. She peered down at the child she had just brought into the world, her breath hitching as her suspicion was confirmed with one look. The baby had his eyes—they were a striking amber green, more amber with flecks of green than anything else.

'Where is my husband?' she asked.

The room fell silent.

'Rosie,' she pressed, 'can you call Gaj into the room, please?'

Maharaja Gaj Singh was neither pacing the corridor nor lounging on his favourite leather couch, smoking a cigar. As the palace staff searched for the father to give him the news of his child's birth, the inebriated man was in the nearby fields, riding Badshah recklessly through low-branched groves, fuelled by speed and alcohol. He finally made his way back to the palace as exhaustion overtook him.

The staff found him sitting alone on the balcony of his bedroom, his eyes bloodshot, his breath heavy, his jaw tense.

'Congratulations, *Hukum*,' said Ram Swarup, bowing. 'The palace has been blessed with a princess.'

Gaj's face betrayed no joy, no sign of happiness; it remained blank as he downed a shot of vodka, as though he had not heard the news.

'Maharani Sahiba is waiting to show you the little one,' said Ram Swarup. When he received no response, he gently repeated the line.

'I do not wish to see the child,' said Gaj Singh in a terse voice. 'I *never* want to see that child,' he repeated, as though speaking to himself.

Staggering to his feet, he left his room and walked back to the stables. Stroking the stallion's mane, he whispered, 'Ah, Badshah, my only loyal friend,' before mounting him and vanishing into the dark night.

★

Days passed, and Aishwarya waited. Eventually, she lifted her baby in her arms and carried her to Gaj, hoping the sight of the child would melt his heart.

But Gaj turned away, his eyes looking out of the window. 'Take her away,' he said.

'Why? She is the princess of this palace.'

'Aishwarya, we both know the truth. She is not mine.'

'You know Jaivangarh needed an heir. We needed a child,' Aishwarya countered.

'That's fine. She has fulfilled her purpose—ensuring the lands and palaces stay within the family in the future. That does not mean I'll accept her as my own.' He paused, then abruptly asked, 'Whose child is she?' His gaze locked into his wife's.

'Don't ask me that. We had a pact, Gaj. Don't forget that.'

'Whose child is she?' he repeated tersely.

'Why? So you can get the man killed?'

'Do you want to protect him?'

'Yes. Because no innocent man should die to soothe your ego.'

'Innocent?' Gaj laughed bitterly. 'Who's innocent here? I am not quite sure.'

'You dare talk of innocence?' Aishwarya snapped. 'You disappeared to the Amalfi Coast with your Italian mistress after asking me to have a child for Jaivangarh.'

'I needed to escape, to find comfort where I could.'

'And I did not object to it, did I? Now you don't have it in you to live with the consequences of your decision.'

'I don't want to hear anymore, Ash.'

'I suppose you have forgotten that along with your family title, we have to give her a name that is her own.'

'Call her whatever you like, Ash. She is yours. Only yours.'

Aishwarya looked out of the window, her eyes drawn to a solitary star shining brightly in the night sky. 'Tara,' she whispered. 'I would like to call her Tara.'

Gaj said nothing. His wife was right—she had given him the heir Jaivangarh needed. But his Rajput pride was lashing out, striking him across the face. He felt a sense of deep indignation that his wife had borne the child of another man. She would always be a reminder, that child.

★

Tara remembered vividly the day she first noticed him. The man with amber green eyes had come to meet the maharani with a request to build a school in the village. He was tall and slim, with sharp features and a black mole on his chin. Wearing a thick tweed jacket to combat the biting chill of the desert winter, he had also draped a shawl around his neck. The line of red vermillion on his forehead marked him as a quintessential Rajput.

As she passed him in the corridor, his gaze followed her and he called out in a warm, almost affectionate tone. 'Tara baby, how old are you?' he asked.

She froze, too shy to answer, his wide eyes searching her face before she bolted down the corridor. Just before turning the corner, she glanced back. She was flattered to notice that he was still looking at her, a faint smile playing on his lips.

Later that evening, as she sat curled up beside her mother, she asked, 'Who was that man who came to see you today, Mummy?' Aishwarya looked away, her expression guarded.

'Oh, no one important, dear,' she replied, flipping open Tara's favourite book of bedtime stories.

As Tara's eyelids grew heavy, she mumbled sleepily, 'Mummy, the prince in the story sounds just like the man who came today.'

Aishwarya switched off the lights and hoped the darkness would erase Tara's memory of the tall man with amber green eyes.

Once Tara was fast asleep, Aishwarya picked up the phone, her fingers trembling slightly as she dialled. 'Shantanu?'

'Yes, Aishwarya,' came the soft reply.

'Tara noticed you today.'

'Well, she has sharp senses. Just like her father.'

'It's best if you don't come to the palace anymore.'

There was a long silence on the other end. Finally, Shantanu spoke. 'Take care of my baby, Aishwarya. And give her a blessing from me every day.'

Shantanu Malhar sat back in his chair, stunned by the coldness in Aishwarya's voice.

His mind drifted to the first time he'd seen her. She had walked into Jai Janami Jewellers wearing Polo jeans and a pink T-shirt, her hair pulled back in a tight bun.

'Can I see that bracelet?' she had asked, pointing to a ruby and diamond-encrusted piece.

'Ah! It's a beauty,' she had murmured, examining the piece and then looking up at him. 'Could you bring it to the palace this evening?'

'I most certainly will, Maharani Sahiba,' Shantanu had replied. Little did he realize that she hadn't come shopping for jewellery that day.

That evening, as he stood before her, explaining the intricate details of each stone, he had even added observations on their astrological significance.

The man was intelligent, and Aishwarya was quite sure he was a Rajput. She leaned back, studying his face. His eyes were the same shade as Gaj's. *Perfect*, she thought.

Several jewellery-viewing sessions later, Shantanu Malhar was no longer just the manager of Jai Janami Jewellers. He had become Aishwarya's secret lover.

15

Growing Pains

Tara's search for her father remained, even though he was present in the same home—even if that was officially a palace. It had been her childhood ambition to sit on his lap, but her finely tuned instincts, even as a child, told her that she was not wanted. His eyes were cold and uninviting when they met hers, and at the dinner table, she noticed how he avoided glancing in her direction.

As she grew older, Tara became increasingly obsessed with finding ways to attract her father's attention.

One day, Miss Graham, the British governess who acted as a part-time teacher and full-time maternal figure, was carefully combing Tara's hair into a tight plait.

'No, not like that, please, Miss Graham. I want the bow at the top of my head,' Tara declared.

'Why ever would you want that?' Miss Graham asked, amused.

'Because when I put the bow up real high, Daddy always notices me.'

Later that day, Tara crept up behind her father, holding a colourful edition of *Rumpelstiltskin* in her small hands.

'Daddy,' she said, opening it gingerly. 'Can you read me the story?'

Maharaja Gaj Singh looked at the young child, and for a moment, he was touched by her innocence. He reached out for the book.

'Now, sit there quietly,' he said, his tone brusque but not unkind, and began reading the story.

But the young girl was not listening to the tale of straws that turned to gold or the gnome-like man's cunning bargains.

Instead, her eyes were fixed on her father's face, watching his expressions intently. She was fascinated. The red bow had worked! For the first time, her father was actually sitting with her, and she basked in the rare moment of attention, even if it was for just a short while.

Encouraged, she tried to strike up a conversation with him. 'Daddy, Ganesh ji looks very nice sitting around your neck,' she said, her eyes on the talisman hanging from its thin gold chain.

'You like him?' he asked.

She nodded eagerly.

Gaj Singh removed the locket—his mother's keepsake—and placed it around Tara's neck. 'He will keep you safe,' he said.

That was a rare gesture of affection.

But Gaj didn't like the softening of his resolve. He spent more and more time in the plush apartment he had created on the top floor of the museum he had built—a long-time passion of his. Immersing himself in the restoration of old paintings and artefacts and studying new techniques to preserve paint from cracking, Gaj allowed his passion for history and art to consume his time.

In the palace, he moved to the east wing, turning it into a fortress of solitude. The sprawling quarters were secluded and private, filled with his collection of rare books and the hefty ledgers of accounts from his charities.

Meanwhile, Aishwarya was left to regret the child that had become a wedge in their relationship, which sliced through its once heady days and left behind a hollow shell. Tara had drained the light from her life.

One evening, Gaj poured himself a stiff drink. The tawny liquid glistened in the Belgian crystal glass, the ice cubes clinking softly as he lifted it to his lips. The fiery single malt burned as it went down, but he welcomed the sensation. His eyes wandered to the painting above the fireplace. The tiger's gaze stared back at him, frozen, menacing and fierce.

Aishwarya made her way to his private space and walked into his room reeking of cigars and alcohol. She just stood there, her eyes welling up with tears. She needn't have spoken. Gaj knew why his wife was there.

'Every time I see Tara,' he muttered to Aishwarya, 'she reminds me of my inadequacy. She is your child, not mine. And one more thing, Ash. Don't ever enter my area unannounced. I have moved here for my privacy.'

'Privacy from your wife?' she asked, indignant.

He stared back at her. 'Leave, please,' he said.

With that, he drained the rest of the 50-year-old Glenfiddich single malt on the rocks, his fingers tightening around the fragile glass until the tendons stood out starkly.

Aishwarya had realized by then that reasoning with an injured ego was futile. *The male ego is primal*, she thought bitterly—its instinct and rules deeply embedded in the DNA, like a blueprint replicated billions of times over. Nothing could alter this nature. Tara would never find a place in Gaj's world. It was best, Aishwarya decided, to keep her daughter away from him.

The hill station of Nainital was a small, picturesque haven for holidaymakers. With its lake stretching across the valley and tall mountains standing guard around it, the town seemed like a painting brought to life. Lovers and honeymooners, under the warm winter sun, floated lazily on boats that glided effortlessly across the waters, with occasional ducks following them playfully. During the summers, the Boat House Club bustled with activity, as the elite descended to claim the waters for their races and regattas.

Gaj enjoyed being out on the waters, where it was just him and his boat. Nothing else existed; nothing could, in this perfect oasis where he came to rest every year. But that year was different.

The months slipped by, and he had not the slightest inclination to return to Jaivangarh.

The winds were perfect, and the white sails holding aloft his royal emblem fluttered furiously against the breeze, their fibres taut, challenging the winds. Gaj took a deep breath and felt a strange sensation of completeness—almost whole, but not quite. A nebulous void gnawed at him. He longed to round off his day with a good gallop on Firefly, the handsome stallion he kept at his holiday home in the hills. The riding track that circled the lake beckoned him.

After a quick shower, Gaj changed into his riding gear and was about to step out when the phone rang. He answered with an impatient, 'Hello'.

'Gaj, it's me,' came the tired voice.

'I am stepping out for a ride, Ash.'

'Wait, Gaj! Come home, please.'

'Ash, I am at peace here,' he sighed.

'I will send Tara away to a boarding school. Then it will be just you and me again,' she offered.

Gaj was silent for a long moment before surprising himself with his reply. 'She is still a child. She needs a mother... No, Ash...no!' he protested as Aishwarya persisted. Finally he relented, 'Maybe...maybe I will come home.' He hung up.

Perhaps, he thought, *it's time to return*.

Outside, Firefly was ready. Gaj mounted his stallion, and with the commanding ferocity that his forefathers brought to battlefields, they galloped off with unbridled power.

A streak of lightning split the sky, drawing Gaj's gaze to the thick clouds rolling in layers overhead. The wind howled, a sharp harbinger of the storm brewing. Firefly, attuned to nature's wrath, jerked his head in agitation. Gaj felt a few piercing drops of rain sting his skin, and then the skies opened up, releasing a torrential downpour.

He knew he needed to slow down, but he felt compelled to keep going. Another bolt of lightning illuminated the track, and the clouds began to dip towards the lake. Gaj looked up, and it seemed as though the sky were drifting down to meet him. Nature was tightening its grip on him, and he was succumbing willingly. He felt a rush of adrenaline and a sense of reckless excitement.

Firefly's neck stretched, veins swollen and throbbing, reaching for eternity. In that fleeting moment, his hooves skidded on a patch of drenched green moss, sending both horse and rider into a tangled mess of weeds. Gaj was a capable swimmer, instinctively moving his arms in a desperate attempt to save his life, but his feet were still stuck in the stirrups.

When he was finally pulled from the waters, Gaj was found still hugging his stallion's neck, the animal's mouth open, entangled in the thick mesh of lakeside fauna.

Tara mourned her father—a man she adored but barely knew. She had seen him so infrequently that his death felt surreal, strange. Those who are present go away; those who have been away remain etched in the soul, untouched by time.

She preserved her father in a dreamland, solid and unchanging, iron-cast in her memory. *No, Daddy had not died. That man in the lake was merely a lookalike. Daddy had gone to fight a battle like his brave ancestors. He would come back one day, perhaps as a victor of war—to surprise her on her birthday.*

She waited.

Every birthday.

But he never came.

16

Sunshine in the Courtyard

She stared at her reflection in the mirror, stepped back slightly and smiled. *Yes!* She loved what she saw. Smearing soft pink lipstick on her perfectly bow-shaped lips, she pouted just a little. Being 19 and gorgeous wasn't easy, but that day, she didn't care. Her inhibitions were set free.

This was the day she had waited for, fantasized about and envied her friends who had got there before her. It was the day she would join the ranks of the free—the day when the 'Writ of Home' would dissolve into the 'Independent State of College Life'.

With a flourish, she let her hair down, brushing it with all her energy. Tossing it back in place, she sprayed on a streak of fluorescent hair colour.

An emerald green top paired with ripped jeans seemed perfect for her first day of college. She replaced her oversized solitaire earrings with simple hoops, swapped her precious rings for understated costume jewellery and gave herself one last look in the mirror. *Ah! Perfect*, she thought.

Unfortunately, Aishwarya did not agree. Her daughter's concept of fashion seemed bizarre to her.

'Tie your hair up, Tara. I don't want the boys whistling at you.'

There went the lush mane, pulled obediently back into a plait by Miss Graham, who carried on with her usual commentary about the dangers posed by 'evil boys' Tara needed to protect herself from.

'Rosie aunty!' Tara called out in protest. 'Look what Mummy's doing to me on my first day of college!'

She stormed out of her room, visibly upset, her plait swinging behind her.

'Come on, Aishwarya,' said Rosie, stepping into the room. 'Tara is just experimenting with her style.'

'I can't take those shredded jeans and that razzle-dazzle makeup on her.'

'She has spent most of her life in boarding school, Ash. It's only natural she'd develop a sense of independence.'

'Frankly, I don't care. Tara is a project that I have to see safely through.'

'You sound unnecessarily tough, Ash. Especially now. She needs you, now more than ever.'

'She took Gaj away from me,' Aishwarya said bitterly. 'She changed my life. And I can sense that she's searching for *him* all the time. In every man she meets, she looks for some thread that might lead her to her father.'

'Don't blame her. It was Gaj who messed it all up.'

'I blame the commoner's genes that keep showing up in her, Rosie.'

'Oh come on, Ash,' her friend replied disapprovingly.

'When she was a little girl, she would run away to the village at every chance she got. Only I knew why.'

'Every royal family has its secrets. Keep that under your breath, Ash.'

✻

Tara went straight to pick up her friends Meher and Divya, who were waiting outside Meher's home.

The drive to Jaipur took a while, and Tara used the time to undo the damage of her mother's interventions—goaded on by her two friends. With one hand still on the wheel, she pulled open the braid and let her hair flow free. She tugged her top slightly lower, admiring her chiselled collarbones in the rear-view mirror. *Jaipur Law College, here I come!*

'Be glad your mum is in Mumbai, Divya. You will get to be a free bird.'

'I was sent here because she felt Mumbai would spoil me,' Divya replied with a giggle.

The three girls walked in, their faces lit with excitement. They looked around and the first thing they noticed were the boys loitering in the corridors. While Meher and Divya seemed pleased enough, Tara was not impressed. A week later, she had shut her mind to ever dating anyone on campus. Their barely sprouting beards, excitable voices and gawky, awkward demeanours left her quite uninterested. Their ability to twist a perfectly innocent compliment into a lurid pass irritated her to no end. She preferred the peace of the classroom to the chaos of what she saw as unruly mobs masquerading as students in the corridors.

'So, how does college life feel, Tara?' asked Aishwarya one evening. 'I haven't heard you speak about it.'

'I can't take it, Mummy. It's not me.'

'Of course you can't,' Aishwarya replied, a trace of triumph in her voice. 'The point of going to a public university is to understand the ways of the masses. Something your posh little boarding school clearly didn't teach you. This is your father's legacy. It's what Gaj's family has always done. They all went to public colleges.'

'You're the one who sent me there!' said Tara accusingly. 'That place is not me.'

Aishwarya smirked. 'So, tell me. What *is* you, then?'

'Oxford. Oxford is where I belong.'

Aishwarya couldn't resist rolling her eyes. 'It's a pipe dream. Stop dreaming, Tara.'

'I have been accepted at Oxford. Do you even know what that means?'

'It means me emptying out our banks for three years, breaking into the savings, and then you'll come home, marry a handsome Rajput boy and lock away your degree in the cupboard for safekeeping.'

'This family, Mummy, is not short of money. Pity my father didn't leave an education fund for me.'

'He wasn't expecting to leave so soon, dear.'

'Mummy, Oxford will be a part of who I become! It won't be something I can lock away. It will run in my veins, fill my mind with knowledge and shape my conversations.'

'Tara, don't forget that in our community, a wedding costs much more than an education.'

'You never compromise on a "no", Mummy, do you?'

'Well, I don't say "no" until I have thought things through. You have to live your life with restraints and rules. You know this.' Aishwarya raised an eyebrow.

'Fine! Someday, I will break every rule. I will break them so completely that they'll never return to my life again.' The defiance in her voice unsettled her mother. Perhaps the years away at boarding school had created a gap—a daughter Aishwarya barely knew stood before her. Just then, the phone rang.

'Aishwarya,' a voice said softly, familiar yet distant, like an echo from another life.

'Who is this?' she asked.

'It's Shantanu.' There was a long silence on both sides before he spoke again. 'I do keep my ear to the ground, Aishwarya. Let Tara go to Oxford.'

'You were not meant to come back into our lives, Shantanu,' said Aishwarya, her voice laced with tacit disapproval.

'I went to Oxford on a scholarship—pity they paid for just a year, else I wouldn't have returned to work as a store manager. It seems to run in the genes. Do me a favour. Send Tara to my old college,' Shantanu said, before hanging up.

Aishwarya sat, pensive. There was something about that man—he always seemed to be around.

★

She chose to sit in the last row of the classroom. When she wasn't sketching caricatures of her professor, she was flipping through magazines featuring her heart-throb, Vivan Mehta. She stared at his image and wondered. His eyes were just like the ones in the painting of her father hanging on the wall at home.

Professor Krishna, or Krish sir, as he was fondly called by his students, was a unique man. A professor of law and an ardent theatre enthusiast, he headed the college dramatics society. His glasses balanced precariously, and somewhat miraculously, on the very tip of his nose throughout his lectures, as he paced the room with arms raised dramatically whenever a topic excited him enough, his deep and resonant voice echoing with Shakespearean cadence.

His classes, dubbed 'Hamlet's Hour', were more performances than lectures. He often donned a black lawyer's robe for dramatic effect and proclaimed, 'All the world's a stage!'

Despite his theatrics, it did not elude him that one of his students, Tara Kumari, often looked bored—and he did not like that.

'Meet me in the staffroom, Tara,' he said one day as he left the lecture hall.

She stood in front of him as he regarded her over a pile of hardbound legal tomes.

'I work extremely hard on my lectures, and you seem completely disinterested. Is there a reason for your apathy?'

'To be honest, sir, I have been accepted at Oxford, but my mother refuses to let me go.'

'That's a pity,' he said, his expression softening. 'Tell you what, Tara. I will make a deal with you. You give me a chance—show interest in my classes—and I will see if I can help make Oxford happen for you one day. Even if only for a couple of semesters. I am not promising anything, but who knows?'

'Sure, sir,' Tara said, her face lighting up with a broad smile.

'Miss Tara,' he called after her, 'remember, I expect you to give me your best.'

Tara turned around and nodded. 'A hundred per cent, sir.'

From that day, Tara moved to the front row, positioning herself squarely in close view of his bifocals. She hung on to every word he said, asking questions so intricate and probing that he often had to admit, 'Tara, I will have to consult my reference books to answer that.'

Before long, she became the star of his class and often joined him in the staffroom for discussions on points of law.

On a cold winter evening, Tara and Meher were huddled together on a sofa, their voices hushed.

'Krish sir is sexy for sure, like guys at 36 normally are,' said Meher, scrolling through his college profile.

'I so, so love him,' Tara declared dramatically, falling back on the couch.

'Then give him a sign,' Meher suggested.

The idea brewed in Tara's mind until she decided to dig into her mother's vault of Colombian coffee. After crafting what she believed was a hypnotic blend, she inhaled its aroma deeply, her eyes closed, her lips forming a soft smile. *Why not,* she thought.

With Meher in tow for moral support, Tara drove to Krish sir's campus residence. He was easy to find—lounging on a cane chair on the grassy patch outside his house, dressed in an indigo kurta.

Leaving Meher in the car, Tara walked hesitantly down the cobbled path and waved awkwardly.

'Good evening, sir,' she greeted.

He looked surprised.

'I was wondering if you could explain a few concepts for my thesis.'

He smiled. 'Tara, you seemed pretty confident in class.'

'Ummm… I also want to join your theatre classes, sir. I acted in every play back at school,' she blurted out, searching for excuses.

'Really? That's good. Lawyers do need to act in courtrooms,' he quipped. 'Come to the class. But first, let's see—what is confusing you in the law books?'

'I want to go beyond my book, sir,' she said. 'I am thinking of doing my thesis on ethical violations in the legal profession and how they lead to judicial misrulings. I want to focus on judges in particular. If humans are fallible, what right does a judge have to play God? To what extent should we rely on a single person's discretion?'

'Your questions show the intense depth of a very curious mind.'

Tara looked confused, not sure if it was a compliment.

'I like your mind, Tara. It shines, just like your name. And I really like the subject of your thesis. Go for it.'

Her face lit up. 'You know my favourite quote, Krish sir?'

He shook his head.

'I am, so I ask why.'

'Who said that?'

'Me,' she giggled, awkwardly lifting the bright red flask she had brought. 'I made some amazing Colombian coffee for you.'

'How did you know I like coffee?' he asked.

'I know a lot about you, sir,' she said, tilting her head back impishly.

★

Tara began visiting Krish sir frequently, animatedly discussing her theories about the perfect form of justice. She was making him rethink several ideas he had taught with conviction for years. Her mind was fascinating, constantly challenging and questioning limits and barriers.

'So, is there a way to quantify a judge's obligation?' she asked one day.

Krish found her idealism infectious. Slowly, he began to look forward to the rich aroma of Colombian coffee that accompanied her visits every evening.

In time, it was clear to both that there was chemistry between them—subtle, quiet, but undeniable. He was 36 and she was 19. Yet Krish sir became a friend and confidant to Tara, a companion in her mental expeditions to utopian justice.

One afternoon, Krish sir addressed her with a knowing smile. 'Miss Tara Kumari, do you remember I had promised to get you to Oxford if you took my classes seriously?'

Tara nodded, holding her breath.

'Well, the opportunity is here. I have been invited as a guest lecturer to Oxford, and I can take along a group of four students.'

17

Wings of Freedom

The British Airways flight circled over London, cutting through the dense cloud cover that had gripped the skies, struggling against the Atlantic winds. Below, rows of tiny cottages looked like dollhouses, their symmetry enchanting from above. Even at this altitude, she felt the magic of London, a city that seemed to sit at the edge of fairy tales.

While the cabin hummed with quiet tension, Tara leaned towards the window, excited and blissfully unaware of those long moments before landing—a time when one often reflects on mortality and yearns to step foot on solid ground. When the wheels touched the tarmac, a palpable sense of relief swept through the cabin; the lights flickered on and mobile phones were switched back to active mode.

'Hello, dear! Harmeet here. Just landed,' said the man beside her into his phone as he wrestled with his oversized hand baggage and polythene bags bursting at the seams.

Tara adjusted her satchel bag across her shoulders in what seemed like a perfect fit. This trip marked a series of firsts—starting with flying economy!

The gust of cold air that hit her as she stepped outside the airport left her shivering. She shoved her hands deep into her pockets and joined the queue to catch the famous London cab.

'To Oxford,' she told the cabbie with a bright smile.

He returned it warmly. 'Oxford students are always welcome in my cab.'

The drive to the university town of her fantasies was the longest hour of her life. As the cab turned into Oxford's high street, the ambience changed dramatically. Students dominated the town, clustered in animated groups along the pavements or filling cosy cafés that looked like extensions of libraries.

This is where I'm meant to be, she thought as the cab stopped in front of a quaint cottage with a wooden board swinging gently on rustic ropes. It read: 'The Oxford Inn, Est. 1820'. Thin vines adorned with tiny white flowers clung to its walls, and for a moment, Tara just stood there, transfixed, taking it all in. It was everything she had imagined. The little British inn was straight out of a film.

Inside, the man at the counter greeted her with a friendly smile. 'Welcome to the Oxford Inn! You must be Ms Nayan Tara Kumari.'

'That's me,' she replied, smiling back. 'I have a booking for a single room.'

'With our scrumptious continental breakfast and evening tea,' he added cheerfully.

'That's making me hungry already,' she quipped.

'Well, help yourself to some of our freshly baked scones while I finalize your check-in,' he offered, his eyes fixed on the computer screen.

Tara looked around the small reception area, which felt like a family living room. A fireplace crackled in the corner, the pleasant aroma of burning wood mingling with the faint smell of cigar smoke. Just then, she heard a familiar laugh.

Seated on a high winged chair, surrounded by students, was Krish sir.

'Hello, Tara,' he greeted her formally. 'How was your flight?'

'It was exciting, sir—because it was headed to Oxford,' she said, grinning.

'Well, that's good to hear. I am sure Oxford will not disappoint you,' he said, though his voice carried a rasp. He coughed lightly.

'Sir, you don't look well,' Tara said, concerned.

'You have no idea how tough I am,' he replied, though his

flushed cheeks and sudden sneeze betrayed him.

'Sir, you are clearly not as tough as you think,' she teased.

'Perhaps not,' he admitted sheepishly. 'But tougher than the robust Indian virus I have probably brought along.'

Tara leaned over with a worried look. 'You look very flushed. Do you have fever?' she asked. Before he could wave her concern away, Tara placed a hand on his forehead, startling him. 'Oh my God! You are burning up!'

'I will be fine,' he assured her, quickly rising. 'You need rest.'

'We'll talk in the morning, young lady.'

★

Tara couldn't sleep that night. She tossed and turned, unable to stop thinking about him. At last, she slipped on her robe—the one with the royal insignia embroidered on the lapel, a piece her mother had insisted she bring—and padded quietly down to the lobby.

There he was, by the fireplace, nursing a glass of cognac. That night, they talked for hours. Krish sir became her friend as he shared anecdotes from his early years in college, drawing mirthful giggles from her. She confessed her hidden desires to him, including her dream of acting in a Bollywood film before she died.

His eyebrows shot up in amusement as he lit a cigar, chewing the edge thoughtfully before drawing on it and exhaling a plume of smoke like a pro.

'You are certainly pretty enough, so why don't you go for it?'

'Simple. Mummy is so terrified at the thought that she's barred me from even thinking of it.'

'Oh no! Then you are definitely going to get there one day,' he said, his laugh deep and throaty.

'Yes, that extra motivation comes when you feel like a rebel with a cause!'

'What a strange combination of ambitions—a student at Oxford and the leading lady in a Hindi film.'

'To be or not to be,' she mused, 'that is the question. Life constantly throws choices at us. To leave or stay, to love or walk away, to say yes or no. Shakespeare fits into every situation with the ease of a man who saw life as a continuum,' she said, sighing. 'A never-ending stream of consciousness that convinces us it will never change—until it does.'

'Never say yes when you want to say no,' he replied, 'and never say no when you want to say yes.'

Their eyes locked briefly before she quickly looked away. The cognac's warmth was waning, its intensity failing him just when he needed it most. A soft glow of the rising sun filtered through the lace curtains, and somehow, they both understood that some things end with the night. Daylight, stark and ruthless, had a way of stripping away the fantasies that flourished in the dark.

Tara rose, her steps unsteady. 'How are you feeling now, Krish sir?' she asked.

'Was I ever ill?' he retorted, a glint of mischief in his eyes. 'I think I have talked myself out of the fever.'

She smiled sweetly at him. The night had passed, but some part of it lingered. Nothing is ever entirely lost.

★

After a long day at the Oxford Faculty of Law, Tara walked back to the inn. All she wanted was a hot meal followed by a steaming bath. She had been sneezing all day and felt increasingly unwell. The flames in the fireplace leapt and crackled, its warmth enticing; she sank into a large upholstered chair and suddenly felt flushed, followed by the unmistakable throbbing of a terrible headache. Feeling dizzy, she climbed the stairs and collapsed on to her springy bed, sinking into the soft duvet and pillows.

She fished her mobile phone out of her pocket and dialled. 'Divya, this is Tara.'

'How are you doing?'

'I have got a terrible fever.'

'Oh no, that is awful.'

'No,' Tara murmured, 'it's beautiful.'

'What do you mean? How can a fever be beautiful?' Divya sounded puzzled.

'You won't understand. It's just the flu; it's special because I caught it from Krish sir! Imagine—this tiny germ lived in him until yesterday, and now it's in me. It's so…romantic,' she said, her voice delirious with joy.

'You are a crazy girl!' Divya replied, sounding both amused and worried. 'Honestly, I could think of a million better ways to romance someone. Have you taken any medication?'

'I don't want to cure it too quickly,' Tara murmured as Divya hung up and immediately dialled Krish's number.

'She doesn't sound well at all, sir,' Divya said, alerting him. Krish rushed to Tara's room, finding the door ajar. She lay on the bed, her teeth chattering, her face flushed, her eyes glassy.

'Tara,' he said, alarmed. 'This is terrible.'

'Krish sir, I have your virus in me—it could never harm me!'

He frowned as he noticed two miniature bottles of cognac lying empty beside her. She had swallowed them as if they were medicine.

Tara knew she might regret her behaviour later—or perhaps she already did, in the recesses of her mind. But in that moment, she felt completely uninhibited.

'Hold me, Krish sir,' she whispered breathlessly.

He was drawn to her; it was an irresistible pull that defied reason. He tried to step back, but his body betrayed him, rooted in place. The desire between them was magnetic, immediate and unapologetic.

He bent forward, kissing her forehead lightly at first. She responded with unexpected passion, her lips finding his, strong and insistent, as if she never wanted to let him go. She surrendered herself to the moment with reckless abandon, her hair falling in soft waves as he stroked it gently.

Krish tempered his passion, his movements careful and deliberate, as though he were making love to something fragile, something precious.

'Look,' she said softly. 'It's snowing.'

Krish propped himself on an elbow and looked out of the window. A million little snowflakes, illuminated by the golden haze of the street lights, danced gently to the ground.

'This is magic,' she whispered. 'Tonight is a dreamer's most beautiful dream.'

As if on cue, the sun appeared like an unwelcome intruder, its sharp ray cutting through the dim room. It sliced between them, breaking the shroud of anonymity and the liberation that the night had brought.

'Krish sir?' she asked, her voice tentative. 'Are you married?'

He turned and looked at her, smiling faintly before shaking his head.

'Professors,' he said softly, 'have a hard time finding wives. And you can stop calling me "sir"—at least, outside the classroom.'

'I would marry you,' she said without hesitation.

'You are a princess,' he whispered back, leaning closer. 'You need a prince.'

She grinned. 'Krish sir, can we drive down to Stratford-upon-Avon for the theatre festival?'

★

That evening, they sat in the Blue Fox pub in Stratford, sipping red wine after an open-air performance of *Macbeth*. Their conversation meandered through the nuances of Shakespearean tragedy and the subtleties of different intoxicants—topics that conveniently masked the undercurrent of the night's unresolved emotions.

'There are moods in these bottles,' he explained with thoughtful seriousness. 'White and bubbly gives you a high; red has a mellow character; sherry is sweet and soothing; brandy warms the heart. You have to know how to sip them—slowly— and savour every note.'

Her eyes had glazed over, and her cheeks were flushed from the wine. 'Don't worry, Krish, I am not about to become an alcoholic. Thanks to your tutelage, I shall aspire to be a sophisticated connoisseur of wines and spirits—like the truly civilized.'

'Sure, you will. Alcohol can be a cultured pleasure, but it's so easily abused.' The humour drained from his face as his tone shifted abruptly. 'Last night,' he said, 'was not right of me, Tara.'

'The line between right and wrong,' she countered, 'is a matter of perception.' She had hoped to be calm, but could hear the decibels of her voice rising. 'I believe in following my conscience, and my conscience tells me it was right.' Her throat tightened, her heart hammering in her chest. She swallowed the lump in her throat, willing herself to stay composed.

'I am your teacher, and much older. I am supposed to be your caretaker…'

Tara abandoned any attempt at nonchalance, her words tumbling out in a rush. 'But, Krish, it was your virus that slipped into me…'

They both giggled at the absurdity of the statement. 'Yes,' he said with a smile. 'Let's just blame it on the virus.' At that moment, the cab driver poked his head into the pub. 'Is that you, ma'am, for the ride to Heathrow?'

'Yes, coming,' she said, rising reluctantly.

Krish walked her to the door, carrying her satchel on his shoulder and her suitcase in his hand. They stood there for a moment, their eyes locking in the evening glow. He noticed the tears brimming in her eyes.

'Bye, Tara. Take care of yourself,' he said.

'Goodbye,' she managed to say softly as she climbed into the cab. As it pulled away, her tears flowed freely. She looked back and saw his silhouette fade into the misty evening.

'Krish,' she typed into her phone, 'I love you.'

Krish smiled as he read the message; it was short and simple, but it brought the most heartfelt smile to his face. He stood by his window, watching as the night quietly embraced the town.

He stood there until he saw a blue car pull up outside the motel. His heart dared to hope.

Moments later, there was a knock at the door.

'I missed my flight,' Tara said simply.

'Did you? And what will convince you to go back home?' he asked, smiling.

'A train to Dover, a ferry across the English Channel to Calais and then a bus to Paris?' she offered with a mischievous grin.

★

Aishwarya Devi was elated to have her daughter back home.

'You look good, baby. Look at those rosy cheeks—the British air has done you good! And as for missing your flight, I hope Paris was everything you dreamt it would be.'

'Paris is poetry, Paris is love, Paris is art and music,' Tara gushed. 'Paris is a dreamer's greatest dream.'

Aishwarya allowed her daughter her moment of excitement, though she found the exuberance a little overboard. 'Yes, Paris is a sort of urban paradise,' she agreed calmly.

At dinner, Ram Swarup filled the table with Chhoti Madam's favourite dishes. As Tara devoured the pungent pleasures of Rajasthani food, her mother quizzed her about Oxford.

'Oh, Mummy, it was an enriching experience,' she said

enthusiastically between mouthfuls of spicy home-cooked food she had missed so much.

Tara knew she would have to bring it up eventually. *Better now than never*, she thought.

'I have something to tell you, Mummy.' Her voice trembled slightly, teetering between nervousness and defiance. 'I know you will not be happy, but I am hoping you will understand,' she blurted out everything in a rush, like ripping off a plaster to get it over with.

Aishwarya Devi set her fork down and waited for Tara to continue.

'Mummy, I am in love with Krish sir.'

Aishwarya was silent, then reached out to put her hand on Tara's. 'How dare he?'

'"How dare he" what?' protested Tara. 'I have always been smitten by him. It was not he who made the first move, Mummy. It was me. Trust me.'

'You are 19, Tara, and he must be at least 15 years older than you. What do you even know about love at your age? Love at the Eiffel Tower is an illusion. It's not real, Tara!' Her voice dropped, her tone measured yet cutting, as though reasoning with a naïve child. A young girl in love with an older man is the most illogical of all creatures. 'Darling, at your age, every infatuation feels like love. You won't know the difference—often until it's too late.'

'I want to marry him, Mummy,' Tara declared, her eyes steady, her voice firm and unfaltering.

'He is years older than you!'

'That's exactly why I love him.'

'I know you've never stopped searching for your father, but this is not going to help.'

'So if I find a man who gives me some part of what I never had, is that a problem for you, Mummy?' Tara said, her voice rising.

'Let me make one thing very clear: age aside, don't forget who you are. You are a Rajput—not just any Rajput, but a princess. And you *cannot* marry anyone other than a Rajput.'

Tara stood up abruptly, leaving her plate half-full, tears streaming down her face. She had always known her mother was tough, but she had never known her to be this cruel and coldly unyielding.

A week later, Krishna Kumar Sinha received a letter in the post. The message was curt, clinical and devastating: his services were no longer required at Jaipur Law College.

Sitting alone in the empty classroom, he stared at the rows of vacant seats, contemplating his life ahead without a job. He had a passion for teaching; he remembered the echoes of his students' voices as they questioned, debated and argued with him, spellbound by their teacher's dramatic style and explanations. It felt as though his reason to live had been snatched away.

After several days of reflection, he began to plan his next move to escape the wilderness of unemployment and the fear of confronting his future. It was evident that his interlude with Tara was having a domino effect on his life. In all certainty, there would be nothing but pain for her as well in pursuing a relationship that had little hope.

He wrote a short email to Tara, letting her know that he had been dismissed from his job at the college and that he was moving to Delhi, where an old classmate had offered him a partnership at his law firm.

I will find my bearings as a lawyer, though I will always miss my days as 'Professor Krish'. You, Tara, must marry a handsome young man, someone your own age—a Rajput, perhaps—if you want to keep family harmony. No harm in that, I'd say. You are young and will meet many men; I hope you choose someone who keeps you happy and at peace.

As for me, I will remember you as you were the last time I saw you, that memory frozen in time forever.

Take care, always.
Krish

18

Pink Champagne in Pink City

'Rosie, darling,' Aishwarya whispered. 'Who is that young man?'

Rosie followed her friend's gaze and smirked. 'Ah! The rajmata always did have a thing for younger men. You really want to know?'

'Don't be ridiculous, Rosie! He is perfect for Tara.'

'Oh, excuse me. You just look so young, I almost forgot,' Rosie teased. 'Well, that is Vikramjit Rathore, if I'm not mistaken. Not a born royal like us, but he is a Rajput.'

'That clears the first hurdle,' Aishwarya said with a satisfied nod. 'And his family?'

'They run a hotel in the centre of town. Nothing grand, but the boy himself is brilliant.'

'Education?' Aishwarya pressed.

'What do you think I am? An encyclopaedia?' retorted Rosie.

'No, darling, you are far better.'

'He is studying at the London School of Economics on scholarship. Rumour has it he may have to drop out because of this damned recession. His family is bankrupt.'

'That's perfect. He can handle the family assets.'

'Ash, Tara can marry into the best royal families. Why him?'

'I don't want to be left alone, Rosie. In fact, I need a man in the house.'

'Ash, you should let Tara have an independent life.'

Aishwarya waved off the comment. 'Now, be a dear and arrange an introduction,' she said, ignoring her friend's advice.

Aishwarya played life like a chess game. Every move was carefully calculated, its implications thoroughly considered; her eyes were always set on winning the game she started.

Rosie walked up to the tall, handsome man and whispered something in his ear. He turned, glanced at Aishwarya Devi, and walked over with a polite smile.

'A pleasure to meet you, ma'am,' he said.

'I am told you are studying at the London School of Economics.'

'Yes! Working hard for a piece of paper,' Vikramjit chuckled. He sounded as good as he looked—his voice rough and gravelly, with a hint of baritone.

Tara, noticing the tall, handsome man standing next to her mother, joined in.

'Hi, I am Tara,' she introduced herself.

Vikramjit smiled back. 'Hi, Tara. I am Vikram. Have we met before?' he said, looking at her with rapt attention.

'So, where were we?' interjected Aishwarya Devi smoothly, redirecting the focus back to herself.

Tara excused herself, leaving her mother and Vikram deep in conversation.

★

'Rosie, that was a perfect start,' Aishwarya said later, like a woman on a mission. 'Now, your next move will be to host a cosy party at your home. Let us all be invited. The food is on you, the booze on me. Deal?'

'Oh, is it now?' Rosie said, arching an eyebrow. 'Well, if the "deal" goes through, I am claiming your sapphire earrings as my fee.'

'Darling, the way I see it, everything in life is a deal,' replied Aishwarya, smiling.

She loved the quiet thrill of exerting control over those around her, often without them realizing it. The rajmata revelled in this subtle display of power, moving people like chess pieces to suit her plans—even her closest friends weren't exempt.

A month later, she sat in front of her vanity, trying on heirlooms from the Jaivangarh family to select pieces for her daughter's trousseau.

'Ah, can't give this one away. It looks gorgeous on me,' she murmured, admiring herself in the mirror as she draped her grandmother's ruby-encrusted necklace around her neck.

'That's perfect for Tara,' said Rosie, watching from afar. 'She will look beautiful in it.'

Aishwarya, however, wasn't listening. Her eyes were fixed on her reflection. 'Exquisite! This one stays with me too.'

She leaned back and remarked, 'I have worn every piece I own, and you know what, Rosie? I am far too young to give any of it away. I'll have some new pieces made for Tara instead.'

'And what happens if the new ones look good on you too?' Rosie demanded.

'Ah, now that would be a real problem.'

'Ash, I have known you since we were kids, so I'll put this bluntly—you have become self-obsessed. This isn't about Tara; it's about you. Even the boy was chosen for your convenience.'

'You've always had a soft spot for my little girl.'

'Yes, and I can't wait to see her as a bride,' said Rosie, a pang of nostalgia surfacing. She remembered how fiercely Aishwarya had clung to her arm the day Tara was born. But now, she felt exasperated with her friend.

Two months later, all of Rajasthan was abuzz with the news of the royal wedding. Ornate invitation cards accompanied by boxes of sweets arrived at select addresses.

On a full moon night, the Jaivangarh Palace gleamed like a jewel as it hosted the wedding of Princess Nayan Tara Kumari and Vikramjit Rathore. The celebration saw royalty from around the world arrive in droves.

Aishwarya's childhood friends had made it to her daughter's wedding, and she was pleased to see them. Lady Izabel Griffin, who had once attended boarding school with the rajmata in Switzerland, arrived in a blue foil print dress that fit her like a second skin. In the sultry heat of the night, she looked like a sculpted mannequin. After her sixth glass of pink champagne, she was open to every conceivable possibility. The drummers created a hypnotic rhythm that filled the atmosphere. The music broke through the night, slipping into silent spaces and knocking on doors till they opened.

The bride's clothes were the talk of the town, her image splashed across the centre spreads of every major magazine. The night unfolded as a postcard-perfect tribute to Rajput traditions, carefully preserved and nurtured in this part of India. Tara sat silently—an image of a Rajput bride, her head lowered under a chiffon veil—yet her eyes peered to take in the details of her wedding. She saw her mother standing in the centre, wearing a magenta lehenga—in a shade similar to Tara's—and greeting the *baraat*. Then, in the teeming crowds, she suddenly spotted him. Vikram, looking dapper in his designer traditionals, walked in with his family. He flung his arms out and hugged his mother-in-law. Tara looked down—it was best today if she kept her eyes shut.

In the shadows of the revelry, few noticed the tall man in a shawl lingering in the background. His face bore the fine lines of a life spent under the desert sun, his amber green eyes piercing as they scanned the scene. Although he had not received an invitation, he felt this moment of pride belonged to him more than anyone. He watched the groom with a steady gaze, then turned his attention to the bride. His face softened as a warm smile spread across it, and he closed his eyes, murmuring a prayer. Then, like the drifting desert sands, he faded into the black night.

★

The small tea shop with a clear view of Windsor Castle served the finest strawberry tarts in all of England. Vikram scooped a spoonful of the creamy dessert and brought it to his young wife's lips.

As he looked around, he noticed the old lady at the counter, fast asleep. He pulled the spoon away, tasted her favourite dessert himself and then kissed her deeply.

'Delicious,' Tara gushed, her eyes still shut as he let go of her.

The old lady suddenly stirred from her nap. 'Did you call me, sir?'

'No, but we could do with one more strawberry tart with double scoops of ice cream, please.'

Tara felt more married with each passing day. She had begun to take care of Vikram in small ways—checking his laundry, ensuring he took his vitamins and managing other little details of his life. Although memories of Krish came back to her often and she wished it were him she was doing these things for, it wasn't to be and she quickly chased the regrets away. She had married Vikram, and now she would do her best to be a good wife.

Walking back to their hotel—once a small 18th-century home—their fingers entwined; the honeymooners giggled and chatted with the exuberance of two people starting out on an adventure.

'Vik, do you think life back home could be as idyllic as this?'

Vikram replied with a carefree smile. 'Why not?'

'Hmmm,' she said. 'If I could, I would start a tea shop here. We'd serve strawberry tarts and scones. I'd never have to leave Windsor then.'

'If you did, we would be out of business because I would feed all the tarts to you—and without cutlery!'

★

It was the perfect day to visit Covent Garden. Tara and Vikram caught the underground train, which whisked them away from Windsor's quiet streets to the vibrant heart of London. As they emerged into the bustling square, they were greeted by a lively crowd of weekenders and eager tourists, cameras slung around their necks.

Once a fruit and flower market, Covent Garden was now a cultural tapestry, alive with street performers, singers, entertainers and craftsmen. Instant shops popped up on Sundays, with wooden racks and stalls, creating a charming flea market. Open spaces transformed into mammoth theatres, where magic seemed to unfold at every corner. It was a haven for artists yearning for applause yet waiting to enter the doors of the many theatres around.

Tara paused to listen to an opera singer, her powerful voice soaring above the noise of the crowd. As the haunting melody faded, it was replaced by the soft strains of a violinist's gentle notes floating in the air.

Soon, Tara and Vikram found themselves at Covent Garden's iconic merry-go-round. She hopped onto a horse excitedly and Vikram got on behind her just in time. The merry-go-round moved, first laboriously and then faster. Its bright lights and vivid colours of the painted acrylic horses made Tara feel giddy, yet she threw her hands open wide, as though she were flying.

'Hold me tight!' she squealed. 'I am going to fall! Hold me tight, Vik!'

Vikram tightened his grip around her, and she loved the feeling of a man's large, protective hands holding her. When the ride finally came to a stop, he leapt off and, with an effortless movement, caught Tara by the waist and helped her down.

They wandered into the open-air foyer, where a clown's performance had drawn an enthusiastic crowd. His face was painted with a smile he couldn't remove. He balanced himself precariously on a tightrope while juggling glass bottles. His fingers deftly caught each fragile piece before it crashed to the floor.

Vikram stood spellbound by the masked performer's artistry until he noticed Tara's face. 'What's the matter?' he asked.

'I hate clowns. They give me the creeps,' she admitted, looking tense.

'Why? Look at him. Poor guy's just trying to make everybody laugh.'

'One never knows what lies behind the mask,' she said. At that moment, her phone buzzed. Slipping her hand into her pocket, she pulled it out.

'It's Mummy,' she said excitedly, answering the call. 'Mummy, we are having so much fun! I want to have a honeymoon every year.'

'I have called you six times in the last five minutes,' snapped Aishwarya, her voice as cutting as glass.

'We are at Covent Garden, Mummy,' explained Tara. 'The noise here is deafening.'

'Two days left before Vikram's term at LSE begins. You should get packing now,' Aishwarya said, her tone brisk and business-like.

Tara fell silent. It felt as though the threads of magic suspending their dreamlike reality had suddenly snapped.

'Can I speak to Vikram?' Aishwarya asked impatiently.

Tara passed the phone to Vikram.

'Hello, Rajmata,' Vikram greeted his mother-in-law. 'How are you?'

'I am keeping fine, but not a single call from either of you in 10 days.'

'I am sorry, we were just—'

'Never mind,' she cut him off. 'I have sent in your forms and the fee for LSE. It's time to focus on your final year there.'

'That's so kind of you. I don't know what to say. I am so grateful. Thank you.'

As the call ended, Tara looked away, lost in thought. Or perhaps it was more than thinking—she was feeling. Feeling an unease she couldn't quite articulate.

'Let's get something to eat, Vik,' she said, steering them towards the baked potato stand, where queues of hungry weekend revellers waited patiently.

That evening, Vikram was unusually quiet. 'I don't want you to go, Princess,' he said.

Tara smiled at him wistfully. From their hotel balcony in Windsor, the strains of a violinist drifted up from the street below. Vikram took Tara's hand and pulled her close, swaying to the tunes of an old Frank Sinatra number.

The next morning, Vikram kissed Tara while she lay half asleep.

'I would like to come along to drop you.'

'No, you cannot,' he said. 'Your car will be here to get you to London in an hour.'

'Goodbye, Vikram,' she whispered, holding back her tears.

'No, don't say that. Just say, "Till we kiss again".'

19

Impurities of Love

Tara returned to Jaipur, and though her life did not seem to have changed much, she felt different; she sensed a strange warm glow within, as though she belonged to someone and that someone belonged to her. She spent hours scrolling through her phone, staring at the photographs they had clicked on their honeymoon. The months without Vikram felt as though her life were on pause, as though she were sitting alone in a waiting room to catch a flight to a new life.

One evening, Tara rushed to the dinner table, drawn by the familiar aroma of home-cooked food she had yearned for while in England. She sat upright as Ram Swarup placed her favourite dishes on the table and then, as always, lit the candles at the centre. Her eyes drifted to the empty chair; she couldn't start before her mother arrived, but on the other hand, she couldn't stand the temptation.

Ram Swarup, noticing her dilemma, smiled indulgently and placed a helping of crispy bhindi on her plate. 'Quick, this is your favourite, I know.'

Tara giggled and tucked in with the glee of a child, savouring the flavours. Ram Swarup still made her feel like a young kid.

The sharp clatter of pencil heels against the marble floor announced her mother's arrival. Aishwarya entered, perfectly dressed, and gave her daughter a cursory look before signalling to Ram Swarup. 'No soup for me today,' she declared.

Then she turned towards Tara and added, 'Vikram called. He just wouldn't stop talking.'

'He did?' asked Tara, surprised. 'I needed to speak to him about my new project at the village.'

'He won't be interested, Tara. He's too preoccupied with his own plans.'

Tara lowered her gaze, focusing on her plate, stabbing her fork into the china. 'So, was it a video call?' she asked.

'Yes, dear, it was.'

She got it now. Her mother had dressed up for the video call.

The rest of the meal passed in strained silence, Aishwarya's words echoing in Tara's mind. *He just wouldn't stop talking... He won't be interested, Tara...*

In the days that followed, a strange distance crept between her and her mother. Even as they sat together at the breakfast table, there was little to say. Unease hung in the air. The silence grew, speaking a language of its own. The palace became claustrophobic for Tara; she longed to drive down to Jaivangarh, take a walk through the museum and then escape into the sheer innocence of the village.

Aishwarya's coldness towards Tara had become second nature to her, so she was surprised at herself when she greeted Tara with unusual warmth one morning.

'It's Mother's Day today,' she announced. 'Aren't you going to wish me?'

Tara gave her mother a tight hug. For a fleeting moment, the distance between them vanished. Tara felt the comforting warmth of the womb that had once held her, and Aishwarya felt a tug at the invisible umbilical cord that still connected them. 'Come with me today, my darling,' said Aishwarya.

'What's the plan?'

'I am the chief guest at an exhibition showcasing Rajasthan's dying arts. Afterwards, we can have lunch together.'

'Sounds perfect,' Tara replied, smiling.

The two shared a perfect girls' day out, and for the first time in months, Tara dared to hope. Perhaps this was the beginning of a new chapter in their relationship. But of course, that was just wishful thinking.

★

Tara grew restless, counting the moments until Vikram's return. She longed to truly begin her married life, and spent sleepless nights imagining what it would be like to have him sleeping next to her. She clung to hope, dreaming and believing that her life ahead would be brimming with happiness.

Vikram's final term at LSE was gruelling. Between classes and assignments, he still managed to call his wife at least twice a day.

'Good night, love,' Tara whispered tenderly into the phone one evening during dinner.

'Tara, I need to speak to Vikram,' Aishwarya interjected, reaching for the phone.

'Vikram, there is a proposal from the Hilton Group of Hotels for the Summer Palace.'

'Rajmata, did you say Hilton?'

'Yes, dear, but it is beyond me. I think I will just refuse it.'

'No, no, don't do that. I will help you through it.'

'Are you sure you can manage?'

'Of course. This business degree has equipped me for just that.'

'Oh, that's such a relief. Thank you, dear.'

'I should be thanking you, Rajmata. Trust me—you didn't waste your money on my education.'

Tara listened quietly, hanging on to every nuance of her mother's words. When Aishwarya finally asked Vikram if he wanted to say goodnight to Tara, she hesitated and then walked away. 'She just walked away. Well, I will tell her you said goodnight,' she replied casually.

The calls soon became a daily ritual. Animated discussions about family properties, business possibilities and grand schemes filled Vikram's conversations with Aishwarya. Tara tried to join in, speaking with interest about the palace and the surrounding lands, but Vikram brushed aside her contributions as naïve and inconsequential. Slowly, she began to feel their worlds diverging. They were like two drifting islands, her love slipping farther away each day.

Determined to bridge the growing distance, she masked her feelings and put on her best for Vikram. 'Hi, Vik, are you eating well?' she asked one evening, hoping he would have the courtesy to at least pretend to show some semblance of care.

'Can you pass the phone to your mummy, please? There's something really important I need to discuss with her.'

Tara passed the phone to her mother and left the room. She didn't feel that warm glow anymore. Vikram had stopped feigning concern for her and always cut directly to the chase. The feeling that she belonged to him was fast fading. She was alone, as always.

The day Vikram returned home from England, he stepped into the house and went straight up to Aishwarya's room. Touching her feet, he reached into his bag and pulled out his degree, presenting it to her.

'I am so proud of you, Vikram,' said Aishwarya.

'You put your faith in me,' he replied, his eyes shining with gratitude.

Tara stood in the shadows, her heart heavy. Her pain deepened and tears welled up in her eyes. She rushed to her room, frantically dabbing at her smudged make-up.

'Tara, my darling Tara,' Vikram said as he burst into the room.

'Vikram, you're finally home,' she replied, forcing a smile.

'Why are you crying?'

'Tears of joy,' she lied, hugging him tightly. She willed herself to forget the hurt and make her fairy tale a reality.

The next morning at breakfast, while Aishwarya and Vikramjit were deeply engrossed in conversation, Tara remained silent, her thoughts spiralling. She sensed that her light-hearted, girlish days had become a distant memory. The dysfunctional marriage she was in made her claustrophobic, as if her proprietorship had changed hands; now, there were two claiming her—her husband and her mother. She no longer felt like a person, but rather an asset. Perhaps her pain was also a part of the Jaivangarh legacy. It was time to escape to her haven of peace.

Aishwarya and Vikramjit did not even notice when Tara got up and left the table. They failed to see her pass by them. She was dressed in a fluorescent Rajasthani lehenga and a short block-print kurta. Her traditional leather *mojari*s made no sound as she moved through the halls, leaving behind the montage of flawed relationships.

20

Shifting Sands

Tara bounded down the steps, her feet moving as if in flight, and made her way to the porch. Ram Swarup flung the car door open and she slipped into the front seat, grateful for the refuge. He peered into her face and she knew that in his silence lay a deep disapproval of the happenings at Jaivangarh Palace.

Tara turned on the ignition and expertly manoeuvred the car through the narrow streets, soon finding herself on the main highway leading out of the city. Her thoughts stayed rooted at the breakfast table that morning—she remembered not being heard or noticed. It was yet another reminder of her nothingness, a reinforcement of the growing belief that, in their world, she simply did not exist.

She glanced at herself in the rear-view mirror—perfectly put together as always, yet somehow diminished. Her mother's image lingered on the windscreen—Aishwarya's bright pink lipstick, a shade too vibrant in the morning light, had surely commanded Vikram's attention. He had been listening intently, captivated by her every word. Tara felt a sharp twinge of irritation and adjusted the mirror, trying to push the moment out of her mind.

Her foot subconsciously pressed harder on the accelerator, surging the car forward. Her knuckles whitened as she gripped the steering wheel, and tiny beads of sweat formed on her forehead. The speedometer needle flirted between 110 and 120, its motion like a spinning roulette wheel. The sudden rattle of a truck startled her, snapping her back to reality. She eased off the accelerator and turned the car through the repeated archways leading to the grand, ancient structure that housed the Gaj Singh Museum and Art Conservatory.

Tara stepped out and headed up the sprawling steps. The doors were open and she walked in. Pride flushed through her, as it always did, when she entered this place. Rows of her ancestors adorned the walls, their eyes following her as she passed by. Their portraits, trapped in ornate frames, stood alongside a collection of rare paintings dating back several centuries.

The faint musty smell that greeted her irked her senses. Mental notes formed quickly: she'd need to look into moisture control for the museum's delicate artefacts. She moved through the arched entrance into a long hall with ceilings that soared higher than a two-storey building. Passing the 16th-century Persian carpets depicting hunting scenes and mounted riders, she finally reached the far end of the hall.

Tara gripped the handle of the iron-grilled elevator and pulled it open. The relic, adorned with a small brass plaque reading 'Otis Elevators, 1892', could easily serve as a display piece. When it was first installed, visitors were often more fascinated by the experience of being elevated than by the exhibits. Stepping inside, she ascended to the top floor, added years ago by her visionary father.

While the museum was dedicated to preserving and displaying ancient artefacts, the conservatory was an open workshop. Here, artisans continued age-old crafts, breathing life into fading traditions. Tara paused to take it all in, her eyes lingering on the skilled hands at work, each artisan absorbed in their craft.

Walking up to a small marble alcove, she lit the brass oil lamp before the deity and bowed her head in quiet devotion. It was something her father had been particular about, and she made sure to uphold the tradition. Perhaps this connection to customs was the only positive thing to emerge from her dysfunctional relationship with him—an unexpected by-product of her angst. *Life has its trade-offs*, she mused.

Her gaze moved to the wood and brass plaque at the door, on which was simply inscribed 'Director'. She stepped inside, settling into the plush leather chair behind the mahogany desk where once Gaj had sat. Tara began counting silently—one, two, three... She could count to nine and expect a knock on the door; she wasn't wrong again today. There was a soft, almost respectful knock.

The door opened to reveal Mehta ji, a grey-haired man with a slight stoop. His glasses perched precariously on his nose as he greeted her with a respectful, '*Khamma ghani*, madam.' He set a thick ledger on the desk and adjusted his glasses. 'I have updated all the listings here, madam. The paintings, the crystals, the silver artefacts and the statues are under separate headings.'

'Mehta ji, I appreciate your work, but I think it's time we got them all on a computer.'

'Madam, computers can make errors. I will never make an error.'

Tara smiled. 'I have someone coming in today—a technology whizz-kid. Let's see what he can do for us.'

Mehta ji's face stiffened, indignation creeping into his expression. Without a word, he closed the ledger, gave a slight nod and walked away.

A man with a slight build walked in with a swagger. 'Anand,' he introduced himself, gripping Tara's hand with unnecessary firmness before promptly setting up his Apple laptop, eager to get on with his presentation. A group of men, led by Mehta ji, walked in and sat down, looking a bit condescendingly at the young man.

'Now, let's begin,' Anand said with a touch of loftiness, drawing their attention to the lit-up screen. 'The museum is about the past, but your systems need to move into the future if you want to effectively preserve the past.'

Mehta ji squirmed in his seat, but Tara looked excited.

'Let me start with a walk-through of our module,' Anand continued. 'For every visitor who steps into the museum, there are 20 more who intend to visit but never do. With the virtual walk-through, they can explore the museum remotely. Some may even be inspired to follow up with an actual visit. Speaking of outreach—you could have visitors on your virtual tours logging in from the US, Africa or just anywhere on the planet…for the moment, that is,' he smiled.

The room was quiet, all eyes fixed on the screen as Anand demonstrated. 'You can stop at any painting, enlarge it and access its full history!' The initial scowls softened; encouraged, Anand moved to the next module. 'Here is the inventory data plan. Every artefact will be catalogued digitally, complete with photographs, dimensions and historical context. Now for security—each object will have a chip embedded beneath it. If tampered with or touched, an alarm will sound. This means total safety and tracking of your collection.'

He turned to Tara. 'From your office, you will be able to monitor every piece, madam. How's that?'

'It's amazing,' she said, extending her hand.

'Are we rolling, then?' he asked, grinning expectantly.

Tara nodded and asked Mehta ji to show Anand around the museum and find him a suitable workspace. They settled on a small desk at the end of the corridor—a perfect spot where Anand's mouse clicks would not disturb the tranquillity of the museum.

The rapid flapping of his leather slippers echoing down the halls on days he arrived late always amused Tara. 'Salaam, Rajkumari ji,' he huffed.

'Salaam, Hari,' she responded warmly.

Hari was the most educated boy from the small hamlet bordering the museum. Despite having studied only till 12th standard, Tara had appointed him as her secretary after a year of training. Her intent was clear—she wanted to encourage the youth in his area to pursue their education.

That morning, Hari beamed with pride as he displayed his latest system for organizing paperwork. 'This is "Urgent File One",' he announced, 'followed by "Urgent File Two" and "Urgent File Three".'

Tara smiled. 'Very inventive, Hari. That's very clever of you.'

'My idea, madam, is that all papers are not the same urgent. Some very urgent, some very less urgent and "Urgent Three", madam, is…well, useless!'

'I think you mean all papers are important in some way, except perhaps category three?'

'Exactly, madam!' Hari exclaimed and left.

Picking up the intercom, Tara instructed, 'Mr Jain, Hari needs a few extra classes in spoken English.'

Just then, the door opened and Tara's face lit up. 'Meher!' she screamed, rushing to hug her close friend and confidante. 'Let's get some winter sunshine on the terrace,' she said, leading Meher to the lush balcony that overlooked the sprawling landscape. Although years had passed since they'd last met, it took all but a few seconds to bridge the time. Meher still looked as beautiful as ever, but there was an exhaustion in her eyes that Tara was quick to notice. 'Tell me, is all good with you?'

'Not really,' admitted Meher. 'Abba has been hearing about builders eyeing our land. What's happening here, Tara? Is your mother selling us off?'

Tara looked as though the ground beneath her feet had shifted. 'I won't let that happen.'

'You don't own it, do you?'

'I do, partially. I won't let it happen,' she repeated, her eyes blazing with determination.

Meher's words echoed in her mind long after her friend had left. Tara slumped into a chair, staring out at the rows of homes and farmland in the distance. She instructed Hari to make sure no one entered the room, then lit a cigarette, puffing hard on the filter—as she always did when she was worried.

Her promise to Meher weighed heavily on her. Meher was probably right.

She stubbed the cigarette into the ashtray with a twinge of guilt. Smoking was perhaps the only thing she had in common with her mother—an unhealthy compulsion to light up. *I must give up smoking*, she thought. *Tomorrow*, she promised herself, *for sure.*

21

The Muse

The sound of a car door opening made her get to her feet. 'We have a very important visitor today, Meher. Let's see if you are still as good at seducing guys as you were in college.'

'Is that a challenge?' Meher giggled, her old carefree smile momentarily back on her face.

Tara walked out to receive her special guest. 'Mr Vardhan, thank you for making it!'

Suraj Vardhan's sharp eyes narrowed slightly, as though sizing her up. 'I have come for the artists and to see the genius you claim to have discovered,' he said rather dryly.

His reputation preceded him as one of India's most committed custodians of art and heritage. Author of numerous bestsellers, Suraj Vardhan was a towering figure, standing just over six feet tall. He wore khaki pants, a tie-and-dye shirt and leather slip-ons. A large African pendant hung casually around his neck and tribal earrings adorned both ears, completing the image of a man who treated himself as a living canvas to champion the craftsmen of the world.

Tara took a moment to absorb his personal style, then quickly recovered. 'This is my friend, Meher. She is an art critic,' she said.

Vardhan extended his hand. Meher clasped it, her grip lingering just a little longer than needed, her gaze locked on to his, a slight smile playing on her lips.

Tara caught the look and stepped in. Meher had taken her challenge seriously. 'Let me take you around the project.' Leading the way, she asked, 'How long have you been back in India?'

'Oh, about a week now. Came back after almost a decade,' he grunted.

'Well, I'm glad. There's so much to see,' Tara replied, unfazed by Vardhan's brusque tone.

As they stepped into the workspaces, Tara's excitement became palpable. Pure white marble plates were laid out in neat rows, engraved with brightly coloured patterns. Women adorned fabrics with tiny mirrors and intricate embroidery. Artisans crafted leather mojaris and polished chunky metal jewellery destined for high-end stores. Tara noticed how Vardhan's expression softened as he observed the artisans, and soon, he seemed visibly in awe.

He stopped at a young man whose fingers nimbly fused fine strands of liquid gold onto a small piece of glass. 'How long will that take him?' Vardhan asked lowering his voice as though not wanting to disturb the artist's trance.

'One month,' Tara replied, 'working eight hours a day.'

'Intricate craftsmanship,' Vardhan remarked, bending closer.

'This is Thewa art,' Tara explained. 'It's over 300 years old, practised by a single family and passed down through generations.'

Vardhan studied the young artist, whose eyes seemed glazed, and he wondered if the boy was exhausted or had merged completely with the art.

'It's sad, really. This boy has so much talent. The preservation of an entire art form practically depends on him; yet, he'll probably have to find employment in a few years as a peon or bellboy just to support his family,' Tara said.

Vardhan interrupted firmly, 'No! I will take care of this boy. He will get on to my scholarship programme.'

Tara smiled faintly and continued leading him. Stopping at a rectangular work table, she gestured to the intricate miniature paintings. 'These are the Mewar and Deogarh styles, dating back to the 17th century. Preserving them isn't enough—we need to make sure they remain relevant in the future. Now, let me show you something else.'

With Hari close on her heels, Tara opened the door to a vibrant space alive with colour and sound. It was as though a rustic village festival had been transported into the room. Folk musicians played traditional instruments, while women dressed in brightly coloured lehengas twirled like spinning tops, their faces veiled in delicate chiffon. A rope walker deftly displayed his craft, and the air buzzed with infectious energy.

'This is the spirit of Rajasthan,' Tara said, her voice brimming with pride. 'It is what has kept us going in the hot desert sands for generations. If we don't nurture this culture, we lose not just heritage, but also people.' Tara paused, then continued. 'Every artisan here has a social media presence. We provide incentives, organize competitions and book them for performances at hotels and weddings. We make sure they get paid their dues.'

Pointing to the dancers, Tara explained, 'This is *ghoomar*. It was originally performed as an offering to Goddess Saraswati before finding its way to the royal Rajput courts.'

Suraj Vardhan was trying to absorb everything he was seeing and hearing. He had travelled the world in search of traditional art forms, but India, with its abundance, felt like a treasure chest brimming with master artists and artisans. His initial aloofness had now been replaced by curiosity and interest.

Tara noticed the change in his expression and pressed on, her voice carrying the pride she felt in her work. 'We patronize any artist who walks in here and preserve 10 to 12 different dance and music forms at any given time.'

She picked up a brightly coloured puppet with a long, bushy moustache. 'Look at this. This is the protagonist of the *kathputli* dance. It's controlled with just a single string. Amazing, isn't it?'

'Fascinating,' agreed Vardhan, a slight smile finally appearing on his face.

'Puppetry originated in Rajasthan over 1,500 years ago,' Tara continued, watching his reaction. 'The songs you hear during the performances are ancient tales passed down orally through generations.'

'That's extraordinary,' Vardhan said, gesturing to a group of women singing while balancing pitchers on their heads.

Tara's face lit up. 'Ah yes, that's *panihari* folk music. Centuries ago, in our parched deserts, women travelled long distances in groups to fetch water. They endured searing heat and hardship, and the songs they sang spoke of flowing rivers and cool waves to encourage them to keep going, to fight thirst and heat. They had to keep going because they needed to return home with water for their families. The music was their way to hypnotize themselves into pushing forward.'

Vardhan seemed mesmerized, the history and artistry casting a spell over him. Tara realized that he was won over. Deciding it was enough for a first visit, she led him to the elevated patio under a shady tree, used as an outdoor theatre for special guests. 'Some chai?' she offered.

'Tea would be good,' he said.

Meher joined them and Vardhan greeted her with a smile. 'Where were you?'

'Giving you the opportunity to miss me,' she replied, her tone flirtatious.

'Well, I did miss you. I was hoping you could share some opinions on art forms.'

As they sipped steaming chai from earthy, handmade cups, accompanied by crispy snacks, Vardhan turned to Tara. 'Tell me, Tara, would you like me to become your main patron?'

Tara's eyes widened. 'Can I start by thanking you already?' she quipped with a soft laugh.

'I am part of a conglomerate of art lovers. I'll present your project at our next board meeting. I have a good feeling about this, since this is in complete sync with our mission to support traditional artists.'

Encouraged, Tara handed him a gift hamper wrapped in tie-and-dye printed handmade paper. 'Mr Vardhan, take home a part of us,' she said warmly.

'Tara, this is not necessary.'

'It is just a sample of what we make here. And do try the cookies and pickles,' she added hastily. 'They are part of a new initiative for farmers to create value-added products from their produce.'

'That's an excellent extension to your work. I am sure our hotels will be happy to try them out.'

Tara's passion spilled over as she explained, 'Mr Vardhan, I am attempting to build a complete chain of productivity for families: the men work in the fields, the women process the produce into packaged food and the youth design the packaging.'

'Tara, I wonder if anyone has told you this,' Vardhan said, a hint of admiration in his eyes, 'you have the makings of a leader.'

22

Hot Evenings

A bottle of red wine had been left open to breathe in the warm desert air. Ram Swarup moved with practised efficiency, placing an assortment of *namkeens* and wafers in silver bowls for Vikramjit to munch on with pegs of his favourite whisky. The evening routine at the palace was in full swing and Tara winced at the all-too-familiar tableau.

'Hello, madam,' Aishwarya greeted her with an overly affectionate tone. 'How was your day?'

'The ruby-encrusted pill box is missing. It's not there in the museum, Mummy.'

'Don't bother yourself with what's not your business, Tara,' Aishwarya replied dismissively.

'The museum *is* my business,' Tara said, then walked out.

Something did not feel right.

She rushed up to her room and went straight to the window, pulling the curtain aside just enough to catch a glimpse of the courtyard below.

Her mother sat resplendent in a rich crimson sari with a delicate gold border that shimmered in the moonlight. The perfectly cut rubies in her ears glinted as she smiled—a knowing, mysterious smile that made Tara's chest tighten. There was an ease between her mother and Vikramjit, a banter that seemed effortless.

Then Aishwarya reached into her bag and pulled out a velvet box. Vikram's face broke into a smile as he opened it to reveal a glistening Cartier bracelet. He grinned broadly as she leaned forward, helping him fasten the clasp around his broad wrist.

From her vantage point, Tara realized that her honeymoon sweetheart had been recast, transformed into a son-in-law entrusted with managing her family's real estate empire. More than that, he had been given the opportunity to dream of becoming a tycoon—as long as the mother-in-law stayed happy.

He wanted it so badly—to stand among the big players of India's business dynasties, to belong to the elite circles he had once only admired from afar. Now, he quoted astronomical numbers, name-dropped with abandon and lived in a world where nothing mattered more than the net worth of a man. She watched him and felt a lump rise to her throat.

Vikram was in his usual muslin kurta, tailored for summer evenings like this, the gauzy fabric barely concealing the perfectly sculpted body he had acquired at an expensive gym. She stared at the ripples, tracing the ridges of muscle, and was overcome by an irrepressible desire to reach out through the glass window and touch him. *Vikram, turn around,* she thought desperately. *Look at me... Hold me...*

Her fingers tightened around the curtain's edge, twisting the fine silk fabric into a knot. Her gaze lingered as he bent forward to refill his glass with more whisky, and in that moment, the brass rod holding the curtains gave way with a loud crash.

'What was that?' called out Vikramjit sharply.

Ram Swarup rushed into the room. 'It was nothing. The curtain rod was loose,' said Tara.

Ram Swarup looked at his young memsahib. For a fleeting moment, their eyes met—something he normally wouldn't do—and in that look, Tara saw understanding. He knew she was in pain.

Downstairs, her husband and mother had resumed their banter, laughing and talking as though nothing had happened. Tara watched them, the lump in her throat growing heavier. At times, it seemed as though they were soulmates. They certainly had much in common.

Vikramjit was ambitious and had a clear mission: to become a millionaire like all his wealthy friends at LSE—the sort who always flew business class—while he had spent years scouring the cheapest tickets and haggling with agents in seedy streets, barely scraping by. Now he was flying high.

The rajmata was intelligent, elegant and worldly-wise. She was also too old to play the field but too young and well-preserved to be put on the shelf. *No*, she told herself often, she was definitely not past her prime; she had a lot going for her. She was accustomed to being desired and was not quite ready to give it up. Although time had etched faint lines on her face, she refused to be cast aside and sought the company and attention of men more than ever, even if one of them happened to be her daughter's husband. It was the good old ethos of keeping things convenient and within the family.

As far as bets went, for Vikramjit, this was a good one. He knew she was his magic carpet, lifting him to the height of his dreams. He was bright and capable by most standards, but it didn't take him long to realize that without a steady hand on their shoulders, very few ever made it big in this land of politics, corruption and godfathers. Besides, Aishwarya's innate intelligence drew him deeply. He had never been attracted to women his age—they talked too much, teetered on pencil heels and paired low necklines with rising hemlines. Ah, he had seen so many of them. They somehow lacked the ability to hold his attention long enough, or perhaps he had grown so accustomed to this elegant and astute woman that comparisons no longer held weight.

Tara barely crossed his mind anymore. The lovable girl he had once adored was now just a wife—a title that came with obligations she should be content to fulfil. In his mind, her purpose was to bear the next generation. That was as much as she could expect from him.

By his fourth drink, his voice had turned rowdy, his laughter echoing off the palace walls and ricocheting against the glass windows beside Tara's bed. She pressed a pillow against her ears, but the sounds of their revelry grew louder, carried on by the alcohol that fuelled them.

Sleep eluded Tara. She sat up in bed, holding her throbbing head, then walked to the cabinet and switched on the television—her only escape. She pulled out a bag of wafers from a drawer and settled back against her pillows.

Holding out the remote control, she fast-forwarded the film impatiently. She could barely wait to see him. And then, there he was. Vivan Mehta flashed his signature smile and Tara felt lighter. There was a moment's relief. He never failed to transport her to another reality, to ease her pain. What had begun as a schoolgirl crush had evolved into a one-sided relationship with a celluloid illusion.

She smiled as he kissed the gorgeous actress on screen, her lips curling into an involuntary pout. As the scene unfolded—his body entwined with the actress's—Tara found herself slipping into bed, breathing deeply, her face flushed. She shut her eyes, letting her fantasy take over. She had long learnt to pepper her reality with illusory escapes.

But the sound of Vikramjit's uproarious laughter, mingled with the somewhat shrill, slightly hysterical giggle of her mother, snapped her back to reality. Tara felt a wild urge to throw open the window, jump into the courtyard and crash their perfect evening by landing right on their table.

Maybe, I will do that one day and then they will notice me, she thought.

Tara remained restless that night. How could she sleep knowing her husband was enjoying the company of someone else so intensely, even if that someone was her mother? She tossed and turned, staring into darkness, her mind swirling with thoughts.

She heard the door creak open, the light from the corridor flooding the room. Vikramjit staggered in, his steps heavy, dragging. He slumped on to the bed, muttering her name in a slurred drawl. His hand reached out for her.

Tara cringed and moved away but he persisted, dragging her towards him. She couldn't fight his grip on her shoulder, but driven by instinct, she bit his hand.

He yelped in pain, a weak moan following his scream. 'Morning. Wait till the morning, and I will get you for this,' he managed to say.

Tara was shocked at herself. She was changing. She was learning to fight back. She smiled. It was a small victory but it felt good.

Light filtered through the curtains and she still lay awake. She glanced at the bedside clock—it was time for her morning ride with Firefly; an exhilarating ride through the desert sands always worked for her. It was one of the few things she had inherited from her father. The steed was named after Gaj Singh's horse, the one he had ridden to his death. Aishwarya Devi had thought her choice in name was morbid, while Vikram had found it ironic; for Tara, it was a precious memory.

The Thar Desert at sunrise was majestic. The layered ripples of sand, the tiger-striped etchings carved with divine precision, seemed like the handiwork of a celestial artist, as though God's hand had stretched down and scratched its crust. Firefly broke free in the paddock and galloped towards Tara. She patted him warmly, then whispered in his ear and he shook his mane happily. Tara pulled on her riding boots and Firefly lifted his hooves, restless for a ride. With one smooth leap, she mounted him, her movements confident, honed from years of equestrian training at Jaivangarh Palace.

As she tore through the desert, her raven-black hair caught the wind like an indigo sail, whipping and twirling with her thoughts. The rhythmic pounding of Firefly's hooves echoed the race of her thoughts, replaying her conversation with Vikram again and again.

'Are you planning to build a hotel in the village?' she had mustered enough courage to ask Vikram one night.

'What did you just ask me?'

'You know what I asked.'

He stepped close enough for her to smell the alcohol on his breath. 'I am going to say this once. That is none of your business. Do you understand?'

'But—'

'No. This conversation never happened, as far as I'm concerned.'

His words had left a sour taste in her mouth. The land on which the village stood was invaluable—not only was it surprisingly fertile, but also strategically placed. It was close enough to the highway to attract commercial interest yet far enough to maintain an air of privacy—perfect for a luxury hotel.

Suddenly, Firefly reared up, hooves slicing through the air. Tara clung to his reins, steadying the startled stallion. Something had darted past the sand—perhaps a snake.

In the distance, a low rumble pierced the stillness. Through the haze of dust, a figure emerged, riding recklessly, cutting through the undulating sand dunes. In one swift move, he brought his horse to a stop and dismounted. He approached her and stared straight into her eyes. She stared back until she felt a chill run down her spine. She recognized the face. He used to sit in the last row at Jaipur Law College. When he wasn't making impassioned statements during debates, his gaze would often wander to her. She had once even thought her mother had arranged for him to be sent along for her protection.

'Tara Kumari ji,' he said respectfully. 'I know your family plans to sell our lands, but you can't. These lands are neither mine nor yours, they are His,' he said, pointing to the sky.

The voice brought her back to her days at college. She remained silent, a little stunned.

'He has chosen us to take care of this land, to keep it as He intended—for humanity,' the man continued in a deep voice. 'We will not let anyone take it, plunder it, destroy it. Our community is committed to protecting nature and we will die before we see it lost.'

His commanding tone sent a rush of adrenaline through Tara's veins.

'Madam, I want to say—'

'I am with you, Jai Singh,' Tara interrupted.

'You remember me?' he asked, surprised.

'Of course I do. Jaipur Law College, class of 2005. Third row from the left, last bench.'

His face softened for a moment and he smiled. 'I am glad you are with us because one day, it will all be over. There will be no more land left—just concrete skyscrapers crumbling over arid, lifeless soil. The poor will be swept aside like an inconvenient nuisance, paid a pittance and left with nothing. We will be left without our land, our farms and our dharma.'

Tara felt the sting of tears welling up in her eyes. She took a moment to steady her voice. 'I will read up on our legal rights to keep our land with us,' she said.

'With us?' he asked.

'You heard me. With us. It's a promise.'

23

A Flight of Sharks

He was the most dapper man on the flight that navigated the dusty skies over Jaipur. The morning flight from Mumbai often carried a touch of glamour, but even by those standards, Dhruv Jhabwala was overdressed. Among the workaholics in sober business suits—most of whom would probably take the evening flight back to dine with their wives or perhaps grab a drink at the club with friends—he stood out dramatically.

The all-black suit he wore, accentuated with fine maroon stripes, shimmered faintly in the early morning light. The suede-trimmed collar and emerald green satin shirt tucked over a generous belly might have been more fitting for an evening premiere of the latest blockbuster than a 7 a.m. flight. A pair of sculpted glasses bearing the Dior insignia completed the look of fashion anarchy. The fact that he had an image consultant, who was known for pocketing a 10 per cent commission on all purchases he made for clients, might explain why Dhruv Jhabwala wore everything outrageously expensive. There was no doubt he had truly 'arrived' in life.

As the wheels of the aircraft scraped against the runway, he flicked open his pure gold Vertu phone.

'Good morning, Vikram sir. I am here.'

The announcement sparked a flurry of activity at Jaivangarh Palace. The breakfast table was adorned with a pure white Chantilly lace cover, and a carefully curated selection of exotic fruits was arranged like an artistic centrepiece. Some might consider it too perfect to touch, almost forbidding.

'Get the breads and cheeses on the table, Ram. And don't forget the juices,' instructed Aishwarya Devi in an excited voice.

'Hukum,' Ram Swarup replied, bowing reverentially.

Vikramjit, dressed in his British best, glanced at his watch with increasing impatience.

'Don't look too keen, Vikram,' said Aishwarya Devi. 'These men we are meeting today are not businessmen. They are sharks. And they can smell you out.'

'Don't worry,' he replied, attempting a stiff smile that failed to mask his tension. 'I have dealt with my fair share of sharks in England.'

'Ah!' Aishwarya Devi giggled. 'English sharks, darling, are vegetarians. These are a different breed altogether—carnivorous, and very hungry.'

The remark did little to calm Vikramjit, who looked even more anxious than he had before the rajmata's little morale booster.

Outside, a screech of tyres announced the arrival of Dhruv Jhabwala's car. As he stepped out, Aishwarya Devi felt confident this man would be able to manage the complex job she had in mind for him—he seemed every bit as shrewd as his reputation suggested.

'Hello, my man,' Dhruv exclaimed in an overtly friendly tone, hugging Vikramjit, who, however, responded stiffly, barely leaning into the embrace.

'Namaste, ma ji,' Dhruv greeted Aishwarya Devi, turning to her with a broad smile.

She squirmed at his choice of words but offered a gracious smile. 'You may call me Rajmata,' she said firmly, thinking, *If he must call me anything, let it be my title.*

Tara, dressed in her work clothes, entered the room, looking distinctly ordinary. She smiled at the guests and joined them at the table.

'Mr Jhabwala, meet my daughter, Tara Kumari.'

'Hello, Tara ji,' Jhabwala greeted, flashing her a broad smile before turning his attention back to the map spread out in front of him with unconcealed excitement.

'So, this is the 500 acres of land we are talking about?' he asked, his voice shaking a bit. 'Vikram, *yaar*, this land is gold. Give me the chance, and I will turn every grain of sand here into pure gold.'

'I will throw in the museum, if you give me an irresistible offer,' Vikramjit replied.

'It's heritage property. We can't bring it down but it would make a perfect high-end boutique hotel.'

The two men accompanying Jhabwala were like silent shadows, barely speaking as they sat at the table. Their dark glasses reflected the light, hiding their expressions as they prodded at their laden breakfast plates and scribbled notes in old-fashioned leather diaries.

'I want the museum as it is,' continued Jhabwala, 'with every piece on display—every single one.'

He pulled something out of his pocket and grinned. It was the ruby pill box.

'I am not paying you separately for this,' he said to Vikram. 'Every piece on display is part of my deal.'

The sight of her father's precious pill box in Jhabwala's stubby fingers made Tara squirm. She cleared her throat and stretched out her arm, placing it firmly on the centre of the map. Jhabwala's eyes followed her movement, lingering for a moment on her well-manicured fingers, where a solitaire sparkled daintily. *Brave*, he thought. *Brave for hands that clearly belong to a thoroughbred.*

'Mr Jhabwala,' Tara began, 'this is not just land. These are people's homes and lives. Over 1,500 families live here—women, children and elderly people who depend on this land. What do you plan to do with them?' She paused, her gaze steady. 'And as for the museum—that is sacred to me.'

The inflexion in her voice made everyone look at her. She noticed Vikram had paled visibly and her mother had grown still.

'As for the pieces in the museum,' Tara continued, 'they represent our family's honour—paintings of our ancestors and artefacts collected through generations. And honour amongst us is non-negotiable.'

With a tight smile, Aishwarya said, 'Tara, go ahead with your day. This will take some time, and you need to reach the museum for your appointment this morning by 10 a.m.'

'I don't need to get there so punctually—Mehta ji will take care of it,' Tara replied softly but firmly. It was a side of her that her family had never seen before, and both Aishwarya Devi and Vikramjit looked puzzled.

'Mr Jhabwala, I run a foundation that supports the livelihoods of 600 families. There's a thriving arts and crafts centre on this land. I have also built a school for children that will hopefully change their future. To displace these families would destroy their world and bring absolute misery. You don't want that on your hands.'

Jhabwala leaned back in his chair, a faint smirk on his lips. 'Ah, young Miss Tara Kumari,' he said, his tone patronizing. 'We will give so much money for your charity work that you will call me a great man.'

Tara's expression didn't falter. 'Mr Jhabwala,' she said, her voice patient but strained. 'These people are rooted in this land. If you uproot them, they will wither away. If you take this land from them, there will be no more music, no more art. I cannot support that.'

'Madam, your family invited me here,' Jhabwala replied, his irritation seeping through. 'I am not here to grab your land.'

'Mr Jhabwala, my next project is also tied to this land,' Tara persisted. 'We will create processed food from farm produce, with a share for the farmers. Their wives will be the ones making these products to sell to retail stores, so they will also have a stake as shareholders.'

'Tara,' Aishwarya Devi's impatient voice interrupted her daughter. 'Please leave us to handle these matters without your interference.'

Tara turned to look at her mother in the eye—something she had never done before. The anger exchanged between them was stronger than any other feeling. It felt like a war within the family. This was not about taking Vikramjit away from her; it was about stripping her life from her hands. Tara walked out of the room. Moments later, the screech of tyres echoed through the palace as her car sped off.

'You have to handle your young lady,' said Jhabwala. His focus was no longer on the map but on the words Tara had spoken, which replayed in his mind. He lit a cigarette and exhaled generously.

Aishwarya Devi waved a hand in front of her face, coughing lightly. She was a smoker herself but couldn't tolerate the harsh, acrid smell of Dhruv's Charminar brand. *Some habits die hard*, she mused. *Even money can't erase them.* 'Let's drive down to see the land,' she suggested.

'Not today,' replied Dhruv Jhabwala. 'Tell your daughter we have returned without a deal on the land.'

'What?' exclaimed Aishwarya Devi, looking worried. 'Surely you don't take the girl seriously?'

'She is your idealistic daughter, Rajmata,' he said, raising his eyebrows as he uttered her title. 'And trust me when I say this—there is nothing I fear more than idealists. They are dangerous. I prefer men who can be bought. They are easy to handle—friends of businessmen, prosperity and progress. All they ask is a share of the pie, and they will make you a king.'

'So, you are not interested in working with us?' asked Vikramjit.

'Of course I am. But let your wife feel she has won this round. Once we handle the villagers, we'll make them tell her what they want.'

Relief washed over the rajmata and Vikramjit. Dhruv was a master tactician, and what had seemed like a lost cause now felt salvageable. 'I brought some earnest money,' he added, 'but I will hold on to it for now. Convince your wife not to stand in the way of your plans. I try not to interfere in family matters, but this one is linked to our business partnership.'

'Don't worry about Tara. She is my wife and a Rajput wife at that. She knows her duties. Or I'll remind her of them.' The finality in his words echoed in the room.

The team of investors stood up abruptly.

'What about some Rajasthani breakfast?' Aishwarya Devi asked in a desperate attempt to hold on to them.

'Let's keep that due for our next trip,' Dhruv Jhabwala replied. He was a player and this game had just begun.

★

At dinner that night, Rajmata Aishwarya Devi sat at the head of the table. Her son-in-law sat to her right and her daughter to her left. Tall white candles flickered in ornate silver holders, their flames leaping and wavering with hot gusts of desert air whenever the door opened. The tension within the walls was palpable. The unbroken, untouched silence could have stretched endlessly through the evening, but Aishwarya realized that it was time to extend herself to her daughter.

'You are not eating well tonight,' she said, her tone almost concerned.

'No appetite, Mummy,' Tara replied flatly.

'She eats with the villagers,' Vikram remarked caustically.

The Rajmata silenced him with an angry glare. Turning to her daughter, she said, 'Tara, I know you are upset about the lands and your museum.'

'You are right, I am.'

'You need money for your projects. The poor remain poor if you don't let money reach them.'

'There are always justifications for everything; anything can be explained away if you twist logic enough.'

'Tara, I am going to make you a partner in this project.

The money that comes in will be yours to use however you like, though I can't imagine what you would do with it.' Aishwarya smiled expectantly, confident that she had handled the situation, but the mirthless expression on Tara's face warned her otherwise.

'I can't believe this. You want me to sell my soul? Don't insult me with this offer, Mummy. I know we are not struggling. Our bank accounts are lush with the investments Daddy left us. This is not need, Mummy—this is greed,' Tara said, her voice rising.

'Tara,' snapped Vikramjit. 'Even the wealthiest monetize every opportunity.'

Aishwarya's fingers tightened around her fork, pressing it into the edge her empty plate. Her calm exterior cracked slightly, but she restrained herself from saying what was burning on the tip of her tongue—the truth about Tara's father. That revelation would hurt too many, including herself. Instead, she forced herself to stay composed, swallowing her anger as Ram Swarup entered the room. He carried the fruit platter, his eyes downcast but absorbing everything. Little did the royals know that they were inching towards a major revolution that night. Ram Swarup was seething with anger. He had served his masters as part of a legacy—just as his father and grandfather had done before him—having sworn his life to the loyalty and devotion of one family. Now, he was ready to revolt. He saw the emptiness and Machiavellian ministrations that threatened to take away from him and his children the only home they had ever known.

'Ram,' Aishwarya's voice interrupted his thoughts. 'Finger bowls, please.'

'Yes, Hukum,' he replied, bowing slightly, though his voice carried a faint tremor of defiance.

As he left the room, the tension lingered in his wake, unnoticed by the royals, who were too absorbed in their private battle to sense the quiet storm brewing just beyond their gilded walls.

24

Anchor

Sunday afternoons at Connaught Circus had an uncharacteristically balmy air. The sound of wheels and horns was replaced by a silence broken only by the occasional flutter of a bird landing near the edges of the old signage that lined the exteriors. The stores stood shuttered, and the mannequins behind the frosted windows seemed like frozen remnants of a city paused in time.

Tara's hands rested lightly on the steering wheel as her misty eyes stared at the road ahead, though her mind lingered in the past. She remembered that day clearly. It was the end of winter, and a light drizzle had been falling over Connaught Circus, making people scurry for cover. Vikram had driven her down for a good time in the big city. They had danced all night at the Sheraton Lounge Bar, ignoring anxious calls from Aishwarya.

'What if your mother changes her mind?' Vikram had teased, driving her back.

'I will elope with you,' she'd replied impishly.

'Then I hope she does.'

'Let's elope now,' she had said excitedly.

'I'm all set.'

'Can I take the wheel?' she'd asked.

He'd smiled, indulgent. 'All yours, my lady. Guess you are driving us straight into married life.'

Sliding into the driver's seat, Tara had hit the pedal, guiding the car in wild circles around Connaught Circus.

'What are you doing?' Vikram had yelled over the screeching tyres, caught between confusion and delight.

Finally, she had slowed down and giggled.

'What was that?' he'd asked. 'That was our *saat pheras*. We are married now!'

That was the last time she had driven around the circle with such carefree abandon. Now, years later, as her eyes rested on the familiar 'United Coffee House' signage, she realized she was running late.

Inside, the air-conditioning greeted her with a chill, prompting her to wrap her scarf around her neck. The waiter with a rather exaggerated bow tie walked up to her with a huge smile. Ah! It had been years, yet the place stood like an unchanging island amidst a sea of change. The white concrete carvings, foggy crystal chandeliers and static menu all exuded a sense of timelessness.

As her eyes adjusted to the dim lighting, she scanned the rows of patrons sitting in groups. A pang of disappointment tugged at her chest until she spotted the familiar mop of black hair. She moved towards the table a little tentatively, flushed and nervous.

'Krish,' she said, her voice barely audible. 'It's been years.'

'Yes, it has, Tara. It has.'

She slipped into the maroon velvet booth, silently taking in the changes that time had marked him with. Stray bits of grey had appeared at his temples and his face bore the faint lines of age. Yet his black eyes still held the intensity that had once enamoured her.

She tried to speak, but her lips remained frozen. The man she had loved and lost was sitting in front of her, and she was unable to say a word. *Perhaps words would spoil this moment,* she thought.

She took a deep breath and finally said, 'You still wear the same cologne.'

'You remember,' he replied.

'It's the one I gave you in London.'

'Well, I have been refilling the bottle ever since.'

Their eyes met, and Tara felt a flutter in her chest. The faint flicker of an old passion shone in his eyes, stirring something deep within her. Memories washed over her—Oxford, the warmth of cognac and the intimacy of a small inn where time seemed to stand still.

'I ordered cold coffee for you,' he said, bringing her back to the present.

'You remember,' she said, pleased.

'I do,' he said. 'Although in winter, it was always espresso.'

'And those wine appreciation lessons you gave me at the Stratford pub? I remember every note of them,' she said wistfully.

'I remember you often, Tara. I never stopped checking on you.'

'Then why did you leave me and go away?'

'Your mother…' Krish shook his head, hesitating. 'She would have made your life very difficult.'

'I would have faced her, if you had been by my side.'

'I loved you too much to put you through that. You come from a world where rules are never broken.'

'You should have asked me if I was ready to break them.'

'I knew what your answer would be, Tara.'

'I am glad you did,' she said quietly, letting the matter rest. She realized there was no point dwelling on paths that could never be walked again.

The waiter placed two glasses of cold coffee on the table. The creamy indulgence shimmered under the light, the thick dollop of fresh cream floating like a sinful promise atop the famed cold coffee.

'They don't count calories here; they weigh pleasure,' Krish said with a grin.

Tara took a sip, savouring the rich flavour. For a fleeting moment, the sweetness drowned her worries. 'Any more orders, sir?' asked the waiter, pulling out his writing pad. The pencil balanced perfectly behind his ear, ready for action. Noticing the two engrossed in each other, he discreetly moved to another table.

'You once promised you would become the Chief Justice of India one day. Any ambitions left in that direction?' he asked.

'Well, that was a bit far-fetched, but I did write a thesis on "The Injustice of Justice".'

'Ah! I remember that brilliant title! And what about your exceptional acting talents? You were passionate enough to make a trip to the Stratford theatre festival for inspiration.'

'To put it plainly, I simply followed in the footsteps of Rajput girls before me and married a boy of my mother's choice.'

'Not yours?'

'You know who my choice was.'

There was a pause as the air between them grew heavier; this was never going to be an easy conversation.

'So, princess,' Krish broke the silence, 'you mentioned enough on the phone for me to check your legal options. I am sorry, Tara, but you have very few.'

'I have to stop this, Krish,' she said, her voice resolute.

'You are walking on thin ice, Tara.'

'Perhaps, but so are the builders. The land belongs to my father and to the villagers, and they are devoted to preserving nature. There is no one who can remove them from it without risking a revolt.'

'You are going to find yourself in the centre of a storm.'

'I have faced worse, Krish. I grew up playing on those fields. My father rejected me; my mother didn't seem to care too much about me. The village has always been my real home. Those people are my family.'

'Have you spoken to your mother about this?'

'Well, I am the invisible woman. No one in the house notices me. A conversation won't lead anywhere, but she's aware that I am against it. It's my legacy!'

'Okay, Tara. I get the picture. Legally, your mother has sole rights to that land. If she decides to sell it, she can.'

'Krish, there has to be a way to stop this.'

'The only way is to rally the villagers and draw public attention. Use the media. Highlight the environmental impact and the plight of the marginalized. Force the builders into the spotlight.'

'Will you file a case against Jhabwala?'

Krish hesitated, then nodded. 'Sure. I will file a case, but legal action alone won't be enough. You'll need the villagers, the media and public pressure to make it work. The builder lobby is ruthless. They stop at nothing.'

'I will make that happen.'

'But you are still living in your mother's home.'

'It is my father's home.'

'Think it through, Tara. You need to be very cautious. Jhabwala is dangerous. You're up against powerful people with no moral compass.'

'I have my Rajput genes intact. I can face them. They can't have my land.'

'They will stop at nothing to clear their way.'

'Nor will I, to save the family museum, the village and farmland.'

'Tara, be practical for God's sake! Just go home and forget about this entire plan. If your marriage is what's stressing you, I will help you find a job in Delhi. Start afresh and build a life.'

She looked at him, unwavering. In that moment, Krish realized she wouldn't go back on her decision. Tara was a woman who would walk right through the fire—whether she emerged unscathed or scarred wasn't the point. The point was that she would walk through it, no matter what.

'Krish, this is a fight I have to fight. The question is, are you willing to help me?'

He wanted to say no, simply because he did not want to encourage her down the dangerous path she was choosing. He knew it was going to be a murky fight.

He meant to say, 'I cannot take this case,' but that was not what he finally said. He took her hand in his and said, 'I will do this for you, Tara. I would be lying if I said it was for the people of Jaivangarh. I will do it for you, just to make sure you don't get into trouble.'

She gave him a dazzling smile. 'Thank you, Krish.'

Years ago, she had accepted the wrong man to marry. But her hero—he had been perfectly chosen.

Krish withdrew his hand, standing abruptly. 'I have a client coming in, so I must leave.'

'Krish,' she called softly, her voice faltering. 'Did you ever marry?'

He shook his head and left before she could ask any more questions.

The drive back to Jaivangarh seemed to stretch endlessly. As she drove, she had an overpowering desire to never stop, to follow the road wherever it led, chasing the mirage of an unknown destination. She was not sure where 'home' was anymore—or whether she had a home at all—a place where someone would be waiting for her.

Slowing down, she watched the sun set over the desert. She had never quite gotten over sunsets on the sand, but that day, there was something menacing about it. She noticed the cracked, dry earth in the evening glow, shining like damaged ceramic.

★

Far away, in a plush office room overlooking Mumbai's skyline, Jhabwala strategized his next move. Behind the sheet of glass, the city's chaos blurred into abstract streaks of light. His fingers tapped rhythmically on the desk, mimicking the keys of a piano, a habit that somehow made him think faster.

The drought had sparked a flurry of excitement. The failed monsoon was fertile ground for Jhabwala and his team—the perfect moment to lure starving villagers into selling off their ancestral lands and disappearing into obscurity. He needed to make his move now.

'Tara Kumari has to be outmanoeuvred. She has no idea who she is dealing with. She needs to be careful, very careful,' he said in a sinister tone.

'She will back off, sir. I am sure she will,' Myra chimed in. Dressed in a blue striped dress, the voluptuous girl knew that being Jhabwala's secretary meant being a cheerleader for him. With an earnest expression, she nodded dutifully through every meeting, and Jhabwala enjoyed being surrounded by those who agreed with him. Myra had the added advantage of being beautiful.

'Asim, strike a deal now. Get them out before it rains. They will not be interested in their princess's idealism for too long. Come on, she really thinks they will spend their lives resisting selling their land when they have no food?'

'Hunger is like no other weapon,' said Asim, reminded of the days he had been at its mercy.

Jhabwala smirked. 'I want to build a hotel with an artificial lake for water sports—a paradise for those who can actually afford it.'

'A water park, sir?'

'It's called marketing, Asim. What is the one thing people crave in a desert?'

'Water, sir,' said Asim meekly. He hated the aggressiveness with which Jhabwala exploited the vulnerable. Although he had admired his boss's arrogance and abrasiveness once, now, he had begun to feel nauseous.

While Jhabwala fantasized about his project, Tara was thinking through her plans to stop the man. Krish's advice about rallying the media played on her mind.

'I am already working on your plan,' she messaged him.

Then, she leaned back against the soft leather seat, letting the music on the stereo soothe her nerves. The solitude of the car brought clarity. As the world outside blurred, a sharper picture began to form on the windscreen of her mind.

Tara started the ignition. The engine roared to life, sending a thrill through her. She shifted into top gear and sped back toward Jaivangarh.

Well, she thought, *everyone's in for a shock.*

25

Tara's Dance

The stage lights changed from dim to bright, then to fluorescent. A voice boomed through the hall: 'Good evening, ladies and gentlemen. We welcome you tonight to the fundraiser for the people of Jaivangarh.'

There was an enthusiastic applause.

The evening was a sell-out. The top media agency roped in by Divya had managed to draw in an eclectic crowd. Dressed, for a change, in a traditional lehenga, she had flown in with an entourage of friends and journalists. The audience fanned themselves with their ₹10,000 donor cards, curiosity sparkling in their eyes. The elite from Delhi had motored down in luxury cars—business tycoons, politicians and social activists were all seated in prime spots. Then there were the glitterati from Mumbai, some having travelled in their private jets. They were all there for a good cause—or, at least, to look the part.

Conspicuously missing were the many estranged members of the Jaivangarh family who kept a distance from Aishwarya. But then, there were no ties that survived the lust for land. Yet Tara's support structure was all around her. Familiar with the area and its people, Meher had managed every detail on the ground. As she walked around, looking occupied, she heard a voice that seemed faintly familiar.

'Hello, Meher, I am here for the event.' She turned around and then burst into a spontaneous smile.

'Just for the event?' she asked impishly.

'No, I can't lie. The event was an excuse,' said Suraj Vardhan.

At the entrance, an archway of marigolds welcomed the guests, while village girls dressed in colourful Rajasthani lehengas scattered flower petals. College volunteers moved through the crowd, offering bottles of mineral water bearing the message: 'Share one drop with Jaivangarh'.

'I want every person to know they are here to quench the thirst of Jaivangarh. I want to create a connection between the audience and the people, a sort of umbilical cord,' Tara had told the young event manager who had offered to lend a helping hand to the people's princess.

Thirst was Rajasthan's Achilles' heel. Irrigation was a promise no government had delivered on. Those who fed the nation lived at the mercy of the clouds and winds—both fickle and unforgiving.

She noticed him weaving through the crowd, his eyes scanning the backstage mayhem. 'Krish!' she called out. 'You made it! Thank you, Krish. Thank you!'

'I will be rooting for you.'

A warm smile played on Tara's face. 'I can't believe the turnout,' she said a little breathlessly.

'Well, you are simply more popular than you realized,' he smiled back, flashing a victory sign.

'Ladies and gentlemen, presenting to you "Thirst, Part One",' came the announcement.

The audience settled in, silencing their phones as traditional performers took the stage, their rhythmic movements enthralling the spectators.

As the evening wore on, came another announcement: 'And now, it's time for the star performer of the evening. Please put your hands together for Princess Nayan Tara Kumari, who is taking the stage tonight for Jaivangarh. She will be playing the lead in a piece titled "It's Our Land".'

A spotlight pierced the darkness, following Tara's poised steps onto the stage. Dressed in a flowing green silk lehenga embroidered with gold thread, she was a vision of regal defiance. Her kohl-smudged eyes gleamed through a delicate net veil speckled with glitter.

She stood still for a moment, before stamping her feet in perfect rhythm, creating music with her *ghungroo*s. Dancers swirled around her, scattering dry mud into the air. From the speakers, came a haunting voice:

It's my land.
Grab it if you can.
Landlords and bureaucrats,
Politicians and middlemen,
Our time has come.
It's our land…'

The chorus erupted, repeating: *'Yes! It's our land. Come, grab it if you can!'*

Sitting in the audience, Vikramjit frowned, his eyes tense, his fist clenched. This was not just music. Tara was speaking to him directly, defying him from the stage. The girl had spunk. He knew she was not fooling around. She was smarter than he had thought. Jhabwala, seated nearby in an electric blue shirt with garish purple, diamanté-tipped collars, reached for his hip flask and took a nervous gulp of neat Blue Label. He looked far less celebratory than he had at the beginning of the evening.

Unable to stomach the embarrassment, the rajmata slipped away to the restroom to have a quick smoke. She wished Vikramjit had not insisted on inviting Jhabwala. She dragged on her cigarette as though it were a stick of oxygen. 'Tara can never be trusted,' she muttered. 'Dancing like a gypsy, not like a royal. It's her father's genes—this girl was made from the clay of the village earth.'

Back on stage, Tara had entered the kathak dancer's meditative zone. This was not just another dance performance for her. With Sufi-like fervour, she spun faster and faster, her arms stretched out in surrender. The crowd watched, mesmerized, as she completed 50 flawless spins.

Vikramjit got to his feet, concerned she might collapse.

As if on cue, a jagged streak of thunder illuminated the night sky and the music rose to a deafening crescendo.

Tara felt euphoric at nature's dramatic appearance. The elements had created a strange *son et lumière* that could not have been planned or replicated by the finest stagecraft.

Her feet, heavy with ghungroos, stamped the ground, its lilting tinkle audible even over the angry rumble of the sky.

Suddenly, the skies opened, drenching everyone and everything. The musicians spontaneously changed rhythm to festive notes and Tara broke into steps of unbridled celebration. The audience surrendered to the rain's magic. Women in stilettos and men in their stylish best joined her in an impromptu mass rain dance. The energy was infectious.

Jhabwala sat frozen, his confusion evident. This was not the evening he had anticipated.

From the distant fields came the sound of villagers rejoicing. Their voices, carried by the wind, merged into a harmonious cry of relief that reached the concert venue. Temple bells rang—their prayers had been answered. There would now be bounty.

*

Aishwarya's vice-like grip on her daughter's hand said it all. It wasn't the touch of a loving mother; it carried no trace of affection, no warmth.

As Tara opened her eyes, she gently freed her hand.

'Why, Tara? Why did you keep your pregnancy a secret? For five months! Even from your husband!' asked Aishwarya sharply.

Tara ignored her mother, turning instead to the grey-haired doctor in a sterile green coat. 'What happened to the baby?'

Dr Mishra had been through this painful moment many times, yet it never ceased to affect her. She cleared her throat before answering. 'The baby aborted itself.'

'Was it a boy or a girl?'

'A boy,' replied the doctor, placing a comforting hand on Tara's shoulder.

But Tara was not looking at her. Instead, she gazed into the distance, a strange smile playing on her lips. 'Have you told my husband?' she asked.

'Not yet.'

'Tell him, and don't forget to mention that it was a boy.'

Dr Mishra was surprised. She had seen many bitter pregnancies and fractured relationships, but something in Tara's words unsettled her. Noticing the tension in the room, she turned to Aishwarya Devi. 'I think Tara needs to rest. Perhaps we should turn off the lights and let her sleep?'

In the visitors' lounge, Vikram sat slumped on a sofa, watching a replay of the evening news. His butler discreetly handed him whisky on the rocks, poured into a steel tumbler to bypass hospital rules.

He looked defeated and tired, like a warrior of too many lost battles, as Aishwarya entered and sat beside him. 'The nurse told me everything,' he said.

'Did Tara ever tell you?' she asked, turning towards him.

'Not a word,' he replied. 'Not a single word.'

The drive back home was steeped in heavy silence, with Vikram behind the wheel of the BMW Aishwarya had gifted him on his last birthday. Neither spoke, but the unspoken truth hung between them. Tara could no longer be ignored.

As the night deepened, the stillness of the hospital became oppressive. The corridors were dark and silent, except for the occasional moans from a distant room. The overpowering scent of disinfectant filled Tara's room, making her feel stifled.

Restless, she climbed out of the elevated hospital bed and searched for her handbag. She sighed with relief on finding her Marlboro Lights intact. Walking to the window, she gazed out at the sheets of rain. She felt drained, tears welling in her eyes as she mourned her unborn child. The reality of her loss hit her, overpowering her hatred for Vikram. Her emotions intertwined mercilessly, leaving her head spinning. Finally, she broke down, sobbing in pain for her loss, while also feeling a strange sense of satisfaction at having lost the child of the man who had insulted her night after night.

Leaning against the cool glass, she sobbed, mumbling, 'My baby, I am sorry. I am sorry. I didn't mean to lose you, my baby. I am sorry.'

In her private mourning, the bereaved mother felt a deep pain that surged through her body—an intense and personal grief that no one could share or alleviate. It was just her and the soul of her child, and she could feel his presence. She clung to it, not wanting to let go.

Suddenly, the skies crackled with lightning, forming a strange shape that resembled a hole—an entry into the heavens. Tara looked up, comforted by the thought that her baby had passed through it and arrived in the arms of God.

She looked around, lit a cigarette stealthily and inhaled deeply. She then noticed the raindrops on the window glass. Nothing would revive her soul like the waters that fell from the skies that night. Tara shut her eyes and imagined the utter bliss in the villages and fields—the relief etched on every face, the rhythmic drumbeats of celebration echoing from every home, the children diving gleefully into instant ponds. The image soothed her, the exhaustion ebbing.

At the nursing station, Sister Shanti was absorbed in the latest copy of *Manorama*, reading the true confessions page. Tara peered out from her room and smiled casually at the nurse before walking down the corridor.

'Where are you going, Tara ji?' Sister Shanti asked, confused.

'Oh, just to the balcony for some fresh air.'

The nurse nodded. 'Okay, but don't take too long. You will feel weak for a while,' she said, then quickly returned to the climax of the story she was reading.

Outside the hospital, a car was waiting at the porch in response to a call Tara had made earlier. It carried her swiftly out of the hospital gates.

She rolled down the window, letting the rain drench her. The cool droplets mingled with the tears streaming down her face. She remembered her favourite quote from college, one that had comforted her when she was healing from Krish's loss: 'I love walking in the rain because no one can see my tears.'

As Tara walked up the steps of her home, she felt like a ghost. Her heart clenched at the sight of Vikramjit sitting with her mother, drinking. The whisky bottle gleamed in the soft light, the wafers rested in crystal bowls and white napkins lay in their holders—as though nothing had happened. They both looked up at Tara, shocked to see her standing there.

Vikramjit rose unsteadily, swaying in his drunken haze. 'Murderer!' he screamed. 'You murdered my child!'

Tara stared at him, defiance flickering in her eyes.

'That child was Jaivangarh's legacy,' Aishwarya chimed in.

'Children are legacies to you, Mummy. That was my child. Never forget that.'

'You forgot me, Tara. It was my child too, and you murdered him.' Vikramjit's hand rose to strike Tara, but Aishwarya's voice rang out, sharp and commanding.

'Vikramjit!' she snapped. 'Don't ever touch my daughter.'

'Your daughter?' he sneered. 'Right, now you want to act like a mother. Tell me, Rajmata, do you remember the nights at Dhan Mahal? Were you being a good mother then?'

Aishwarya looked as if she had been slapped. Without another word, she walked away before Vikramjit could say any more.

'Can't hear it, can you, Rajmata?' Vikramjit shouted after her. 'Tonight your daughter has murdered my son. You will have to hear me!'

He turned back to Tara and grabbed her by the thick braid of her waist-length hair, yanking her face close to his. 'Tell me,' he hissed, 'why did you dance like a maniac? If you knew you were carrying my child, why were you so reckless?'

Tara stared back, unflinching.

'Answer me!' he screamed, tightening his grip on her hair.

'Let me go, Vikram,' she said in a voice so steely that he released her almost involuntarily. But his rage was unrelenting—this time, his hand rose and struck her across the face. The sharp edge of the hexagonal-shaped solitaire on his finger tore her skin from the corner of her mouth to her jawline.

Clutching her bleeding face, Tara bolted up the stairs and locked herself in her room. Standing on the low balcony, she peered out, her heart pounding. She was certain he would follow her, but he did not. Instead, she saw him pick up his flashy phone. What she heard would change her life forever.

'Rajang, I am sending you a picture from another phone. I want her dead by tomorrow.'

She watched him slip the phone into his kurta pocket, a smug smile playing on his lips. He stood, and she heard his footsteps, heavy and deliberate, as he ascended the stairs.

Her heart raced wildly as she scanned the room. In a desperate bid for self-preservation, she slid under the thin quilt on her four-poster bed, trembling as the doorknob clicked. The light from the corridor spilled into the room before the door slammed shut.

She felt his presence—the weight of his footsteps as he moved closer. Her heart lurched. She heard him swear as he pulled off his kurta, and then with a force that made the bed shake violently, his body fell beside hers with a thud. He rolled towards her, his fingers searching for her.

'Come on, princess,' he growled. 'Let me make love to you one last time. Tomorrow, you will pay for my son's death.'

His words were laced with menace, but as he mumbled, the alcohol finally claimed him. He fell back on his pillow, and she turned her head cautiously to look at him. Tara had made up her mind.

Part Three

26

When Time Stood Still

It had been an hour, and he hadn't looked up. Vivan Mehta flipped through the pages slowly, and Tara could feel her heart thumping against her chest. She had never felt so completely exposed in front of any man—as though she were standing bare, her arms wrapped around herself. Her eyes flickered to the doorway, and for a moment, she wanted to get up, walk away and pretend this had never happened.

And then, Vivan finally looked up. He leaned forward and placed his hand gently over hers. He had read the last line; Tara waited for him to speak but he remained silent.

'Tara,' he said finally, 'you are a star, and you are on fire. You are burning yourself every moment, as though your energy exists only to give, never to preserve.' He paused, then pensively added, 'It's a compelling story and must be told.'

Tara was relieved. It all felt surreal, as though she had stepped into the screen and become part of the film she had been watching. The moment teetered on the edge of fantasy.

'I didn't know you were a princess, but I sensed you were someone special—I have a sense for people.'

'Special is relative.'

'Okay, let me try again. You have the aura of holding back, even while giving everything away. That comes from class.'

'I haven't held back anything in that,' she countered, pointing to the file Vivan held in his hands.

'If the story had come to me in the post, I would still have grabbed it.'

'You came into my life for a reason, Vivan. You can make a difference to thousands of lives—generations ahead.'

'I have acted in 127 films, and in every one of them, I wanted to entertain, be acknowledged, maybe win an award or two and make more money than I could ever spend.'

'Vivan, entertainment should never be undermined. It's a precursor to happiness and peace. In subtle ways, it moves the stream of consciousness until it affects popular culture.'

'Perhaps, but too many things are doing that already. This film will be different, historical—woven into a moving reality, a fluid one. I hope it can change lives.'

'It will. You will save 1,500 families from being uprooted.'

'I am glad to have the opportunity. I will go for it.'

Vivan extended his hand, and Tara placed hers in it. It was sweaty, but he held it gently, as though he appreciated its softness. She pulled her hand back quickly and caught her breath. She'd have to get used to his presence—if that was even possible.

'Will you act in this production?' he asked.

'I could. I was active in theatre as a student.'

'And you have the looks,' he said, his eyes narrowing on her face. 'There is a shoot in Pushkar next week. It will be a chance for you to face the camera. I won't be there, but they will take care of you.'

'Pushkar... Close to my home,' she murmured wistfully. 'Just tell me what I need to do, Vivan. As long as the film tells Meher's story, I will do it.'

'Meher's story?' he asked, puzzled.

'Meher has been my closest friend. I grew up in her home and took her mother's blessings on the first day of college. I promised her my mother would never tear their home down.'

'I sensed your special connection to the village.'

'It is my real home—where my soul has lived, not just my body.'

Vivan smiled, studying her as though she were a character in one of his films. The energy in the room had shifted.

'The watermelon martini looks rather diluted,' he said suddenly. 'Can I offer you a fresh one, or maybe something else?'

'It's getting late,' she said, rising. 'Kabir is waiting for me.'

Vivan leaned back, his face momentarily distant. *Three is never a great story*, he thought wryly. *May the best man win.*

A helicopter floated down to the helipad. 'Let me give you a ride to town,' he offered, leading her to the open clearing. 'It will get you to Kabir faster.'

Vivan seemed relaxed as he navigated the chopper through the sky. 'Tell me more about this man you chose to marry?' he asked.

'Someone who wants to kill me. That says it all.'

'What a loser.'

'He will trace me to Mumbai.'

'This is my city. No one will lay a finger on you here,' he said confidently. 'Go back to Rustom's and act as though nothing happened.'

'What if he finds me there?'

'You will be under my watch. Leave it to me.'

★

After a sleepless night reliving her trip to Vivan's island, the aura of his presence and the suspended feeling of floating over Mumbai in the chopper, Tara placed her hand on Kabir's. She knew who she loved.

Kabir slept soundly, oblivious to the shifting sands beneath her feet. Restlessly, she got out of bed and put on a loose dress and slippers.

The beach was within reach and she was tempted to get closer to the shoreline. As she walked barefoot on the wet sand, the waves brushed her toes before receding, the moist breeze healing her conflicting thoughts. Exhausted, she sat on the sand, watching a new day rise. She shook her hair loose, clearing her head of all thoughts.

Her phone flashed and she wondered who it could be. There were just a handful of people who had her new number. Hari's shaky voice reached out to her from the other end. 'Hukum, the villagers want to sell. '

'Tell them to hold on.'

'They feel abandoned since you left.'

'I have not abandoned them,' she said, her voice trembling with emotion. 'Tell them I will send them enough money to develop the land if they don't sell.'

She scooped up a fistful of sand, letting it drift away with the wind.

27

Journey to Freedom

Tara leaned back in the recliner and shut her eyes. Her hand reached out until it found Kabir's, and she held on tight. For a moment, she remembered the night on Kamala's terrace. She had felt so utterly alone—the sounds of the party and the music filtering out as she stood staring at ships in the harbour. She had been unhinged until he appeared and extended his hand—that strong clasp, her resistance and his quiet patience that made her believe in love again.

A small smile played on her lips, and he could see them curl at the corners.

'Are you dreaming a beautiful dream?' he asked.

'Yes,' she murmured, her eyes still shut. 'And the dream is mingling with reality.'

Life is a perfect circle, she thought. *It keeps turning like a wheel, returning to the same place, yet it's the dichotomy of movement and stillness that propels it forward.*

She had escaped her home in Rajasthan, but between Vivan Mehta and her destiny, she was heading back to the only place she had ever called home.

The train to Pushkar was packed to the brim with jostling travellers, yet Tara found the crowd comforting. Her stomach was tied up in knots at the thought of a screen test for the film. Kabir had taken over the long and complicated discussions with Vivan's team of professionals. He understood this was not just a film for her—it was her life, her anguish, her vindication. It was about preserving her family's land and, most importantly, creating a bulletproof shield for her safety. He also sensed her unease in Vivan's presence, and hoped she would eventually move past treating him as her childhood hero and focus on the professional relationship.

For Tara, the train journey felt like a vacation from real life. Journeys always made her feel as though time had pressed the pause button.

She glanced around at the sea of faces in the crowded compartment. The travellers represented India in all its vibrant diversity. Boys in ripped jeans sat next to women in traditional saris, some of whom had their heads covered. A young girl carrying a guitar perched next to a slim woman in a full veil, her eyes barely visible. An old woman seated a few rows away was smoking a *beedi*, flouting every rule.

'Maa ji,' said a young clean-shaven boy hesitantly. 'You are not allowed to smoke inside a train these days. Also, it's not good for your health,' he added.

'I have been smoking for 40 years,' she snapped. 'I have been smoking beedis from before you were even born. And I will smoke them till the day I die. Let the government come and arrest me. Even in jail, I will light up my beedis!' She puffed with a vengeance, glaring at the boy, who quickly sank back into his seat, intimidated. He returned to his copy of Gandhi's *The Story of My Experiments with Truth*—his attempt at intervention having failed miserably.

The old woman continued to shoot him hostile looks, ensuring he kept his head lowered, reading through the rest of the journey.

Kabir chuckled and pointed his camera at her. 'Picture okay?' he asked.

'Okay,' she said, swinging her head from side to side with a toothless grin. She seemed flattered as he clicked away.

'You are a charmer,' Tara said with a smile.

'There is no charmer like the camera. Honestly, this is one lucky guy,' he said. 'Everyone smiles at a camera. The rich, the famous, the poor—they all stop and look into it with expectation, even reverence. On the red carpet at Cannes, they pause to pay a moment's obeisance to it. No other gadget ever made holds that kind of power over human nature.'

'Hmm, you are right,' Tara agreed. 'It worked on the angry lady too.'

'Recognition and appreciation, a desire for immortality, a wish to freeze moments in time and, of course, the tendency to gloat over one's self-image—these are some of the most tempting human instincts that my Nikon brings out,' Kabir said, patting the camera affectionately. 'One day, I shall write an ode to my Nikon.'

'I think you just did,' said Tara.

The landscape outside the window began to change. The blue of the sky grew paler, the lush green palms gave way to sparse foliage as the train moved away from the ocean and towards the desert.

'I am going to sell this one to *National Geographic*,' Kabir declared, expertly capturing a languid village against a setting sun.

Tara reached over and gently took the camera away from him. 'Now look at it without the camera.'

He turned to her, surprised. 'But that is my job, Tara.'

'Even so,' she said softly, 'if you can, take time to absorb each sight without the lens first. Your pictures will have a soul.'

Kabir turned his gaze to the sunset and felt its quiet serenity.

Tara put the camera back in his hand. 'Now click. Do you feel a difference?'

The view had changed. Now he saw it differently. The sun seemed more fiery, the colours more vibrant and the poetry of the sky more profound. He realized, with a pang, how robotic he had become over the years, obsessed with capturing the perfect shot. Tara had reminded him to connect with the moments he was capturing, and somehow that transformed his work forever.

She curled into his arm as if he were a bolster pillow and

fell into a deep sleep. Kabir glanced at Tara. She looked so tired and frail that he felt a sudden urge to take her somewhere no one could find her.

He gently manoeuvred himself out of her embrace and opened his laptop, relieved to find that he still had network. His fingers moved deftly over the keyboard, his mind working out a plan to bring attention to Tara's fight to save her land. He combed through his database of media contacts, selecting the most influential journalists in New Delhi. After crafting a carefully worded email, he sent it off. Then he began drafting a blog post.

As he scrolled through his blog, Tara stirred in her sleep, her eyes fluttering open. She peered at the glowing screen.

He smiled at her. 'Do you want to see more?'

She nodded sleepily.

'Then get up and take a look. I am famous,' he teased.

'You are famous? But why didn't you tell me? I thought the blog was just a hobby!'

'Well, famous in a way.' He tapped a few keys and turned the laptop towards Tara. 'See that? That is my blog page. It gets anywhere from 70,000 to a million hits, depending on the post. I share photographs, articles and opinions from my travels, that sort of stuff.'

'Let me see,' she said, her voice tinged with childlike wonder.

She leaned closer, scrolling through images of Kabir chasing an ostrich in Africa, sailing along the Rio Grande and sipping tea in an Egyptian coffee house. Then her eyes stilled as one photo caught her attention—a beautiful, red-haired woman with tanned skin and green eyes lounging on a beach, her shapely legs stretched out, her face glowing in the sun as she rested her head on Kabir's bare chest.

'Now,' Kabir said abruptly, shutting the laptop, 'let us get some sleep.' He stretched out on the reclining seat, his long legs cramped in the small space. Tara lay awake, tossing and turning, reaching out towards his shoulder only to hesitate and pull back. Finally, she gave in and whispered, 'Kabir?'

'Yes, love?' he replied softly. 'You haven't slept?'

'That girl in the picture with you, Kabir… Who is she?'

There was a long silence. Moonlight streamed through the train window, casting pale light over Kabir's face. She could see his apprehension, the way his eyes searched hers. Then, with quiet determination, he met her gaze and spoke. 'Do you remember the day on the beach when I told you there was something I needed to say?'

'Yes, I do. I stopped you because I wanted those moments to stay.'

'I understood that, Tara. We both were running away from a past, and perhaps neither of us wanted to face it.'

'The past always catches up, Kabir, in some way.'

'Well, the truth is best told. Showing those pictures was my way of sharing my past.'

'Is she your past, or is she your present?' Tara asked flatly.

'She was my wife. I loved her very much, but she left me a year ago.'

'Oh, Kabir, I am so sorry she left you. I am so sorry.'

He nodded, his jaw tightening.

'Was she in love with someone else?'

'No. Not at all.'

'Well, what then?'

'Jennifer and I were married for four years. We didn't have any children.'

He glanced at Tara's face and knew it wasn't enough. He needed to tell her more.

He tried to think back to the day when he lost the woman he loved. Her memory still choked his voice, and he paused.

She had been lying in his lap, his fingers playing with her hair.

'Have my baby, Jen,' he had said. 'Please, have my baby. I

want to see our child—a baby girl with eyes like yours.'

'Let's adopt then,' she had replied. 'Don't forget our pact, Kabir. When we married, I told you we would never have children.'

'Come on! All women say that. You can't be serious.'

'I was serious, Kabir, and I still am.'

'But babies are divine! More than anything, I want to see what we create together,' he had replied.

She had turned her face away, burying it in the sand.

'What's the matter, darling? Are you crying? Okay, I'm sorry. It's all right. We don't need to have a baby.'

'I *can't* have a baby, Kabir. I said what I said because I don't have a choice. I can't have children.'

Kabir had been stunned. He had reached out for her, holding her in his arms. 'Why didn't you tell me before? That's fine. We can just adopt; it's not a big issue.'

'It *is*,' she had said, sobbing. 'You just said you wanted a child of your own more than anything, and I can never give you that.'

After that, something in her changed. Jennifer was never the same again. She barely smiled. She started pulling away from Kabir. She turned away when he tried to hug her. She felt as though she had let him down, like a woman who was incomplete.

One day, when Kabir returned from his travels, she was gone. She left a note and a bouquet of red roses. He wrote her emails every now and then, but she never replied.

'…and that's when I accepted the assignment in India. I was not ready to love again, but then you came into my life, like an injured bird trying to fly, and I held on to you. Maybe because I wasn't just looking for someone to heal—I was in search of wings too.'

Tara's lips gently brushed his eyelids, and he knew that she had accepted him with love and compassion. Her touch said more than words could: 'I feel your pain; I want to share it. I am here with you; you are not alone.'

His frown eased, his body relaxed and he fell asleep holding her. She lay awake, softly stroking his unruly locks, smiling down at him as though he were a baby in her arms.

She whispered, 'Kabir, do you want me to speak to her?'

He smiled faintly without opening his eyes. Tara knew she was helping him find peace within his pain. Then she quickly turned to the window, so he wouldn't notice her tears. She felt as if her heart were cracking open.

Just when you find love, she thought, *it turns into a fledgling with restless wings.*

28

Pushkar

He watched the video of the party on the ship, replaying the moment when Tara hesitantly took to the dance floor and then set the room on fire.

Shiv observed Vivan with an amused expression. 'So, the shooting schedule wasn't a coincidence.'

'I don't believe in coincidences,' Vivan replied.

'Ah, are you in love with this girl?' Shiv asked.

'No. Just in lust, to be honest. Love is too elevated a term to use lightly.'

'Fair enough. At least you are honest.'

'If I find a woman irresistibly attractive, I don't see the need to dress up a raw emotion with dignified pretence. Attraction is lust. As for love, that's a questionable emotion.'

'I know you too well, Vivan. It is just your ego speaking. You love this girl—more than you will admit, even to yourself.'

Vivan smiled back but kept silent, not because he was hiding the truth but because he wasn't sure of it himself. He hadn't planned on coming but he finally did. *Does that mean something?* he wondered. 'I have invited Tara here for a screen test,' he finally said. 'Ask Rahil to carve out a small part for her in the film. Something to test her acting skills. She will be in my next casting.'

★

Tara had been visiting the Pushkar Mela since childhood, yet its energy never ceased to amaze her. Aishwarya Devi was a devotee of Lord Brahma, so trips to Pushkar had always been spiritual pilgrimages, not mere holidays.

'Can you stop at Pushkar Lake?' she asked the cab driver.

'Of course,' he replied enthusiastically, slowing down as they approached the waterside.

Tara stepped out and descended the steps to the ghat before stepping into the chilly water. Kabir watched her from a distance—her face serene, her eyes shut and hands folded, the winter sun bracing her skin. She dipped into the sacred lake several times. Looking cold and shivery, she stepped out and rushed to one of the many cubicles to change. She returned dressed in a set of fresh clothes, her damp hair left open.

'I feel purified now,' she said, as they walked towards the Brahma Temple by the banks of the sacred lake.

Rows of flower sellers lined the path, and Tara bent to pick a lotus. After queuing patiently, they climbed the 17 steps leading to the sanctum. She placed the lotus at the feet of Lord Brahma and moved aside to let other devotees have their moment of worship.

Seeing Kabir's confused face, she explained, 'Legend has it that Brahma, the Creator of the universe, dropped a lotus here, and from that spot, this lake emerged.'

'That's interesting,' said Kabir, nodding.

'What do you believe in, Kabir?' she asked, noticing his expression.

'I am a humanist. I respect all faiths but can't tie myself to just one. My belief stretches from the speck of dust on my hand to the last star—boundless, like the universe.'

'It's your genetics, I guess.'

'Spot on. My chromosomes are a cocktail. I believe in what I am—a mix of the world's faiths.'

The sun set across the desert, and in the distance, lines of camel riders wound their way to trade their animals at the Pushkar Mela. Travel-worn traders paused for a dip in the holy lake before leading their camels to the bustling marketplace. This was India—where commerce and spirituality coexisted harmoniously.

Every year, the Pushkar Mela transformed into a kaleidoscope of colours, attracting devotees, merchants and tourists alike. That year was no different. The vibrant chaos was alive with Rajasthani dancers in traditional lehengas, tourists attempting their moves and film crews capturing it all.

Inspector Mathur arrived in a jeep packed with policemen, who quickly assumed their positions. 'Why do these film actors disturb our peace every year?' he grumbled. 'At least I'd better get a good photograph with one of them.'

'Unbelievable,' remarked Kabir as he scanned the vibrant landscape around him, capturing the lively chaos with his camera. 'My camera is ecstatic—never seen so many shades in one place.'

Tara smiled at him with a sense of pride. Thank goodness she was born here, where life sparkled in every corner. 'Kabir,' she said as he moved closer. 'The grey weather in Europe, the muted colour palettes—it will probably feel like a monochromatic experience when you get back.' She paused, suddenly uneasy. The words 'get back' unsettled her. She wished he would never leave her—that he would always stay.

The skies over Pushkar were clear on this sacred night.

'Look at the full moon—it's Kartik Purnima, and it's glowing,' said Tara, pointing at the night sky.

'Kartik Purnima,' Kabir echoed, slightly overwhelmed by the celestial energy. The festivities carried on into the night. The shadows brought with them an unmistakable bohemian allure. A fire dancer twisted and slithered under a burning ring of flames, his sweat-slicked muscles glowing in the light, while a curvaceous performer spun and twirled around him, her voice rising in a gypsy song that taunted and goaded him.

A group of revellers sat on the soft sand, passing around a small earthen bowl of country wine in a communal spirit.

The off-white canvas tent Tara and Kabir had booked online hadn't prepared them for the luxurious opulence of its interior.

Tara reclined on one of the loungers, but they were eager to soak in the night's gaiety. Leaving their bags behind, they stepped out into the pulsating crowd.

Kabir handed Tara his hip flask. 'Look what I have here—your favourite Bordeaux red.'

Tara grinned, taking a huge swig before giggling. Familiar stall owners waved at her, and she waved back with warm recognition. This was home—her culture, her life. The wine had reached her head, making her emotions more pronounced. Her body swayed, or was it the earth? She was not quite sure.

★

Vivan Mehta moved through the crowd, the edge of his headgear pulled down to camouflage his face. His entourage of security walked tensely around him, trying to blend into the crowd for anonymity. He was just a few yards away from Tara, but the bustling throng kept them apart. Yet, by some inexplicable pull of fate, their paths began to converge, like two stars on a collision course.

Tara moved towards him, drawn by some unseen force. Vivan felt it too, as though some electrifying energy were dragging him. In a moment of climax, they came face to face.

Tara froze, her heart skipping a beat as she recognized those eyes that attracted her. When he pulled the muslin covering away from his face, she began to tremble.

'Kabir,' she whispered under her breath, as if she were sinking into quicksand. She looked around, but Kabir was nowhere to be seen.

'Hello, Tara,' Vivan said, surprised to have run into her.

'I was not expecting you here,' she managed to say.

'Well, now that I am, may I invite you for a drink? My tent is nearby.'

She wanted to say no but what she heard herself say was 'All right'.

The interior of Vivan's tent was reminiscent of a luxury hotel. Tara felt uneasy as she stepped inside. *I shouldn't have come along*, she thought.

'Let's stick to the screen test, Vivan. I am here with Kabir, so let's keep this purely professional.'

'Really?' Vivan's face fell. 'What a pity. When you find your love, someone else already has her,' he said candidly.

'I think I should go.'

'Wait,' he said, his voice urgent. 'I want you to do more than a screen test. Would you consider taking a role in my film? It's the part of a woman I meet in the desert and become infatuated with. It will help me convince my investors that you can act, and you will leave me with a celluloid memory.'

She looked at him, silent and hesitant, then walked away. Yet, she couldn't shake the urge to look back. Was he trying to make her play out his fantasy? *No,* she told herself firmly. She was not going beyond the screen test.

As she stepped inside the white canvas tent, relief washed over her at the sight of Kabir. He was lying on the bed, a book in hand, French music softly playing on his computer—something he did when he felt homesick.

'Where were you, Kabir?' she asked. 'Where were you?'

'I was on the phone to France,' he replied calmly.

'Vivan Mehta is here.' She didn't need to say more. The look in her eyes told him everything—she was in turmoil again.

'You said he wasn't coming.'

'He told me so, Kabir. He must have changed his mind.'

'Oh! I see. So he told you one thing and did another... Strange man.'

Tara looked away, trying to escape the tension in the air.

'Did he lust after you again?' Kabir asked, his voice taut.

'Not really. He wants me to do a small role in his film.'

'I thought this was just a quick screen test.'

'That's what he said, but now it seems he wants something more.'

'Do you want to do it?' he asked, hoping she would say no, but the silence hung in the air between them like a foreboding of things to come.

That night, Tara lay beside Kabir, her eyes wide open, staring into the darkness. She turned to him, and like an uninvited memory, Jennifer's face flashed before her—the flame-red hair, the sunburnt skin, the joyful smile. It made her feel reckless, desperate and utterly confused.

'You should have told me before,' she said softly.

'About what?'

'That Jennifer is still a part of your life.'

'I tried, but you stopped me.'

'I did?'

'I remember it clearly. "Let us be in this moment. This is the only truth," you told me. And I was tempted to believe it.'

'Glad you did, because the truth hurts, and I was already hurting.'

'Come on, princess, I love you...and nothing is going to change that. We are here, in this moment. Nothing else matters.'

'Except that you love her, Kabir,' she said and looked away.

The morning sun was strong, and rows of foreigners sprawled across the sands, baking themselves in the golden sunshine. Some turned bronze, others ashen, while first-timers turned the colour of ripe tomatoes. Meanwhile, Indian girls slathered themselves with sunscreen, petrified of getting tanned, shielding their skin under fashionable hats and dark glasses. Ironic—each group coveted what the other had. No one seemed happy with what God, in all His wisdom, had given them.

Tara slipped her hand into her cloth bag, pulling out her mobile phone. She dialled a number, and the jingle of Vivan Mehta's latest release filled her ear. A tiny nerve in her temple throbbed, and she quickly disconnected. Almost instantly, her phone rang.

'Tara,' he said softly, 'I have been waiting. We will start your shoot today. Come as you are.'

'I will come,' she replied quietly.

At the breakfast table, Tara avoided Kabir's gaze, nibbling on the edges of overcooked pakoras. Finally, Kabir broke the tension.

'Princess, don't feel so guilty. We come from different worlds—both fugitives from our lives. Wanderers. Our searches may be different, but we met by some magnificent chance. Tara, we are not here to claim or enslave each other, but to free each other from the shackles that held us back. Celebrate, princess. We have but one life to live. Live it. Give in to that deep calling within you.'

'I know you, Kabir. You are jealous!'

'And you are too,' Kabir retorted, laughing.

'Jennifer is beautiful.'

Kabir looked at his watch, then at Tara. 'Don't deny yourself the most beautiful part of yourself, princess.' He lifted his camera as he walked away, his footsteps trailing into the rising dust cloud.

He wandered aimlessly, angry at himself for pushing her, testing her. Then again, he knew he wanted to see the injured bird he had rescued take flight. Healed, free and soaring higher than ever. He wanted Tara to make up for the long days she had spent in fear, in repression.

Inside the tent, Tara sat bathed in the soft glow of a lamp, debating with her conscience. Finally, she got up and walked towards the object of her desire—it was the only way she could describe this compulsion.

★

The swift strokes of a make-up brush tickled her skin, and Tara instinctively sniffed as she inhaled a trace of powder. The make-up artist worked deftly on Vivan Mehta's protégée. Tara's lips were painted a crimson red, her eyes smouldered with black kohl and her cheekbones gleamed with highlighter.

To her surprise, Vivan was nowhere to be found. Instead, she was greeted by a team of professionals.

'Hello Tara ji,' said a young man with a crew cut. 'I am Danish, the dress coordinator.' He held up a red lehenga choli embellished with tiny mirrors. 'This, madam, is your costume, chosen personally by Vivan sir.'

She looked at the dress, tired and strangely compliant.

'Any views on the dress?'

'No. If Vivan has chosen it, I will wear it,' she murmured.

She slipped into the exquisite attire, the choli strings pulled tight against her body. Someone's hands draped a veil delicately over her head, while another adorned her feet with anklets and toe rings. Tara felt like a mannequin being dressed.

When she finally looked up, the reflection staring back at her was not her—it was the darker side of the woman she had never imagined she could be.

'Gorgeous! Absolutely gorgeous, Tara ji,' came a crisp voice.

Tara turned to see Rahil Kapoor, the maverick director behind Vivan Mehta's last four blockbuster hits. With his horn-rimmed glasses and bushy ponytail, he was not a man to waste time.

'Good evening, young lady. Your scene was scripted by Vivan,' he said, pulling up a chair and sitting next to her. 'Tea for you?' he asked, trying to make her feel comfortable.

As Tara nodded, Rahil continued, 'Let me explain your role. You are Vivan's obsession. He meets you at the Pushkar Mela and is simply hypnotized by you. You, however, decline his advances. Vivan vows not to touch you till you want him. The rest...will be improvised. That's how he wants it.' His work done, Rahil got up and walked away.

Tara felt as though she were back in college, playing offbeat roles in experimental films shot on amateur cameras for inter-college competitions. She had been a pro at that, but this was different. She felt unnerved.

★

They shot all day in the desert. Vivan appeared on set but hardly looked at her. Tara wondered why. She was beginning to feel insulted, a bit ignored.

Her role required her to wander through the sand dunes while Vivan followed her in a Land Rover. Tara was exasperated with playing the ignored obsession. *God! Couldn't he give me a scene where I could act?*

By sunset, the desert was an ethereal sight, simmering like an earthen oven.

'That was amazing work,' Rahil said, pleased. 'You didn't look like you were acting at all. You are a natural.'

Tara offered a polite smile.

They returned to the tent for the final scene. Tara was instructed to recline on a lounger and wait.

'This is going to be an improvised scene,' Rahil explained. 'Vivan is on his way. Look, Tara, you may find this a bit difficult as there are no pre-written lines for this scene. Vivan wants you to do what feels natural. Just say whatever comes to mind when he says something. He might not speak at all also.'

'That is very difficult. I would prefer it if…'

Vivan walked in then, his eyes fixed on Tara.

'Everyone leave, except the cameraman, please,' instructed Rahil.

As the crew dispersed, and the cameraman focused his lens, Vivan moved closer to Tara. He leaned in, blowing on the nape of her neck. Startled, she turned to face him. His lips hovered above hers, almost touching but not quite.

Her mouth quivered, and she lifted her hand to cover her face, creating a barrier. Vivan's mouth traced the air over her fingers, his breath heavy, ghosting over her skin.

Nothing made sense to Tara; with her breath out of control, she reached for him, drawing him towards her.

'Please, Vivan, make love to me. Just once, please,' she whispered, her voice barely audible.

'No,' he replied. 'You can never be mine.'

'Just once,' she pleaded. 'Just once, and never again. Let me get over you.'

Rahil Kapoor had never been at a loss when the camera was rolling—until that moment. 'Cut,' he whispered to the cameraman through the headset. The latter silently slipped out of the room, leaving behind an untamed fire that seemed ready to erupt into a blazing inferno of passions.

It was the other side of midnight, and the desert lay silent. Tara burst out of the tent with an urgency that startled the night guards stationed outside. Fires flickered in nearby tents—some dying embers, others still glowing faintly.

'Can we drop you anywhere, madam?' Vivan's security guard asked politely, but Tara did not hear him. She ran like a fleeing deer till she reached her familiar tent. She hesitated at the entrance, wondering whether Kabir would be there. Had he left her, and gone forever? She took one tentative step at a time, her feet sinking deeper than ever into the cold sand. She lifted the canvas door, her breath heavy. She strained her eyes to see through the darkness, trying to see if the bed was empty.

'Princess,' came his soft voice. 'Hope your dreams came true tonight.'

Tara collapsed into the cane chair beside the bed and sobbed. 'I am so sorry, Kabir. I am so sorry to have hurt you.'

'Don't cry, princess. We belong to different worlds. We are spinning stars—always moving, never stopping. Not even for each other. We have to find new galaxies. We have to keep travelling.'

'I stopped in time, Kabir,' she said abruptly, her burdened conscience aching for absolution.

'You did? Well, I guess I am glad you stopped him,' he said, his tone neutral.

'No. I stopped myself in time.'

'I would not have held it against you even if you had gone all the way. To desire is natural, princess... How come men never feel so guilty about giving in to passion?'

'It's over for me,' she said. 'He's gone. Like some Rasputin who cast a spell on my senses. I have driven him out of my system. There is something...evil about him, yet something so compelling.'

'Sleep, sweet princess,' he murmured. 'I love you for everything you are.'

Tara slid into the bed, and from under the quilt, her muffled voice replied, 'Good night, Kabir. I will love you forever.'

Kabir held her gently, kissing the furrows on her forehead until she fell asleep. He then climbed out of bed. Sleep was not easy on this night of emotional turmoil. A hint of suspicion fluttered through his mind before he shook it off.

The night was dense as he stepped out; the desert stretched around him, eternal and unyielding. He walked barefoot, the cold sand swallowing his footsteps. Once back at the tent, Kabir yanked his laptop from its case and sank on to the ground, the device resting on his knees. His face was flushed, his eyes smarting. He reminded himself that their relationship had always been unconditional. No bonds, no promises to hold them together. She was a bird who had flown into his life, seeking refuge for a fleeting moment. She had made it clear that they would live for today—no chains, no permanence. They were nomads, running from conformity and experimenting with life as no one had before.

Yet, the thought of Tara in Vivan Mehta's arms made a vein

twitch in his neck. He was in love with an unstoppable wave—a wave that did not yearn for the shore but avoided it.

The soft light of the screen illuminated his face as he stared at it. He clicked on the Skype icon and pressed 'Call'.

'Hello', came the deeply accented voice. Jennifer's face appeared, her expression touched by serenity and a quiet sadness that only deepened her beauty.

Kabir's heart felt as though it had forgotten its rhythm, struck by the sight of her. He couldn't help noticing the small heart-shaped locket hanging from her neck—a keepsake from years ago, bought at a street market at the foot of Montmartre in Paris. He remembered the moment vividly: she had held her hair aside as he clasped it around her neck.

'Forever,' he had whispered, and she had smiled back, repeating, 'Forever.'

Now, like a flash, she was back in his life, smiling into the camera as she said, 'Kabir, how are you?'

The years melted away and she was his Jen again. 'Fine, darling. And you?'

'I'm well,' she replied softly. 'It's been a while.'

'Not enough to make me forget you.' A little anxious, he asked, 'Any man in your life?'

'No. Not really.'

'Not really? And won't you ask me…'

'No,' she said, a sad smile lighting her face. 'I won't.'

'Why not?'

'I can't say why.'

'Not curious?'

Jennifer looked away from the screen and said, 'Maybe I just want to freeze our last moment and keep it with me.'

The cup of coffee had just touched her lips when he remarked, 'Roasted, toasted…special.'

Her eyes snapped back to the screen. 'How did you know?'

'I can smell it all the way from here,' he said wistfully. 'I am feeling homesick.'

'Really? Kabir, you only feel homesick when you are not on the road,' she said, her lips quirking in a knowing smile.

The thin canvas wall couldn't muffle his voice, and Tara woke, having heard Kabir speaking in the silence of the desert.

She was not looking for the answers that were coming to her. Picking up her blue diary, she wrote: *No man or woman is born to love only one because love, left to its natural self, moves and changes shapes and forms if not imprisoned along dotted lines.*

She felt unhinged. She knew she had damaged her relationship with Kabir, but she was human and flawed. Troubled, she wanted to hear a voice from home.

'Ram Swarup,' she said into her phone. 'I am at Pushkar. Can you bring Firefly to me? I miss him.'

'I will bring him, Hukum,' came the reply.

'Don't let anyone find out,' she added before sharing her location.

At dawn, she waited outside the tent until she heard the sound of hooves. It sparked a sense of excitement in her. She didn't want to ride him; she simply wanted to look into his eyes and pet him.

Firefly shook his head. Tara wasn't sure if it was her imagination, but she saw a glimmer of something—was it moisture? Emotion? She turned away, overwhelmed.

Ram Swarup looked concerned until Tara looked at him and said, 'I am safer being away right now. I am doing fine. Don't worry about me.'

With a nod, Ram Swarup mounted Firefly and vanished into the desert. Tara turned back to find her way to her tent.

★

As the sun streamed through, Kabir woke to find himself curled on the ground. Someone had covered him with a light Rajasthani quilt.

He stepped outside and looked up at the sky. Overhead, colourful hot-air balloons floated across the horizon. He ran back inside for his camera—this was something he needed to capture.

'Tara,' he called out, 'come quickly—we need to get on one of the balloons!'

They rushed to the launch site, where a plump man in a turban stood counting crisp currency notes. He glanced up, clearly pleased with his thriving venture.

'Tickets for two, please,' said Kabir.

The man scribbled on an invoice and handed it to Kabir, who looked at the paper and groaned. 'I could take a flight back to Delhi for this!'

He looked at Kabir squarely till the latter gave him his credit card.

'I will give you my share, Kabir,' said Tara, sounding a little awkward.

'Let this be on me, princess,' he smiled.

They climbed into the woven basket and waited as the balloon operators prepared for the ascent. Few others seemed willing to splurge on the costly ride.

Soon enough, the balloon lifted off the ground, carried by the gentle currents of the early morning wind. They leaned on the edge, watching the sea of sand recede. There was something liberating about leaving terra firma and floating in the sky. They both knew they would return to face a reality that would hurt but, for the moment, the skies were their home.

29

Martinis at Sunset

'Lovely Tara,' he said, as the sun reflected in her eyes, till it slipped into the ocean, leaving behind a warm brown serenity.

The beach house in Goa had become Vivan's creative haven over the years. Close enough to Mumbai for his team to fly in and return within a day, yet far enough from its snarling traffic, it provided the uninterrupted flow of creativity and inspiration he craved. Two months had passed since Tara met him at his house, and they were already knee-deep in the early stages of *The Blue Diary*.

The sunsets and the ocean, though unchanging in essence, remained Vivan's fascination. Every evening, he made sure his bottle of wine was ready to toast the twilight.

'Sir,' Robert interrupted politely, 'just to inform you, sunset today will be at 6.35 p.m., so your drinks schedule might be delayed.'

Vivan smiled at the minor disruption. The sensitivity of an artist coursed through him, attuned to details others often overlooked. Colours, textures, sounds—everything held significance when he was in his creative zone. That evening, he watched Tara as much as he did the sunset. Her hair, caught in the ocean breeze, framed her lightly curvaceous form. As she moved closer, his gaze lingered over her mouth—a teasing enigma reminiscent of the Mona Lisa, a smile that was there, or perhaps not.

He lifted his flute glass and offered, 'Wine for you, Tara?'

'Not today,' she smiled. 'I need my head clear.'

Pushkar was a regret she still carried, and regrets, she told herself, must never be repeated. She had worked on herself—layered herself with a Teflon coating.

'Perhaps a watermelon mojito,' he persisted.

'You need me here to deliver a good story, Vivan,' she replied.

'I do, but a little wine never harmed the imagination.'

'This feels like walking through every room of my life—opening some doors I'd rather leave shut, knocking on others and breaking down the ones I have lost the keys to. It is harder than I imagined.'

Vivan smiled. 'I like the metaphors you speak in, and I understand your angst. But have you decided? Do you want to show the negative side of your mother?'

'That's the door I can't unlock. For all the pain she brought me, it's not easy.'

'The lawyers will make sure it's legally airtight. It'll be marketed as fiction.'

'The papers are already speculating it is my story. Besides, this has less to do with the law; it's more a tussle between me and my conscience.'

She suddenly seemed fragile, defenceless. Vivan wanted to take her in his arms and kiss her, her lips a constant tease. Instead, he walked away. He was going to be part of her story and he wanted to be a part she would remember fondly.

As he left, Tara felt conflicted. Part of her wished he had stayed, yet another part breathed easier in his absence.

The group of young writers sitting at a logwood table glanced at her, hopeful. Their laptops were open, ready to transform her stories into vivid scenes.

She looked at them and smiled. 'Will you let me take the night off today?'

'Yeah,' they chorused. 'We are hitting the bars on the beach!'

Tara reached for her phone and pressed the last dialled number. 'Kabir,' she whispered, her voice half-choked.

'I am coming,' he replied immediately.

She ended the call and smiled. She understood now why she

needed him so desperately. It was difficult for her to admit it to herself, but somehow, when she was with Vivan, the energy between them always felt as though it might spiral out of control.

She walked to the two-storey house adjacent to Vivan's villa, which had been converted into a quaint guest house. Its original Portuguese architecture was painstakingly maintained, with a covered patio extending into a small garden. Tara smiled as she spotted Divya sitting on the wooden swing and waved to her.

Kicking off her sandals, Tara joined her. 'I am missing Kabir,' she confessed.

'You love Kabir, but there is chemistry between you and Vivan,' Divya remarked.

Tara gazed into the distance. 'It's okay, Divya. Let the oceans flow. Don't stop anything. Walk into the storm, play with the winds…and don't hope to find your way back. That's how I look at life.'

'Will you marry him?'

'Love him too much to marry him.'

'What does that mean?'

'It simply means this relationship is beautiful—too beautiful—to risk. It's not bondage; it's the opposite. It's liberation of the spirit. Marriage would go against the essence of something that happened unplanned and is moving uncharted on a road with no destination.'

'One day, you will feel the need to settle down. It's the nesting instinct.'

'Look at the greatest lovers in history. Can you imagine Mr and Mrs Romeo and Juliet squabbling over porridge at 70?'

They both giggled.

'Stop it, Tara. Don't ruin my romances. Romeo and Juliet will never feel romantic to me again.'

'Besides, we both share a desire to roam and keep moving.'

'You are both escaping life.'

Tara smiled. 'Perhaps. But escape can create the best moments. The reality is, I share his heart with his wife in France.'

'I have noticed the way he looks at you. He is smitten.'

'He is, but what stops him from loving Jennifer as well? Have you seen the little bird charm around his neck? She gave it to him. He never takes it off,' she said, her voice tinged with sadness.

Tara jogged along the beach in her blush pink tracksuit, her eyes tense, her pace faster than usual, her mind spinning with thoughts. Finally exhausted, she slowed down and collapsed on to the sand, stretching her legs till her toes brushed the gentle waves.

Once she caught her breath, she took out her blue diary from her bag. Her mother's portrayal in the film had played on her mind all night. She had tossed, turned and debated with herself endlessly. She couldn't run away from the decision forever.

Opening the diary, she began to write. First, she listed everything she loved about her mother. Then, she scribbled all the things she hated. Her eyes were damp with tears as she spilled her thoughts on to the page.

She did the same for Vikram, starting with their honeymoon and ending with the night she fled for her life. Flipping through the pages, she read them over and over again till she was sobbing. She wanted the anger to stay long enough to see the film through. She didn't want to weaken and let those who had let her down get away with it all.

Her fingers dug into the sand until they ached, trying to anchor herself in a past she wished she could forget.

Suddenly, she was startled by a voice calling out to her.

She turned to see Vivan jogging towards her, dressed in black shorts and a T-shirt, his two bodyguards trailing behind. He sank down into the sand beside her.

'How's my superstar doing?'

'Almost perfect!' she replied. 'And to make it even better, Kabir is coming today.'

'Oh,' Vivan said, his eyebrows lifting. 'I was going to ask you out for dinner tonight.'

'Vivan. Let's save it for another day.'

'That won't be the same.'

'Why not?' she asked.

'Because tomorrow is not today. Never mind,' he said. 'Tara, there are probably few women I cannot have, yet there is only one who will not have me. Such is life.' Before she could respond, he pulled off his T-shirt. She looked away but couldn't help catching a glimpse of his sculpted body, likely the work of the country's best trainers.

'Come, let's swim,' he said.

'I am not a great swimmer.'

'I have read your story, remember? You love swimming.'

And before she could answer, he had vanished into the waves, his bodyguards dutifully following.

★

Kabir was waiting at the cottage when Tara returned and she fell into his arms sobbing. 'Don't leave me, please, Kabir. I need you.'

'Okay, baby. But where's the anger? We need anger to set things right. No more tears.'

She pulled away, straightened her shoulders and smiled. 'Yes. I must fight for Jaivangarh.'

That evening, Tara dressed in a pair of dark blue jeans and a shimmering tank top, ready for Kabir's promised experience of Goa's nightlife.

'Where are we going?' she asked, as they settled into the plush Bentley Divya and Arjun had hired for the trip.

'To the best place in all of Goa,' Kabir replied as the car made its way through the narrow roads.

Tara was excited. She needed a break from the turmoil. The strain of revealing her life for the world to consume was suffocating her. For all her righteous anger, the guilt of exposing her mother's flaws still gnawed at her. And the charged undercurrents between her and Vivan only added to the chaos. The stakes were too high, and she felt like a fragile thread stretched to its limit.

The Knights at Night was Goa's place to be seen. Known as much for its unbeatable music as for its spicy prawns, squids and lobsters, the club housed in an oversized shack had a dance floor that spilled out on to the sands. Retro tunes from the '80s played, giving way to pulsating beats as the younger crowd swarmed in.

As the night wore on, the make-up on the women's faces smudged, the music slowed down again, coaxing the inebriated crowd to cling to their fading sensibilities, their energies waning, and return home. Few realized how keenly they were being controlled by one man—Christopher John Singh, aka DJCJ. With his dancing fingers on the console switches, he completely owned their moods and senses for the next few hours.

Christopher John Singh, the coolest DJ in the country, had a major in psychology, yet DJCJ had abandoned a 'promising' life to master the art of music. Ingeniously, he put his psychology degree to good use. He played with his crowd as if conducting an orchestra, his intuitive grasp of human emotions turning each set into an experience. DJCJ observed his crowds and enjoyed his ability to manipulate them via his console. It had become somewhat of a game for him. His silky hair was left carelessly open, and swayed as he moved to the music. Often, he was spotted in tabloids escorting glamorous girls who wanted to be seen with him.

Kabir and Tara walked in with Divya and Arjun, and Tara immediately wished she were somewhere else, far from this strange hedonism she had long forgotten.

A commotion at the entrance caught her attention. A retinue of black-suited security guards moved in perfect synchrony, shielding a man in a long black kurta and blue jeans. Tara rose on her toes to get a closer look, but the group moved like a jellyfish in a water tank. Suddenly, a streak of blue light illuminated his face for an instant.

Vivan was moving to the music.

Just when Tara began to think she was hallucinating, DJCJ's voice cut through the music. 'Dudes, we got lucky tonight! Thanks, Vivan Mehta, for celebrating your birthday with us! This one's for you.'

Tara abruptly gulped her wine down and Kabir looked at her with an expression that conveyed everything she didn't want to hear. She looked away, trying to avoid his glare.

'Don't, Tara,' he said. 'It's not good for you.'

She responded by ordering a martini and chased it with Divya's freshly poured glass of single malt. Then she stood up, a playful smile on her face, her steps unsteady.

She walked up to Vivan and gave him a hug. 'Happy birthday,' she said softly, her lips brushing against his earlobe. 'You should have told me it was your birthday, Vivan.'

'Didn't I say, tomorrow won't be today.'

'You play games with words, Vivan.'

She stepped back, but he held her hand lightly. 'A birthday dance, please?' he asked.

The music shifted to a tango. Tara hesitated, her eyes searching for Kabir, but her body gave in to Vivan's movements.

Before she knew it, the hesitation had receded. She slipped out of herself to have this one dance on this one night. She was becoming someone else, someone she didn't know.

She was the wine she had drunk, the pain she had endured—she was everything except herself.

The music changed again, and Tara stepped back, her knees wobbling. Vivan looked on, hoping for a repeat, but she turned around and made her way back to the table.

'If you want him that badly, go sleep with him,' Kabir said, his voice tight, barely making it through clenched teeth.

'Really, should I?' Tara slurred. 'You really think I should?'

'We are leaving now,' Kabir snapped. He grabbed her hand and led her through the crowd. Unsteady on her feet, she did not resist. Divya and Arjun followed silently.

The night outside was humid; deep clouds drifted over the half-moon and the salty tang of the sea lingered in the air.

The ride back was filled with tacit silence. The evening had turned out to be a disaster.

Kabir's jaws tightened, his head spinning with anger. Suddenly, he turned to look at Tara, his frustration flaring again. Tara looked at him, her large brown eyes apologetic like a child who had made a mistake, the transparency of her soul endearing.

The Bentley stopped at a red light. Without warning, Tara rolled down the window and reached out slowly to touch a young girl's shoulder. The child's eyes lit up. Her slouching form straightened and she held her head up high, her expression softening into a slight smile that seemed to say, 'Thank you for this moment of dignity.' She suddenly didn't seem to ask for money, she had received something much more valuable.

In a town where sleek cars with humming engines glided through streets dotted with the underprivileged, the dispossessed and the unacknowledged, it was almost unthinkable for the tinted windows of privilege to roll down to embrace a street urchin.

A tangible tension hung in the air until Kabir, in all his French liberality, burst into a hearty laugh. 'Come on, guys. That girl is human too.'

'You don't understand the issues, Kabir,' said Divya. 'It's not about poverty. It is about hygiene, diseases—leprosy, tuberculosis…'

'My grandmother died of tuberculosis years ago. I hugged her every day till her last. In any case, the "dispossessed" often have more immunity than you can imagine.'

'Oh, Kabir, I am so sorry about your grandma,' said Divya, the embarrassment obvious in her voice.

'It's fine. She lived to 90 and drank four goblets of red wine every night. She even had a roaring affair with the village baker in her 70s. Every evening, he would visit her with her favourite butter cupcakes, which she claimed were the secret to her health. She said he baked them with all his love poured into them.'

The mood in the car lightened with his anecdote, but Tara was elsewhere, her mind drifting as she watched the night through the tinted window. Her mother's face, her father's handsome features, Vikramjit's once youthful charm and Vivan's cynical smile—all played like flickering images on a darkened screen. Then her eyes settled on Kabir and she smiled peacefully.

The Bentley screeched slightly as it turned into the steep driveway of the cottage. By the time they arrived, Tara had fallen asleep, her body curled into a foetal position.

With a casual ease that caught Divya by surprise, Kabir lifted his sleeping love into his arms and made his way to the plush bedroom. He placed her gently on the bed, slipped off her heels and covered her with a blanket.

Lighting a cigarette, which he pulled out from her packet, he sat back in a chair, his eyes fixed on her through spiralling smoke rings. *Am I turning into her father?* he wondered. *Am I protecting her from herself, or am I taking refuge in her? Am I her saviour, or is she mine?*

He wasn't sure of the answers, or of the questions. He exhaled slowly, telling himself, *Sometimes, finding the correct question is harder than finding the right answers. Once you know the question, the answer becomes simple.*

'Do I love her?' he murmured aloud.

A faint smile played on his lips *Passionately. I love her with all my passion.*

He had finally found the right question.

30

The Runaway Child

The morning cup of tea was Aishwarya's meditative moment. Holding the fine china handle, she felt deeply rewarded by the first warm sip on the nippy winter morning. At this hour, she always felt pure and serene—her face untainted by make-up, her hair left free. Wrapped in a pashmina shawl, her feet clad in slippers, the cotton kurta and pyjamas she wore were simple and unassuming.

It had been months since Tara had left. Although Aishwarya had never understood her daughter, Tara's absence had left a strange void in her life. *Do I miss her?* she often wondered. What worried her most was that Tara, out and about, might tarnish the family name. Perhaps she did miss the dynamics of controlling her. There were no issues now, with just her and Vikram sharing time, days blending into one another—often filled with boredom.

Seated on the terrace, basking in the early morning sun, Aishwarya debated whether to reach for the morning papers, when her yoga instructor appeared.

'*Padhariye*, Guruji,' she greeted with reverence and stood up, reflecting a culture that placed the teacher atop all hierarchies.

'Vrikshasana,' Guruji instructed, and Aishwarya stood tall like a tree rooted to the earth. She then flowed through the poses—a triangle, a cobra, and finally, the *surya namaskar* to welcome the sun and accept its gift of light.

From his window, Vikram observed his mother-in-law with detached amusement. Her agility still amused him. Whatever feelings he'd once harboured for her had long since dissolved into wry indifference.

Exhausted yet relaxed to the bone after the yoga session,

Aishwarya sipped a glass of lime water infused with Ayurvedic leaves. Reclining in her chair, she finally reached for the morning paper and flipped straight to Page 3. A smile spread across her face as she saw her photograph at the Museum of Modern Art, flanked by the city's elite art lovers. Inaugurating an exhibition of 14th-century royal jewels had been a triumph. She loved the sari she had chosen, perfect for the occasion, and savoured the media's comments about her beauty and style. The Rajmata enjoyed reading about herself.

Immersed in self-satisfaction, she was about to set the paper aside when a headline caught her eye. Hurriedly, picking up her spectacles again, she pushed them on to her nose.

No, she thought. *This can't be.*

'The Feisty Princess of Jaivangarh,' read the bold letters.

'Vikram!' she called out, her voice rising above the palace rooftops.

'Look at this!' she exclaimed, thrusting the paper at him as he reached her, adjusting his quilted robe around himself.

'I told you, didn't I?' Vikram fumed. 'You kept saying not to worry.'

'Don't blame me for your mistakes, Vikram,' snapped Aishwarya.

'My mistakes?' he retorted.

'You should have handled her better. Everyone knows it was your alcohol and anger that drove her away.'

'Calm down, Rajmata. This blame game won't help,' Vikram said, trying to defuse the tension.

He picked up the paper. The article announced Tara Kumari's collaboration with Vivan Mehta to produce a film based on her life. The film, provocatively titled *The Blue Diary*, was already fuelling rumours about the secrets it might reveal.

Vikram's phone suddenly buzzed in his pocket. He answered it, his face turning pale as the voice on the other end grew loud enough to carry beyond the device. His nostrils flared, but he stayed silent and then hung up the call.

'What's happened now?' asked Aishwarya.

'She's speaking at Pushkar next week.'

'How dare she!'

'This is just the beginning, Rajmata,' Vikram muttered darkly.

That night, unease rippled through Jaivangarh Palace. Ram Swarup served Vikram his usual bottle of Johnnie Walker along with a bottle of red wine for Aishwarya. The strains of a distant wedding band in the neighbourhood added to her already frayed nerves.

'You have nothing to worry about, Mr Jhabwala,' Aishwarya tried to assure the developer. 'Tara has always been impulsive. She will come around.'

'With all due respect, Rajmata, I disagree,' replied Jhabwala, his voice flat. He had no patience left for niceties. His nasty mood was evident to the royals.

'What do you suggest we do, then?'

'I am not suggesting. I am insisting because I have already invested.'

'Careful, Jhabwala,' Vikram warned.

'Apologies,' Jhabwala said stiffly. 'We are all tense.'

'Go on,' said Aishwarya.

'We need to accelerate our plans. Every day, your daughter gains more support. Once *The Blue Diary* hits screens and lands on OTT platforms, the game will be lost.'

'He is right,' said Vikram, accepting the wisdom of the seasoned businessman. 'Every media person worth his salt will be there and the trail will lead right up to where we are all sitting today. Pushkar draws huge international attention. This is not Tara's doing; someone very competent is steering her.'

'She's using the family name against me,' Aishwarya seethed.

'We'll proceed with the land acquisition,' Jhabwala said firmly.

'Once the small hutments covering the prime land are removed, we will take over and start the project.'

'Perfect, Jhabwala,' said Vikram. 'If you can pull it off quickly, we will catch Tara before she's ready for the fight.'

'I agree,' said Aishwarya, her eyebrows knitted together.

Jhabwala got on the phone and quickly gave instructions. It was likely Vikram had already spent most of the advance he had paid them. The package had been a confidential handshake between the two men—large enough to buy a small apartment. If the deal didn't work out, Jhabwala planned to get his money back from Vikram for starters, and he wanted the Lamborghini returned. The one Vikram had hidden away so the Rajmata remained unaware of his side deals with Jhabawala.

Jhabwala regretted underestimating Tara—he should have steered clear of this project. However, now that his feet were already dipped in the ocean, the best he could do was take the plunge and swim.

31

Premiere Night at Raj Mandir

A woman with her face covered by her *pallu* approached the entrance, her hands trembling slightly as she pulled her ID and invitation card from a Fendi handbag.

'Show me to my seat,' she commanded, her voice firm with authority.

The usher switched on her torch and led her inside with practised politeness.

Once seated, she waited for the lights to dim before unveiling her face. A woman in a chiffon sari settled into the seat beside her, casually holding a packet of wafers. Leaning closer, she whispered, 'She has your genes, Ash. I have always found your daughter remarkable.'

Aishwarya Devi hadn't been able to resist. She wasn't sure whether to feel pride or anger towards her daughter. But one thing was clear: Tara was moving ahead with a purpose.

'Let's see, Rosie, how remarkable she has been in describing me.' Her hands fidgeted with her ring, while her eyes remained fixed on the screen that was waiting to reveal it all. Although she did a good job of hiding it, she was petrified. There was no exposure more complete than that revealed by a family member.

Rumours had swirled for weeks about what Tara might expose in this film. Fed up with incessant calls and messages, Aishwarya had switched off her phone.

She now looked at Vikram with disdain. *This man is not worth my daughter,* she thought bitterly, tired of his cheeky remarks.

'You know, Mummy,' he had teased one day, 'your daughter once told me she had a pathological obsession with this actor—

what's his name? That Mehta guy. I thought she was kidding, but look at them on that poster.'

Ignoring him, Aishwarya had walked to the cabinet and pulled out an old album. Turning the pages, she found pictures of Tara as a young girl—sitting on her lap, riding her favourite pony or on her first day at school. A wistful smile had flickered across her face. *It could have been different.*

Meanwhile, Vikram had leaned into his phone, whispering, 'She is softening, Dhruv. Get your act together and make it fast.'

The area around Raj Mandir Cinema was cordoned off, with a red carpet flanked by barricades to control the surging crowd. Anticipation crackled in the air, and performers from Tara's project at Jaivangarh worked tirelessly to entertain the restless audience.

A crescendo of excitement erupted as the sound of a pilot car approached. People jostled, desperate for a better viewing spot. A procession of black cars arrived, their darkened windows rolled up, adding to the aura of mystery and intensifying the buzz.

A reporter thrust a microphone towards Tara as she stepped out. 'Madam, there is a lot of expectation from this film. Why have you kept the contents confidential? What is your reason for this secrecy?'

'The film premieres tonight. Until then, the mystery remains. For me, it has one purpose, and that is Jaivangarh. This is my gift to its people.' With that, Tara moved forward, an entourage of security forming a human shield around her.

She paused, searching for Kabir. He stood at the edge of the crowd, his eyes following her possessively. The little injured bird he had rescued had healed; it was now all set to take a flight on its own. He was happy just to stand back and smile.

As Tara walked down the red carpet, the cameras zoomed in, and her face filled the large screens, every nuance of her expression captured. She paused and waved, then impulsively brought her fingers to her lips and blew a kiss into the air. The crowd turned ecstatic and cheered even louder—loud enough to be heard at Jaivangarh Palace.

From the tinted window of his car, Vivan Mehta watched his protégée, feeling pleased. Tara, he observed, had the potential to hold every heart she reached out to—much like the kathputli artists of Rajasthan controlling marionettes. He let her have her moment before stepping out of his car and following the rest of the cast, waving at the crowd that had become hysterical at his sight.

He leaned into a reporter's microphone. 'This one is for all of you to stand up and support our farmers. Popular culture has the power to inspire change, and we can't afford to waste that.'

Vivan was enjoying the new elements of depth that Tara had brought to his work and to his persona with this film. This project wasn't just a film; it was a legacy—one he hoped would go down in cinematic history.

Inside the hall, as Tara sat in the front row, it all felt surreal. She looked up at the ceiling, its intricate carvings conjuring memories of her younger self. She had skipped several classes in college to sneak out and catch a premiere at Raj Mandir Cinema, standing behind the barricades to glimpse a young Vivan Mehta. She remembered feeling faint as he passed her by, waving. In her wildest dreams, she could never have imagined that one day, the crowds would gather here to see her.

How she loved this place—a theatre that had preserved its identity as a plush single-screen hall with sprawling spaces, dramatic lighting and red velvet seats. It was a throwback to the days when going to the films was an experience in itself. Like most things in Jaipur, Raj Mandir was protective of its traditions and she fervently hoped it would remain that way.

'Good evening, Jaipur,' Tara's voice echoed through the

speakers as she addressed the crowd. There was a roar of excitement, followed by silence. She looked at the expectant faces before her and forgot about the prepared speech in front of her on the podium. Instead, she spoke from the heart—of her beliefs, her dreams and her hopes.

'There's one thing I believe above all else,' she said, her voice ringing clear. 'Your home is as precious as any palace in Rajasthan. It is your palace. No one can touch it. Your fields are your livelihood. No one can take them away from you.'

The crowd, ecstatic, erupted into cheers. An old woman in the audience wiped a tear with the edge of her sari.

'I grew up in this Rajasthan,' Tara continued, 'and I am proud of it. I am proud of my family—of my mother and my late father, whose teachings made me the person I am today. This premiere is my homecoming. To all the people who are here or at home, I want to say this: I never left you; not for a moment. And to those who said I abandoned my people—I didn't. I left to survive. And today, I return with a film that will have not just me, but the world, by your side.'

As Tara stepped back from the mic, the crowd rose to their feet and clapped with wild enthusiasm. She turned back and approached the podium again. 'One more thing—don't accept what is given to you as charity. Demand your rights.'

The applause was deafening. At the far end of the auditorium, Aishwarya sat slumped in her seat, tears streaming down her cheeks. Between the excitement and cheers, no one noticed her, but it was the first time she truly felt like a mother.

As the lights dimmed, the front rows were served coffee, and small tables with snacks were arranged. Kabir slipped inside and sat a few seats away from Tara. He gave her a huge smile and a nod—one that said it all. She was tempted to ask the minister seated next to her to switch seats but resisted. She waved to him and smiled back. She wondered if Vikram and her mother were in the audience. They no longer bothered her.

The title *The Blue Diary* appeared across the screen in bold letters. But Kabir was not watching, his attention diverted by the sudden flurry of messages on his phone. His eyes narrowed, and he quietly slipped out of the hall, unnoticed.

✶

Vikram stood on the observatory perched on the terrace of the Gaj Singh Museum and Art Conservatory, his vantage point offering a clear view of the city. He marvelled at the unchecked power of the builder lobby—how every institution had been breached. He had heard rumours of dissenters disappearing for opposing a development, yet his wife had moved ahead undeterred.

Oblivious to the searing heat, he peered through his binoculars. 'Finish it before her damn film is over. I have arranged for a massive traffic jam around Raj Mandir. You have got two hours,' Vikram told Jhabwala.

Dhruv Jhabwala was confident and presumptuous as always. 'It will be over in the next hour. I know how to do this. Nothing can stop me from claiming a good piece of land when I see it.'

While Vikram and Jhabwala remained entangled in executing their plans, Mehta ji hid behind a pillar, waiting. His body trembled with anger as he mumbled, 'I will die before they get their hands on the museum.' His eyes pierced through the two men on the terrace, watching the destruction of homes with voyeuristic glee; the sight was unbearable. His hand moved to his leather satchel, the cold iron feeling foreign to his fingers. He took the small pistol out and aimed it at the men. *Can I do it?* he wondered, unsure.

His grip became firmer as he allowed his anger to surge, giving him the resolve he needed to pull the trigger.

✶

In the narrow lanes of Jaivangarh, pandemonium reigned. Families scrambled to gather their belongings—treasured memories, wall hangings, children's toys and school certificates.

Some villagers regretted not accepting the offers that had come their way. But the land was sacred, passed down through generations. To abandon it wasn't easy.

Inspector Nakul Singh looked unsure.

'Mr Jhabwala, we cannot shoot unarmed civilians,' he had protested earlier.

'Come here, Nakul. You and I need to have a chat,' Jhabwala said with a cold smile.

'You know these people, Nakul. You will be able to handle them better than anyone else and reinforce order.'

He had been chosen deliberately—a move that was clinical and devoid of empathy.

'Sir, it is not easy to raze the homes of families I have known for years.'

'They were offered money and an opportunity to relocate, but they refused,' Jhabwala said dismissively.

Nakul's lips curled into a bitter smirk. *Would any of these rich men accept an order to pack up their families and clear out?* he had wondered.

'Sir, I will not be able to look my own family in the eye if I do this,' he pleaded.

'Don't question your duty, Inspector. No officer of the government has the luxury to do that. You have received orders from your boss.'

Nakul had saluted Jhabwala and left. Leading a convoy of police jeeps into the desert, to oversee the destruction of the village he had grown up in, was proving to be the toughest assignment of his life.

★

In one home, an elderly man was dressed meticulously in his favourite three-piece suit, the one he reserved for important occasions. He took out a red turban, carefully pinning on a stone-studded plume gifted to him for years of service at Jai Janami Jewellers. A red tilak adorned his forehead and a touch of *surma* highlighted his eyes—he was ready.

As an afterthought, he draped a turquoise blue shawl with bright pink paisley motifs—the one Aishwarya had left behind on the fateful night she had visited him, hoping to give Jaivangarh an heir. He smiled at his reflection in the mirror. 'This is how I will enter the gates of heaven,' he whispered.

Mangal Babu lit the candles on the dinner table and stepped back. He bowed to his master of many years, tears glistening in his eyes, and turned to leave. Honour was instinctual in this village, woven into the fabric of its people. The house was eerily silent except for the faint growl of bulldozers in the distance.

Shantanu Malhar sat alone at the table, his favourite meal laid out before him: *laal maas* and *khichdi* with fresh vegetables. He savoured the smell and the colours.

He switched on the radio and turned up the volume to drown the foreboding hum of machinery outside.

The wall shook. A crack appeared but Shantanu remained seated. He gazed at the table, tempted to reach for the last piece of meat. 'They could have waited until I finished dinner,' he said, his voice calm, almost resigned.

Outside, a middle-aged man spoke to the media, clearly agitated. 'That house you see there is 200 years old. It is a part of our history. We have lived here for generations. And now, they want to bring down our homes and our lives to build a water park.'

Kabir adjusted his focus and panned the camera. Through his lens, he saw her sari billowing in the hot desert winds as she emerged. He removed the lens and looked at her again—just the way she had taught him to. She flung the pallu; it slipped from her face and he could see the sheer passion in her eyes, the pure love she had for the land she was saving. Lowering the camera, he saw her—not as an image, but as the passionate woman who had once taught him to see the world differently.

'She's here,' Kabir murmured.

Tara had found out and couldn't stay away from Jaivangarh any longer, not even with her film premiering at the moment.

The media went wild.

'This is history in the making,' cried one reporter. 'The Princess of Jaivangarh, Nayan Tara Kumari, has arrived to confront the bulldozers.'

'Fearless as Durga,' another claimed. 'The police are at a loss at her unexpected appearance.'

'She's a film star, a lawyer and an activist,' added a regional channel journalist. 'Today, she has made all Indian women proud.'

Broadcasts carried her image across the country and the world. In living rooms and offices, people paused to ask, 'Who is that woman? What is she fighting to save?'

Tara's heart raced. She spotted a familiar face and approached him, whispering a set of quick instructions in his ear. Hari was stunned but relieved to see her. He moved ahead, weaving his way through the crowd, with Tara following him, until they reached the front of the protestors.

Hari raised his hand, shouting, 'Nayan Tara Kumari *aa gayee hain*! (Nayan Tara Kumari is here!)'

A roar of excitement arose from the crowd.

Tara looked around and realized that her moment to save Jaivangarh had come. She stood at the head of the protest, waiting for Kabir to give her the go-ahead. She felt a surge of emotions rise through her body. There was fire in the moment and an uncontrollable energy took hold of her.

She stared ahead at the rows of policemen in riot gear and screamed, 'Do not even try to touch my land!'

'Who are you?' a police officer shouted.

'I am Nayan Tara Kumari, the Princess of Jaivangarh, and you are standing on my land.'

Vikram, perched on the terrace, adjusted the lenses of his binoculars, confused.

'Who is that woman at the front of the crowd? What is she doing there?' he asked Inspector Nakul over the phone.

'It's Princess Tara,' came the subdued reply. Jhabwala grabbed the binoculars from Vikram and focused on Tara. 'Break that woman's legs. Arrest her!' he barked into the phone.

'Don't you dare! That is my wife,' said Vikram, his voice laced with anger.

'I've paid you millions. Handling your wife is your job. But if you can't, I will,' Jhabwala sneered.

'Jhabwala!' snarled Vikram.

'And you, Inspector Nakul,' Jhabwala continued, unfazed, 'I do not need to remind you that I have paid you more in one go than I have ever paid any police officer. Arrest her and make sure she never leaves the prison walking.'

Vikram's voice dropped to an icy tone. 'Jhabwala, Inspector Nakul. If you touch her, you both will die at the hands of a Rajput tonight.'

Jhabwala froze. Before anyone could react, a gunshot shattered the air.

Jhabwala slumped to the ground, blood pooling beneath him. Vikramjit turned to see Mehta ji holding a pistol.

'Ask them to stop,' he commanded.

Vikram stood still, hesitating.

'Make the call now,' Mehta ji roared. His behaviour made Vikram squirm as he looked on, frozen in place.

★

Shantanu Malhar stared at the trembling wall, its cracks deepening with each rumble of the bulldozers. He took a deep breath, his lips moving silently as he invoked the name of his God. His mind wandered to Aishwarya Devi's ice-cold eyes when he had visited her with a plea to spare the villagers' homes and land, reminding her of the 'gift' he had given her—a child. She had looked at him without any emotion; he knew then that using people and discarding them was second nature to her. In his frustration, he had promised her that he would be sitting in his chair at the table when they brought his house down.

Suddenly, he was pulled back from distant memories by voices that came through, loud and incessant. Then, as if God's hand swooped down to intervene, the grinding roar of the bulldozers stopped.

The wall, precarious yet solid like its owner, stood firm.

Shantanu's lips curved into a faint smile. He knew Jaivangarh was saved. He could hear people chanting 'Tara Kumari'. He smiled. It was his daughter. He knew she would come.

32

A Drive to Bliss

The new four-lane highway had made it an easy drive down to Gurgaon. He had plans of moving here—perhaps to one of the swish penthouses—once the land deal was over. Jhabwala was dead, but there would always be others like him.

Vikram was conflicted by the unexpected turn of events. Exhausted and restless, he decided to escape to his perfect playground for a night of hedonistic pleasures. The smooth midnight drive promised to wipe away the nightmarish memories of the day, at least for a while. He slowed at one of the brightly lit alcohol vendors; grabbing a bottle of Bacardi, he swigged it with one hand while steering with the other. Anger and desperation consumed him as he pressed harder on the accelerator.

The glowing skyline of India's Millennium City lit up the night, casting mystic hues across the horizon. Gurgaon was the city of the future—a beacon of enterprise, ingenuity and dreams realized. This was where Vikramjit was meant to be. He liked its unapologetic vibe—money here was God, and the brands of cars dictated the road hierarchy. There was something make-believe about this world of excess and artifice. He liked it.

By 4 a.m., the early morning air at the Sunset Lounge had turned heavy and stale. Vikramjit Rathore dragged on his Romeo y Julieta cigar, savouring its flavour. On the dance floor, two women wobbled playfully on their pencil heels. The party had been planned as a private celebration for the launch of his pet development project in Jaivangarh. What was meant to be a celebration had become a night of pure escape.

'This is not right,' slurred Yogi, his friend. 'Vikram, it's very rude to pick one of them, but you must. Blonde or brunette?'

'Both. Rajput men never insult women. I will take on both together,' Vikramjit smirked. The second one was meant to be for Jhabwala but the man seemed to have missed out.

'All yours,' Yogi said, raising his glass, the emerald-cut diamond ring on his finger catching the candlelight. He approached the women, whispered something in their ears that made them giggle, and returned to Vikramjit's side. The two women moved in sync, draping their arms around him.

'Goodbye, Vikram. See you at lunch,' Yogi called out as he walked out of the lounge.

Vikram grinned. 'If I survive these two,' he quipped.

The blonde with the wavy curls reached for the elevator button as Vikramjit was escorted down to the cobalt-blue Lamborghini. The chauffeur stood ready to open the door, but Vikramjit waved him off; he needed privacy. Sliding into the driver's seat, he motioned for the women to hop into the back.

The car roared to life and screeched towards the exit, only to halt abruptly at the barrier. Frustrated, Vikram pressed the horn impatiently, but the blaring sound didn't wake the sleeping watchman.

'Open the gate now!' Vikram bellowed, his voice shaking with anger.

The women exchanged nervous glances. For them, a drunk client meant nothing more than a night of hard work.

Vikramjit glanced at his gold Rolex. It was 4.20 a.m. This imbecile had made him wait too long. His frustration was palpable, but then, as if by magic, the barrier lifted. With a growl, the Lamborghini sped on to the highway, moving towards its destiny.

★

Sanjay Kumar looked out of his window, feeling like a pigeon in captivity at his cramped three-by-three work desk. Night was fading over the city. He glanced at his watch—4 a.m.—the magic hour of freedom was nearly here. His eyes drifted back to the view outside: the enormous wave of concrete and metal surged up the flyover and cascaded down toward the upper end of the city. The screech of steel on rubber, the crunch of tyres on the road—it was the city's evening ragas, the night music of the Millennium City.

He hated the timings of his new job, especially the graveyard shift.

The walk to the cramped parking lot felt like a small victory. His stiff limbs revelled in the stretch, and the sight of his bright yellow Santro brought a sense of relief—it almost felt like he was halfway home.

It was 4.20 a.m.—five minutes more than it usually took him to get to his car. Then, a knock on the window. He turned to see Devi, the office fantasy, once again catching him off guard. He pressed the button to roll down the window, and she greeted him with her effervescent smile.

'Drop me home tonight, and I promise you prawn curry,' she whined. 'Can't stand the company shuttle.'

Sanjay couldn't resist. 'Sure, sweetie,' he said, helplessly charmed by the brown-eyed beauty who seemed to have every man wrapped around her finger.

'This is John,' she said, introducing the young man with her. 'My cousin from Panjim.'

'Hey,' Sanjay said, extending a hand, though part of him just wanted to drive off, leaving them to fend for themselves. But that wasn't something his mother would be proud of. So, in spite of himself, he invited them both into the car, hoping the promised Goan prawn curry wasn't just an empty offer.

Across the highway, Vikramjit adjusted his rear-view mirror to steal a glance at the women in the back seat of his Lamborghini. Their heaving chests and entwined legs performed a silent seduction—every movement deliberate, designed to captivate. His pulse raced, sweat glistening on his brow. The Lamborghini swerved slightly as he veered toward one of the many farmhouses lining the highway. He glanced at his gold Rolex. It was 4.35 a.m.

*

Sanjay swerved into the fast lane and pressed down on the accelerator. Devi's incessant chatter was unbearable. He cranked up the music, glancing at the time on the dashboard. 4.35 a.m.

Like a predestined appointment with fate, it was the last thing both men saw before their timepieces shattered into a million pieces.

*

The morning papers carried a hurriedly compiled piece. A grainy image of a mangled car dominated the page, the twisted sheets of blue and yellow metal barely recognizable as vehicles. Beneath it, a small inset showed a man with perfectly chiselled features and a dazzling smile. As Tara read the report, her hands began to shake. She passed the paper to Kabir and left.

Kabir held the paper, his eyes lingering on the image of destruction. The last line of the report read: 'The palace priest has announced that Vikramjit Rathore's funeral will be held in Varanasi.'

*

Standing on the banks of the Ganga, Tara held the corner of her white veil tightly and sobbed for the man who had died—the husband she never truly had. He was the man she had fled from, but also the man she had briefly loved. With her eyes shut, she prayed for the soul of her husband.

Kabir watched her from a distance. She never ceased to surprise him. The complete dichotomy of her nature fascinated him—the fiercely traditional woman and the absolute rebel existed in her single form. He wasn't quite sure if he had uncovered all her layers yet. The river echoed with rituals of a life departing—chants, temple bells, prayers and the rhythmic rustle of waves mingled with the soft murmurs of the mourners. Boats drifted by slowly, carrying families clutching earthen vessels that contained the ashes of their loved ones. As the remains were immersed in the river, a collective serenity seemed to envelop those left behind, with a fragile belief that their dead were not lost forever, but held in the arms of the sacred river.

In the distance, a procession of mourners in stark white approached, their solemn presence ethereal in the twilight. Tara's eyes scanned the group: Gucci sunglasses perched on aristocratic noses, pale lipstick and subtle make-up ensured that even in grief, there were no slip-ups. Her gaze settled on the jetty where the group gathered.

A pandit circled a smoking urn of embers, chanting hypnotically. The stoic Rajputs stood motionless, their grief contained within. Tara moved forward, stepping amidst them like an apparition.

The murmurs ceased. A heavy, charged silence hung over the gathering as every eye turned to her. Very slowly, she turned and looked into her mother's face.

Rajmata Aishwarya Devi met her daughter's eyes without guilt.

Tara searched for answers in the stoic face she knew so well, her own unspoken question loud and clear: *Why, Mummy? Why did you betray me? Why did you take my husband away from me?*

The rajmata looked past her and Tara knew that a question unacknowledged was not worth asking.

She walked up to her husband's body, and kneeling reverently, she touched his feet before raising her fingers to her forehead. The air was heavy and sombre, the gaze of mourners transfixed on her.

The flames leapt skyward as the funeral pyre was lit. Tara watched for a moment, then slipped away into the dusk, feeling strangely exorcised.

33

Goodbyes

It was the culmination of all his work—the moment he proudly spread out his artistry, laying it bare to be viewed and assessed with critical precision. Meeting his publisher was always the high point of Kabir's assignments, but it also stressed him when he placed his work before a man who demanded nothing short of excellence.

James Gabriel, an expat and consummate Indophile, was a man who put most natives to shame with the wealth of knowledge he had about India. He remembered minute details of its history, cultures and textiles. His home, overlooking the holy shrine of a Sufi saint and the majestic Humayun's Tomb, was a testament to his love for the country. When house-hunting in Delhi, he had insisted on finding a place that resonated with the city's magical history.

In addition, he harboured an obsession with typography. His collection of antique maps was his prized possession, and he often resisted the urge to donate them to a museum in his adopted city. Gabriel's connection to India had begun 30 years earlier when he arrived as a student to work on the Prince of Wales Charity. What had started as a temporary stint had turned into a lifelong love affair with the country.

That morning, Gabriel sat in his study, sipping tea from a handcrafted blue pottery mug while reading the newspaper. A staunch opponent of electronic dependence, he had a simple rule: if you chose to enter his sanctum, your mobile phone had to be deposited in a cabinet at the entrance.

'When we wake up in the morning, we are already switched to "on" mode. We depend on electronics to function; we reach out helplessly to a ridiculous gadget that essentially turns us into our own secretaries and telephone operators,' he declared with disdain.

Kabir, sipping Gabriel's special blend of four teas, smiled at the rant that he had heard on more than one occasion. 'It's a great communication tool,' he ventured.

Gabriel raised a brow, his seniority giving him an air of authority. 'Young man, it all depends on your definition of communication. Most people are addicted to their screens. It's not an option anymore. It's a compulsion.'

'Got the point,' Kabir replied, wisely avoiding a debate with a man who could argue circles around most.

'And don't even get me started on those who send the same message to multiple women at a time,' Gabriel grumbled.

'That sounds like a dangerous game,' Kabir said, laughing.

Gabriel's sharp eyes fell on a photograph of Tara, dancing by a bonfire in the desert. 'Who is this lovely lady?' he asked. 'She seems to appear quite frequently in your work.' The shrewd man's eyes narrowed, a sly smile on his lips.

'You really want to know?'

'I do.'

'She is my muse. Perhaps the reason I have been able to finish half the assignment you gave me.'

'Ah, I see. She is beautiful. So, will she be going back to France with you?'

'When does the book go to print?' Kabir asked, a clear deflection to change the topic.

Gabriel chuckled knowingly but let the subject drop. 'Let me get the editor started. She is very fussy, but I think the pictures are really good.'

'You wouldn't accept anything that wasn't.'

'What shall we call it?' he said. 'Any suggestions?'

'*The Dream Chaser*, perhaps?' smiled Kabir.

✹

The hypnotic strains of a Sufi singer's voice rose from the shrine—a plume of impassioned sound that carried through the night air. It was Thursday, the evening when the *dargah* opened its doors to the mystical allure of spiritual music.

'Can we go to the dargah?' Tara asked as they strolled through the area looking for some of the popular authentic eateries.

Kabir seemed hesitant. 'You will be recognized. The crowd will maul us.'

'I always carry this with me now,' she said, pulling out a black face mask studded with small Swarovski crystals along the edges.

Kabir nodded as she slipped it on. 'Sure, let's go.'

He hadn't learnt to say 'no' to Tara.

They sat cross-legged, heads covered, facing the mystical messiah of music—incidental spectators to a spiritual rising. Ali Akbar Sabri was performing at the dargah and there was a huge crowd.

The Sufi singer's rendition at the shrine of the 13th-century saint Hazrat Nizamuddin Auliya was his offering to God. It was a private communion—him and his singular audience—no one else existed. The crowd became a white blur before his eyes; he felt the light of the universe glowing within.

Ali Akbar Sabri was an imposing figure, his tall form and formidable girth crowned by wavy, oiled locks that framed his face dramatically. His eyes, unable to contain their euphoria, were bloodshot and webbed with fine veins. Swooning to his own voice, he seemed transported, utterly convinced that music was the winged chariot carrying him to God.

Amidst this euphoria, Kabir found himself observing Tara. Something about her felt different that night, and it unsettled him. She looked meditative, her eyes shut. Was it her expression or the way she sat? He knew her well enough to sense that there was something she was dealing with, something she was hiding from him. He watched her for a moment longer before turning back to his camera.

As Sabri's voice rose to a pitch that seemed to cause a vibration on his camera lens, Kabir wondered, for the first time, whether it was possible to capture the intensity of this performance in a photograph. He clicked insistently, moving around the crowded courtyard, and then smiled when he finally reviewed the shots.

One image stood out—a moment frozen in time. Ali Akbar Sabri was encapsulated mid-performance—his eyes bulging, his lips in motion, his veins pronounced, his face tilted upwards to heaven, his forehead glistening with beads of sweat.

Kabir uploaded the photo to his website with a simple caption: 'Can you hear the music?'

Within moments, comments poured in. 'I hear it loud and clear,' one read. Another said, 'Yes. Yes. I think I hear him.'

This was the connection Kabir lived for. When his photographs touched people he had never seen, never met, he felt an indescribable sense of purpose.

The music concluded, and Kabir and Tara joined the long queue to enter the holy sanctum, each holding strands of thread. The shrine's pillars were laden with knotted strings of wishes and hopes. Tara tied hers.

'Don't ask, don't tell,' she whispered to Kabir. 'Remember, if you tell me what you have wished for, it won't come true.'

As Kabir tied his string, she watched his expression. She wasn't too sure if they had both wished for the same thing.

'Kabir, do you think we are destined to be together forever, or are we just part of an adventure that will end?'

'Why should it end? We can keep getting into trains and reaching new places that need to be left behind. We can fly to Africa, to Egypt, sip the best wines in Italy—scale the earth.'

'And then?' she pressed. 'And then what? It has to end somewhere.'

'Don't worry yourself, princess. Remember our promise to

ourselves? We live for today; tomorrow may chase us, but no worries—we are always a step ahead of it.'

★

The narrow streets behind the shrine were dotted with eateries. Tin-roofed establishments exuded the aroma of recipes perfected over generations. Mansoor Ali Qureshi, a fourth-generation chef, worked deftly, twisting long iron skewers over a traditional barbecue with the precision of an artist. The board hanging over him still gave him sleepless nights and he often wondered why he had let himself be bullied by his jean-clad son into changing the name from Nizami Kebab—an ancestral name—to Kebab Corner.

Tara and Kabir sat on one of the long wooden benches set on the street.

'The lady is vegetarian but I will compensate for her,' Kabir said.

'We have the best haryali kebabs for Begum Sahiba,' said the polite waiter, much to Tara's relief.

'Kabir, you should try becoming vegetarian.'

'The steaks in Paris are forbidding. I don't want to resist them,' said Kabir.

She ignored his casual comment but it was one more reminder of their drifting paths.

Through the smoky waft of singeing coal fire, Kabir noticed the eyes he had come to know so well.

'Beautiful, what is it that is worrying you?' he asked.

'Nothing,' Tara replied, her expression contradicting her words.

'I can sense the slightest nuances of your face. Come on, Tara, what's on your mind?' he persisted.

She didn't answer.

'I can hear your silence,' he said. 'So, out with it.'

'Why didn't you tell me before?'

'Tell you what?'

'That your assignment in India was ending.'

'Because I don't believe in that word—never have.'

'Okay.'

'What would you call that?' he asked, pointing to the sky. 'The end of the day or the beginning of the night? There are no endings, Tara,' he said with a soft smile, 'only new beginnings waiting for you out there.'

'Profound, Kabir, as always.'

'Don't worry, Tara, I will find another job. Now smile. Don't think of tomorrow. And if you do, just believe that it will be blissful, and it will.'

'That can't always be a rule.'

'It can indeed. You move towards what you believe will be.'

Tara smiled and seemed to trust the philosophical interlude, at least, for the moment. She held out her hand, and he squeezed it tightly. For a while, it seemed as though the puzzle pieces of their lives had fallen back into place—or had they?

★

Kabir was right. Tara was hiding something from him. She wanted to tell him, but something held her back. She had expected it to be complicated, perhaps incomprehensible, but the simplicity of it startled her. It seemed strange that the coming of a new life should be discovered through a tiny strip of paper with pink lines.

Her eyes misted over as she stared at the result, a sense of wonder infusing her. She held the strip tightly, as though it were her ticket to eternity. Suddenly, she was not alone; she felt part of something larger than herself, entwined with a timeless chain of life—those who had come before and those who would follow.

She stared at the screen of her phone, deliberating, before

finally dialling. Her first instinct was to call her mother, but she disconnected before the call could go through. She dialled again.

'Divya,' she whispered into the phone, 'I have something exciting to tell you.'

'I am holding my breath,' retorted her friend.

'I am expecting a baby.'

'Oh…' came the reply, tinged with apprehension. 'That's wonderful,' she added quickly.

'Divya, I know that tone. Say what's on your mind.'

'Have you told Kabir?'

'No,' Tara replied shortly.

'Will he marry you? I hope he will,' Divya said, her voice edged with concern.

Tara leaned back slowly on her bed, staring at the whitewashed ceiling.

'Divya, that's not what I want from my relationship with him. I don't think I want to tell him.'

'Don't be foolish,' her friend replied, shocked.

'Well, I want to live my life foolishly.'

'This is a very serious matter. He is the father of your child. He has to take responsibility for you and the baby.'

'Oh, Divya… This child…I can feel its presence. I know it's made of the most exquisite love. I won't insult that love by using the baby as a trap. If Kabir asks me to marry him someday, maybe I will surprise him with the news.'

Divya listened, her worry unspoken. Her thoughts drifted to a phone call years ago, from Oxford, when her friend had spoken of Krish with the same breathless idealism.

'It is an amazing feeling,' Tara said, 'as though my body is embracing divinity. I just want to sit here, look at the sky and feel my link with eternity.'

Tara had always been a dreamer, lost in her illusions that often became her reality, Divya thought. She did not ask the one question on her mind: 'Wouldn't it be wiser to abort?' The words stayed stuck in her throat.

Instead, Divya listened as her reckless friend spoke of her unborn child as a talisman of love—the embodiment of the creative impulse.

★

The coffee was getting cold as Kabir's fingers tapped impatiently on his keyboard.

'It's this damn deadline I can't take,' he muttered to himself.

'Relax, you will finish it,' Tara reassured him.

Kabir glanced up, his eyes narrowing slightly. 'Have you been eating too many chocolates?' he asked, looking at her flushed face.

She shook her head, brushing the comment aside, and began flicking through the TV channels. She pressed the remote with impatience, searching for something to distract her, when she froze.

The screen flashed a clip of Vivan Mehta's birthday celebrations in Goa. She stiffened, her forehead slick with sudden sweat. She had locked him away in the recesses of her mind, hiding the memory like a drunken regret buried by the clarity of the next morning. But there it was, caught for posterity, immortalized on camera.

She was taken aback to see the short, sensual interaction amplified for the world to see—its rawness visible to all in extreme close shots. Her hands moved to her face in despair.

'You love him, princess,' came his voice. Kabir's laptop lay forgotten, his eyes riveted to the TV screen. 'Admit it—you love him.'

'I am yours, Kabir. Never say that again.'

'I don't own you, Tara. We only own ourselves. I saw that look in your eyes there. You are smitten, and so is he. That's your good luck. Go for him.'

'You are insulting my loyalty and my love, Kabir,' she said, sounding both accusatory and defensive.

'Maybe if I hadn't seen that close-up of your eyes just now, I would have believed you.'

'I was distraught and drunk! But you, right now, are not, and you are hurting me.'

'No, baby,' he said, reaching out to her. 'I would never do that.'

'We all go through moments in a relationship. I am honest with you. If I wanted to go to him, Kabir, I would.'

'I know, baby. You've been through so much. I should have understood.'

'Let's wander.'

'Are you sure?' he asked.

'One last time, please.'

He held her hand, sealing a fragile bond for one more day together.

Outside, a slight drizzle fell, doing little to wash away the pain as they made their way to the station. Kabir seethed within, and she too was hurting.

In the mayhem and chaos of personal turmoil and the stench of overcrowded trains, they stood holding hands on the platform, as if letting go would mean losing each other forever. Just then, Kabir's phone rang and he let go of her hand to take the call.

The voice on the other end spoke in his native language, its familiarity softening his expression. A smile broke across his face, and for a moment, he looked as though he were home—relaxing against a cushion in front of a warm fireplace.

The train grunted threateningly, preparing to move. Kabir instinctively leapt into its open door, still holding his phone. Turning, he extended a hand to pull Tara in.

But there was no trace of her.

Panic surged through him as he scanned the platform. Then he saw her—standing in the doorway of a train on the opposite side of the platform. It had already started moving, its pace steadily gaining momentum. 'Tara!' he called out, his voice rising above the din of the station.

In an instant, she was gone—out of his sight, heading towards a separate destiny. She had left his life in the same strange and mysterious way she had appeared.

34

From the Minar

Tara lay on the four-poster bed, staring out at the silhouette of the Qutb Minar against the dusky sky. The charming colonial house in Mehrauli, unpretentious and cosy, offered a perfect view of history unfolding in many directions. Its quiet simplicity was soothing—unburdened by opulence and free of pretensions. Its bedrooms opened into a small courtyard.

When she left Kabir at the New Delhi station, it had been an impulse. She had let him continue his conversation with Jennifer; he had been speaking in French with a tenderness that cut her deeply.

Tara felt her body flush with the memory. She felt the burden of being alone as never before. A sudden knot appeared in the pit of her stomach and moved up to her throat. She missed Kabir's presence, his touch of reassurance, the curved pit between his shoulder and his chest, which she had discovered was the best place to rest her head.

Yet whenever she pictured him, she imagined the small bird pendant on his chain, begging to be freed. She loved him too much to hold him back.

On the train, as the city outside blurred into the countryside, her fingers had instinctively dialled a number she hadn't used in years.

'Hello... Hello, who is this?' her mother's voice, softer than she remembered, had come through the line. 'Hello, hello?' she had repeated. 'Tara, is that you? Please speak to me, Tara.'

Tara froze, trying to articulate the words that came to her mind, but all she had managed to say was 'Mum...mummy,' before she cut the phone, her emotions spilling over.

She had sat scrolling through her phone gallery: snapshots of Pushkar, Rustom's garden and finally, one of her, leaning on Kabir's shoulder. In that picture, her eyes held a calm she hadn't felt in so long. Kabir had been her silent blue water—steady and deep. But the memory of his tone as he spoke to Jennifer intruded. Although she didn't understand what he had said, the look in his eyes, the softness in his voice had revealed all.

She looked around the room, taking in its somewhat rustic charm.

'Arjun got this as our secret love nest when my parents were trying to stop us from falling in love "any further",' Divya had said as they walked in. Potted marigolds lined the doorway, and a lemon with chillies hung from the threshold to ward off evil spirits.

She hugged Tara tightly and said, 'I found one of your childhood maids and swore her to secrecy. You're safe here.'

'It is perfect and charming. I love it,' Tara replied with gratitude.

'Put your bags down. Let's grab a bite at Olive.'

They strolled down to the ritzy restaurant, where the hostess at the counter had greeted them with a smile. 'Welcome, ma'am. I loved your film!'

The large sunglasses and brimmed hat did little to hide Tara's face, and she knew that she would have to live with that recognition for a while.

'You are recognized, Tara. It's a cross you need to carry because I know you are private by nature.'

'For a while, I guess. One day, I will grow unrecognizably old.'

'Won't we all?' said Divya, smiling. 'But there will still be beauty in us. The soulful beauty of women who have walked the mile and done it all.'

'And with no regrets,' Tara added with a tilt of her chin.

'And waiting for more experiences ahead,' Divya concluded with a smile.

As the waiter appeared with the menu, Divya scrolled through it and declared, 'Let's start with a bottle of pink champagne. We are celebrating today.'

After giving it a good shake, the waiter ceremoniously popped the cork, sending it flying out of sight.

'To the little baby in a floating spa,' toasted Divya with a grin, her glass raised.

While she crunched a perfectly baked pizza, Tara had stuck to a large bowl of salad.

'Come on, Tara, you have to try their famous Margherita pizza.'

'I am eating for the little one, and I just heard him say no to pizza,' Tara quipped. 'It could be her,' she added quickly.

'Are you sure? No sinful foods?' asked Divya with a laugh.

'No way. I'll be getting kicks soon for bad behaviour,' Tara had said, a twinkle in her eyes.

That evening, Tara opened her diary and wrote just one line:
If I could walk back through my life, how far would I go and walk back again?

★

The sound of azan from a nearby mosque mingled with a bhajan singer's voice somewhere in the distance. Tara paused to absorb the confluence before continuing to type an email to Kabir.

Kabir, my love,

I want you to know that I am doing fine, so please don't worry about me. I am in a safe place. I miss you every moment, but I had to leave. I miss your warmth, yet I had to set you free. Someday, I know you will understand my reasons. We came together to chase a rainbow, but when we got there, our fingers slipped through its formlessness.

You need to find your peace, and I think I know where it
lies. As for mine, I am not so sure.

Yours,

Tara

Kabir leaned back, and took a deep breath. 'Tara is safe. Thank
God she is safe,' he murmured to himself. He could sense her
pain in every word she wrote, underscored by her quiet strength.
Now that she was writing to him, he felt encouraged that he
would find her one day.

He pressed the reply icon, carefully weighing each word. He
feared that if he came on too strong, she might stop writing.

Tara, my love,

I need to be with you. Where are you? I miss you more
than you can imagine. Why did you leave so abruptly?

Her response was short, her words measured as she evaded the
question.

Let there be space in our togetherness—like Gibran had said.

His reply came swiftly.

Should there be space between lovers? Gibran would have
changed those lines if he had seen us together.

Her emails continued to be brief yet layered with restrained
emotion, and Kabir pored over each one, searching for clues to her
whereabouts. Each night, he sent her a photograph he had taken
that day and she sent back a poem. He smiled at the connection
he sensed in her emails, the feelings he tried to detect within them.

Look up at the sky, Tara. Remember what I told you
when we first met: even if you can't see the stars, they are
still shining for you somewhere. I will wait for you till the
last star loses its light. I will wait.

Her reply came slowly.

> Kabir, we live in each other's souls. Nothing has ever parted us. Nothing ever will.

As she typed those words, Tara felt the truth in them. A part of him was still with her. She was carrying his child. Her fingers hesitated on the keyboard. She had an urge to tell Kabir about the baby, but something held her back. She quickly shut the laptop before her resolve faltered.

Ambushed by memories, Tara's mind spiralled into the past: the merry-go-round at Covent Garden with Vikram's hands around her waist; standing atop the Eiffel Tower with Krish holding her hand; Vivan's breath grazing her neck in Pushkar; Kabir appearing on Kamala aunty's terrace that night. She remembered all those wonderful men in her life. They were part of the life she had lived.

Divya's voice cut through her thoughts. 'Six months to D-day. You need to keep yourself busy,' she said, her concern evident.

'You are right, Divya. Every moment feels heavy. I need to do something—something the baby will be proud of.'

With that decision, a room in the house was transformed into a legal office. Tara enlisted law students committed to providing free legal aid to those who needed it most. The hiss of the coffee machine and the rich aroma of roasted beans gave the space a compelling energy. Over steaming cups, they debated cases, determined to create a better world.

The small room soon became a hub for activists and idealists. Some walked in with a fire in their belly to oppose just about anything that fit into their version of an ideal world, while others, it seemed, were still searching for a revolution they were yet to define.

The days bustled with activity—meeting people, sifting through cases worth taking up—yet when the hub emptied at night, Tara was alone. With her face now on every poster and magazine, she had no desire to be seen around the city. Instead, she found herself leaning on Kabir for company. She was excited to tell him about her new venture.

Kabir, I have started a free legal aid centre with law students. We are helping those who need it the most.

His response came with the swiftness of his unwavering support.

Kind Tara, you are like the banyan tree—your roots strong, your branches reaching beyond yourself to give shade. Keep going, Tara. Law was your first love, and they say you always return to your first love.

She read his words repeatedly. They felt prophetic.

Tara's childhood maid became her support during those days. Mornings at the hub began with Shanti Bai's inventive omelettes and cups of coffee. The 'kids', as Tara referred to the students, brought a youthful zeal to the breakfast meetings. They were still untouched by the cynicism that time often brought, their idealism intact. Their motivation was not financial gain but rather the pursuit of a noble cause, which Tara had provided.

✦

Tara cherished her early morning walks through Mehrauli. It was a soothing experience to see time stand still as she passed the Qutb Minar, away from the city's hustle and bustle.

Stepping inside a coffee shop that catered to early morning walkers, Tara scanned the tables and finally spotted him waiting at a corner table.

'Hello, beauty,' he greeted her in his typical style. 'Glad you agreed to meet me, superstar.'

'Hello, Vivan. It's good to see you,' she replied, taking the seat across from him.

As they settled into a pleasant conversation, Tara realized with some amusement what her pregnancy hormones had done to her attraction towards Vivan. *It has practically shut the tap*, she mused.

'The industry is out of breath, waiting for you. You could have been the biggest thing to happen this year.'

'I know it has worked out well for you, Vivan, and I can't thank you enough for believing in me.'

'You did well. But why vanish now?'

She hesitated for a moment, then looked into his eyes, deciding to trust him. 'I am pregnant. And all I want in life right now is to have this baby. I can't think beyond that.'

Vivan looked shocked. 'How did you manage that? Your timing—'

'It was meant to be, Vivan,' Tara interrupted.

Vivan's face softened, though a trace of awkwardness lingered.

'You can call me Mama T from now on if you like!' Tara teased, laughing at his expression.

'Tara, you will lose this opportunity. The excitement won't last forever. This industry thrives in the moment and moves on just as fast.'

'I have thought this through, Vivan. It was a choice, and I chose the baby.'

'Well, that's your decision... I don't mean to pry but I hope the father is taking charge.'

'I am touched by your concern, but honestly, a mother and child make a perfect team.'

'I got a call from a friend in the ruling party. They want to rope you into politics,' said Vivan, his mind still fixed on capitalizing on Tara's success.

'Maybe someday. That's a line of work where age is not a barrier.'

Over cups of coffee, their conversation shifted into a warm, easy rhythm. For the first time, they revealed more of themselves to each other than ever before.

As they shook hands at the end, Tara said, 'Vivan, you will never cease to be my friend.'

'Always your friend, Tara,' he replied with a warm smile.

As Tara walked back, she felt relieved that her meeting with Vivan had gone so well. All the men in her life, except the one she had married, were great people in their own special way. While she was more than the sum of her relationships, she knew each had shaped her in some manner.

The twilight hour cast its soft glow over the Qutb Minar outside her window as Tara lay awake in bed, staring at the towering minaret. She tried to distract herself from the gnawing pain in her hips. A ripple of movement deep within her made her wonder if this was the beginning of labour.

Memories of another child surfaced, but this time it was different. This was her child of love. She felt a determination she hadn't known before. She willed herself to protect this baby—*it would be born healthy and glowing,* she reaffirmed to herself. A part of her sought redemption for the child she had once lost.

Hours later, Tara found herself on a sterile hospital bed, her body wracked with excruciating pain. She dug her nails into Divya's hand, stifling a scream as the pain ebbed and flowed. Then, suddenly, a piercing cry filled the room. Tara's body relaxed, a wave of calm and fulfilment washing over her. She was at peace.

The moment was everything she had imagined. She felt divine—a goddess participating in the creation of life. For a fleeting second, she felt part of an eternal chain that would never break. In her anaesthetized haze, the moment felt surreal. The nurses bustling around her in white coats seemed like angels. One of them approached Tara, cradling a small bundle.

'It's a boy,' the nurse said softly.

'Let me see him,' Tara whispered. 'Let me see my baby.'

She peered at her son in wonder. He was fair-skinned, with a mop of soft brown hair. He craned his tiny head, and she smiled. His deep azure eyes stared back at her. He had Kabir's eyes. He had her father's cleft chin too.

★

Four days later, Tara returned home with Divya, holding her little baby in her arms. The little one was wrapped snugly in a soft blanket, his tiny face peeking out. 'Arjun and I were thinking we could adopt the little one and then leave him with you. That would sort out a lot of questions.'

'Oh! You are a saint! Or maybe just a normal Rajput friend,' Tara replied, laughing.

As the car passed a statue of Lord Shiva, Tara whispered a silent prayer for her newborn.

The blue BMW slowed down in front of the old villa. 'This little place has seen so much love,' smiled Divya. 'Good things have happened here.'

That night, the sky was clear. The Qutb Minar stood timeless under the glowing moonlight. Music drifted faintly from nearby clubs and restaurants, but Tara's thoughts were elsewhere. Her heart raced as she stared at her phone. Finally, she dialled the number she had resisted for months.

'Kabir,' she said. 'Kabir, Kabir, my love…' She repeated his name like a chant.

'Tara, my darling, where are you?'

'Come to me, Kabir.'

'Where are you?' he asked, a trifle exasperated.

'In Delhi. I will send you the address.' Her voice cracked as she ended the call, tears threatening to spill.

The soft cry of her baby startled her. She instinctively lifted him, holding him close. No one had taught her how to cradle her child, how to feed him, how to change him or how to soothe him, yet it came to her naturally—as though it were programmed into her genes, passed down from generations of mothers before her.

'My baby,' she crooned, 'don't cry.' He nestled into her, finding a perfect position, before drifting off to sleep.

In his silence, he spoke volumes—of faith, love, hope and trust. He knew he was in his mother's arms.

Tara sat awake all night, waiting. *Would Kabir come? Or had he made his own path and would not turn up?*

Laying down the baby back in the crib, she put her head against the window and fell asleep. As the morning sun filtered in, a soft caress on her head woke her. She opened her eyes and saw him through the golden haze.

He smiled at her and she knew that nothing had changed. Rising slowly, she fell into his arms, her tears soaking into his shirt.

He kissed her as always, repairing her tears and splits, the cracks and damage. She cried softly as he said, 'I am here with you, Tara. I am here. Don't cry.'

She led him to the tiny crib. Kabir looked down in wonder, then up at her. She nodded.

'Ours,' he said. 'Our little baby,' he said again, his voice cracking.

With a tender smile, he lifted the baby into his arms. 'You have my eyes and your mother's hair, my complexion and her pout, a French nose and Indian lips. You are amazing,' he murmured, his voice filled with awe.

He then turned to Tara. 'Thank you. All my life, I have wanted my child. Thank you.'

Tara smiled back peacefully.

'What is his name?'

'I want you to name him.'

'I will give him a universal name. Do you like Inza?'

'Inza,' she repeated. 'It is beautiful. Inza it is.'

'Years ago, I photographed a man named Inza. It means "flower of heaven". I saved that name in my mind for the day I had a son.'

At that moment, Shanti Bai entered the room. She had seen enough of the world to sense things, and gave Kabir a loving hug before taking Inza into her arms. 'Both of you relax and talk. I will take care of the baby.'

'Inza,' Tara smiled.

'Inja,' Shanti Bai repeated.

'No, Inza with "zee".'

'Injha,' Shanti Bai said with some effort.

The day passed in conversation, filled with laughter and memories they had made together, and then they made love— intense and passionate, as if it were the last time.

He wasn't sure, but he sensed something in her eyes, in her touch. It felt like a goodbye. They still had so much to say, so much love left to share. But finally, Tara said what she had been pushing away from her mind.

'Drop me home, Kabir.'

'What?' he said.

'I need to return. Come with me to the station. I want to take a long train journey with you. I need to have you with me for just a bit longer.'

'I can't do that, Tara. I can't leave you,' he said, looking confused.

'Hari told me Mummy is ill, and I want to see her. My adventure is over. I need to go back to where I belong.'

'And what about us?'

'Did we ever plan anything?'

'But there is Inza. We have to marry now.'

'"Have to"? You know how I feel. We must never do something because we "have to". Let our hearts lead us to what we do next.'

'My heart is with you, Tara.'

She smiled knowingly, like a friend who held all his secrets. 'Ah, I know all about your heart. It is in three parts.'

'What are you saying?'

'One for me, and two for Jennifer.'

'Jennifer will always be a part of my memories, yes, but now we have a child, Tara. We should marry.'

'I have never done what I *should* do.'

She got up to pack her belongings.

Epilogue

The Pink City Express pulled into New Delhi station. Flocks of tourists boarded the train, some with rucksacks and others with overnight bags. Tara and Kabir settled into their recliners with Inza wrapped in a soft blanket, his eyes darting around, curious about the hustle and bustle around him.

'You hold him perfectly,' Tara said as Inza fell asleep, secure in Kabir's arms.

'A father's instincts,' Kabir whispered, then leaned in and kissed Tara's ear gently.

Tara rested her head on his shoulder and felt a moment of peace, but her eyes kept drifting to the bird he wore around his neck.

As the train slowed down and pulled into Jaivangarh railway station, Tara opened her eyes. 'I am getting off here and Inza must go with you.'

'You can't leave him. He needs his mother.'

'He will have a mother—Jennifer. And a father too.'

Tears welled up in her eyes as she stood up; she had to move fast before her resolve melted. She placed Inza's bag beside Kabir and then bent over her baby.

Inza suddenly opened his eyes, as though alerted by some sixth sense. She stared at him, her heart clenched, a sharp, wrenching pain cutting through her. She gave him one last look, kissed his forehead and got off the train.

She wanted to rush back, to grab her baby. But she knew the truth—Jaivangarh would never accept Inza. He would have to live with the stigma of being a child born out of wedlock, and Kabir would never truly be hers. The whistle of the train startled her as she stood contemplating on the platform. As the wheels began to turn, she braced herself and started walking, resisting the urge to turn back and leap on to the train. Kabir looked at her through the window till Tara became a blur—a watercoloured memory, a perfect photograph captured in his mind.

When Tara finally reached the palace, she climbed up the spiral stairway and went to her room. It smelled the same. Nothing had changed, yet nothing was the same. She stood under the shower till it had washed off every other life she had lived. She had been away too long. Too much had happened.

Wrapped in a sarong, she went to her mother's room.

'Who is there?' came a feeble voice.

'It is me, Mummy.'

'Tara. My Tara. Come here,' she said.

Tara sat beside her and held her mother's hand. She noticed how frail the rajmata had become. Kabir had been right. In one life, we live all our reincarnations. This was an avatar of her mother she hadn't seen.

'Sleep well, Mummy. I am back home now.'